SLEEP WITH ME

SLEEP WITH ME

Joanna Briscoe

BLOOMSBURY

First published in Great Britain in 2005

Copyright © 2005 by Joanna Briscoe

The moral right of the author has been asserted

Bloomsbury Publishing Plc, 38 Soho Square, London W1D 3HB

A CIP catalogue record for this book is available from the British Library

Hardback ISBN 0 7475 7995 4
ISBN-13 9780747579953
10 9 8 7 6 5 4 3 2 1

Export paperback ISBN 0 7475 8167 3
ISBN-13 9780747581673
10 9 8 7 6 5 4 3 2 1

Typeset by Palimpsest Book Production Limited, Polmont, Stirlingshire
Printed in Great Britain by Clays Ltd, St Ives plc

For Charlotte, with love

Acknowledgements

Many thanks to Oliver Bennett, Luigi Bonomi, Carol Briscoe, Frank Briscoe, Holly Briscoe, Claire Calman, Edith Clarke, Eleanor Clarke, Ruth Corbett, Cecily d'Felice, Tony Dixon, Peter Grimsdale, Helen Healy, Julia Hobsbawm, Allegra Huston, Carol Jackson, Tara Kaufmann, Nicola Luckhurst, Fiona McMorrough, Charlotte Mendelson, Clementine Mendelson, Rachel Mendelson, Theodore Mendelson, Kate Saunders, Louisa Saunders, Gilliam Stern, Becky Swift, Caroline Trettine, and especially to Jonny Geller, Alexandra Pringle and everyone at Bloomsbury.

ONE

Richard

The day our child was conceived, someone else arrived.
She was there as the cells fused, like a ghost.

We had fucked, my love and I, moments before going out
to dinner. In a hasty, clothes-off scramble as we changed, we
had collided for the sake of romance, aware that we didn't
have time, and that the best sex occurred with self-imposed
urgency. We spent twenty minutes laughing, protesting, trip-
ping over gussets, bellowing curses at the inevitable gathering lateness. How pleased we were with ourselves as we
glanced sly-eyed at each other in the taxi, one snorting and
hushing the other while we called mid-journey to lie about
our lateness.

'I'm full of you,' said Lelia.

I twitched. Though limp and spent, I felt myself stirring
again. I saw swarms of tadpoley cells diving through crevices.
I didn't know which one would swim fastest, like a little
medal-winner.

The taxi came to a halt outside the house, and we bundled
in, still sex-dazed. We were rudely late. I worried that my
skin would smell of her as I kissed our hostess, Catrin. I
could still taste her scent in my nose. Catrin's boyfriend

MacDara came over and shoved me a bit, and I nearly laughed at him in comradeship – the double delight of conveying sex afterwards to your friends – and because it was almost Christmas.

'Come in then, you old bastard,' said MacDara. He turned to Lelia. 'Hello.' He hugged her. 'You look great,' he said.

The guests were already a little inebriated on Christmas champagne. My other closest friend from college was there, beside someone I knew slightly, and there were four strangers – a couple and two other women. We were introduced. I cannot remember her: can't recall the first sighting of her, was entirely oblivious to her. We were all happy to reach the end of a year marked by the increasing disappointment of being in our thirties without the wealth or fame we had imagined for ourselves. Time was running out. Reality was finally dawning. However, the New Year would bring a magical sprinkling of fresh chances, of course, and here was Christmas Eve's eve. We drank quite a lot, until the ice sneeze of champagne bored through Lelia's juices in my nose. She looked fucked still, her dark eyes off-centre, her movements fluid. I nudged her, raising one eyebrow and smiling at her to hint at this. She scratched the back of my neck in passing, and I leaned against her and breathed in the scents of her hair.

We became happier. MacDara and Catrin, being richer than the rest of us, always provided. There were grilled things oozing olive oil on ciabatta which required more champagne, and then red wine to go with the Parmesan, and then inevitabilities in the minor smug-arse world we had somehow embraced without meaning to: rocket, and more Italian bread, and a risotto starter, all semi-familiar from the same cookery books everyone used.

Digression. The ghost was there. I didn't even hear her name.

I was in my bubble. Lelia and I felt passion reignited, we who had only been together four and a half years and sometimes couldn't be bothered to have sex. The glow of our recent activities bled into the glow of alcohol, and I loved her because she was beautiful. I loved her despite myself, despite my patchy relationships CV, my tired neuroses and all the little trip-wires laid across love. She filled me, between sporadic rows and sudden irritations, with a kind of fury of devotion.

I was barely aware of the ghost at all. She was some face in a group of ten. Did she speak that night in her curious catching voice? A little, probably. I dismissed her as dull without even forming a conscious opinion. The others were too highly coloured: the glow of Lelia; uptight old Ren from university; blustering MacDara; his girlfriend Catrin. They were so familiar, I knew their every tic with wincing recognition. The only hook on my memory, slight as a Velcro claw, was a vague recollection of her in the hall, speaking to Catrin before we all left. Something about her, or what she said, made me feel a flicker of protectiveness towards her, as though she needed to be helped.

That first sighting was repainted and lingered over so many times later; but at the time she was a blur. A slick of grey. Nothing. Beware of mice.

TWO

Richard

To start at the beginning, of course, my name is Richard Fearon. I grew up with liberal parents and four siblings near the Cornish coast. It was a wild childhood, fraught in all its freedom, which filled me with excessively urban concerns. I came to London as soon as I could, quietly ashamed of my rural comprehensive school education, to start my brilliant career.

My early twenties were dedicated to fevered bouts of work and masturbation. I reviewed endless novels; I interviewed countless hysteria-ridden authors; I threaded lowly hack work with attempts to become a full-time biographer, my ambition always ill-matched to my haphazard working methods. So I worked and wanked, and fell for largely unsuitable women. Disturbed, rumpled goddesses were seduced from their heights by my exhausting inventiveness. Usually married or unavailable, they spread their joys and casual torments over what was essentially a safe life, leaving me lonelier than I was as a semi-virginal boy.

It was a history of infatuation that only the years cured, and which, by the time I was in my early thirties, spread behind me in a garish sick pattern. Others had squatting and clubbing and dodgy adventures in Thailand to teach them. I, too secretly square or apprehensive, too obsessive at heart, had glamorous old prima donnas. I spent as much time fantasising about their funerals as I did about sex: my starring role, distraught and furtive at the cemetery, avoiding the twitching-jawed husband.

But eventually I turned quite sensible, because, having grown beyond all that, I met Lelia. It was the greatest piece of good fortune. When I was in limbo, resisting the divas and expecting very little, I met the one I wanted.

The day after supper at MacDara and Catrin's, I decided to do a little work, purely in order to soothe my conscience over Christmas. It was afternoon by the time I lumbered into my study and sat myself in front of my computer. The crackle as I went online hurt my hangover. I punched at the volume button. There were a couple of work messages, a few group greetings from friends, and a jangling Christmas card sent by MacDara that I couldn't be bothered to activate. I opened the last email.

I was frightened, all passion spent until I was a hollow girl of glass. I wore my calico chemise, my veins pulsing blue and secret beneath. My petticoats were porous as canvas. Blood would seep into them unless I was very precise.

'*What?*' I grunted out loud. Irritated, I hit the *PgUp* and *PgDn* keys, but there was no more information. The email was sent from a Hotmail address that gave no clue as to its owner.

'Lelia!' I shouted.

'Yes?' she said, after a pause to indicate resistance.

'Come here.'

'Why?'

'Please. Look at this.'

A kiss landed on my head with the warmth of breath in a cold room.

'Ugh!'

'Exactly. It gives me the creeps.'

'What is it?'

'I don't know.'

'What do you mean?'

'Well—' I said. 'I don't bloody know.'

'Shhhhh . . .' she said in my ear.

I edged my head away. 'Sorry. Hangover.'

'Such a *grump*. For God's sake don't turn all strict and horrible at Christmas.'

'Only if you require punishment.'

'Yes, well. So why don't you just email back and tell them to bugger off? Then do some work.'

'Yes,' I said. 'I'll just reply *Fuck off*.'

'Do you want a mince pie?'

'Yeah. Please.'

I pressed *Reply*. I read the email again. It almost affronted me, as though I had touched a stranger's dirty clothes. *Who are you?* I wrote in a rush, and sent it. Oddly embarrassed, I deleted my reply from the *Sent* file, and then from *Trash*.

Lelia brought in a mince pie on a chilled plate and a cup of tea, steaming in the cold.

'Stop pretending,' she said, and kissed my cheek. 'It's so annoying. Do some work if you're going to do some work. Or—'

'You know I won't enjoy myself completely unless I do an hour or something.'

'Pretend work.'

'Yeah, well, you know me too well.'

'Did you tell the lunatic to fuck off?'

'Yes,' I said. I hesitated. After years of game-playing and strategies with others, I could never lie to Lelia. 'No,' I said. 'I wrote, *Who are you?*'

'Oh, you idiot!' said Lelia, indignation followed by amusement rising in her voice. 'What a creep. It's probably some bearded man who sits in internet cafés all day getting turned on by writing as a girl. He probably smells like a tramp. He'll be back to you in minutes.'

'Probably.' I grabbed her by the waist.

'Come on,' she said, her funny, melodic, posh little voice – more precise than mine would ever be, full of North London girls' schools – blowing into my ear. 'Pretend to work for an hour if you have to, then come back to me.'

Christmas was our honeymoon. We were celebrating not yet having a child – or being together in the time before it happened, if it ever did. The mutual misunderstandings and bouts of exhausted snapping that periodically erupted during our working lives were soothed within hours of the start of the holiday by a sense of romance. We would trawl up to Golders Green to see Lelia's mother, but then we were free to spend our time in a shared tent of coats and books and flirtation alone in Pâtisserie Valerie and the Pollo, to wander through the Great Court, and end up in the Bar Gansa or the Coffee Cup. However many plans we made to discover the East End or see some Shakespeare, we somehow trod a known path between Soho and Camden and further into North London.

With Lelia, I chatted far into the night, the most obscure observations liberated by darkness, barely expressible notions hinted at and then pounced upon by the other in recognition. Our conversation was enchanted at those times, running, oiled, into the early hours, so that talking to her was like talking to a better version of myself: our thoughts meshed in counterpoint, and sex was unnecessary, incestuous, and an immense effort. And then, without sex, we grew fractious and distant, and we were obliged to argue and misunderstand each other for a while, minefields springing into life and misery in the air, until, in her subsequent obstinacy, I caught a whiff of the raddled old goddesses who had once kept me erect, and insecurity activated my lust.

That evening, after I had written a sketchy paragraph with a few notes beneath it as an uncomfortable salve to my conscience, I cupped her buttock, slapped it, and told her I wanted to fatten her up. I grabbed the car keys. The old car hiccuped and juddered into life, and we drove to Marine Ices to eat multi-coloured ice cream under strip lighting on the night before Christmas.

'Get mango so I can have some too,' I said.

Lelia's lips parted slightly.

I sensed someone glancing at me from a lower section of the restaurant.

'Get your own,' she said.

'I want *yours*.'

I turned round. There was no one. Only a couple eating pizza and a girl reading a book.

'I'll see,' said Lelia.

This is my Lelia. A glowing creature, moody, anxious yet deeply sweet-natured. She is, above all, altruistic, though she indignantly and quite earnestly denies it. She falls into full-blown bouts of misery and vicious self-castigation as she fails to match up to her own elevated standards and exhaustingly insists that I join her in perceiving the source of her despair. Her moods make me want to bellow in frustration. When she emerges, she is that glorious, stubborn, extrovert self, a bright and chatting beacon in a room, with her arcane adoration of fashion, her honey-milk skin, her eyes bright brown moon-tilts. She makes me laugh. She lets me get away with very little.

She was born a clever, worried girl; an only child striving to achieve. The daughter of an Indian doctor, now dead, and an English classroom assistant, how my poor Lelia drove herself through her modest childhood to succeed: a neat little North London bluestocking with her independent girls' day school assisted places and her strict notions of morality. She is beautiful, yet she knows it only in fragments perceived obliquely, because her beauty needed to grow beyond spectacles and overworn clothes, beyond the chunky little girl my viola-curved love once was. The loveliness bloomed in front of me, her face refining itself into a matching tilt of eyes and cheekbones as her late twenties tipped into her thirties.

When I met her, I knew her. Two souls recognised each other and came together. It was an uncanny sensation, in which all time was lost. When a fortnight had passed, we were confused; for surely time had slipped, and we had known each other for months and years? I wanted to absorb her and protect her from the first day onwards. She came to live with me the following week, both of us shocked by such precipitation, yet knowing it to be inevitable.

We ordered ice cream.

'How gorgeous,' she said. 'Five whole days to ourselves.'

'A little holiday. Let's do fuck all.'

'OK. Except lie around in our dressing-gowns and eat.'

'Let's decide we won't even clear out the bloody cupboards,' I said. 'Just wolf down tangerines.'

'Oh, Richard,' said Lelia, flicking my wrist. 'We said we would.'

'OK, OK,' I said. 'Only joshing. But let's promise to do it in two hours flat, drunk, stuffing ourselves with mince pies.'

'Whatever you want, Richard,' said Lelia with exaggerated tolerance. 'I'm going to the loo.'

I stacked the menu on the table with a satisfying box sound. It caught the strip lighting. I wiggled it to play with splashes of reflection, like a child.

'Hello.'

It was a flat greeting, delivered quietly behind my shoulder, only the faintest indication of surprise lifting the word. I turned. The girl who had been reading at a lower table stood beside me, her expression closed except for a slight smile.

'Hello,' I replied automatically.

'Oh,' she said, glancing to one side. 'It's Sylvie.' She paused. 'We met – Ren's friend MacDara—'

'Oh yes. Of course.'

Fragments of the previous evening flitted through my mind: the low lights of MacDara's, all that food; the wine, still trailing a hangover through my bloodstream. I attempted to recall the faces that had merged at the end of the table. This one seemed unfamiliar under the bright lighting of Marine Ices. Then I thought I caught a fleeting memory of her, talking in the hall, though I wasn't certain. What a rude smug bastard I was, I thought, with my own little circle, a circle gathered and refined after years and years in one place until it was self-supporting, and I could barely be bothered to meet anyone new. Yet once, newly resident in London, I had been so lonely. I felt sorry. I wanted to apologise to this reserved person alone at a table, who had remembered me and said hello.

'Sylvie,' I said.

'You didn't remember,' she said quietly, levelly and her

mouth moved into a smile. 'Did you?' Her voice had a catch in it, a faint sweet cloudiness at odds with its quietness. She glanced at me for a flickering moment.

'Oh, I—'

'It doesn't matter,' she said calmly. She looked at her book on her table. The fact that she was out, alone, on Christmas Eve struck me. Her book lay beside a single glass of water, the pages weighted open by an unfinished bowl of pasta, and, glancing at her — her grave, steady gaze, her reserve, the austere design of her clothes — I realised that she must be new to London, or socially unpractised, or simply solitary. She looked very young. She was plain to the point of invisibility.

'I — have something to read,' she said, following my eyes. She had a slight accent: something indefinable and not quite English. 'I mean, something I must,' she said simply. 'By tomorrow.'

She smiled at me.

'Tomorrow is Christmas,' I said.

'Yes—' She paused.

I nodded. I smiled at her. 'Of course,' I said.

She was silent.

She stood still. She was so quiet that I became awkward, trying to fill in the conversation instead of enjoying my own contrasting self-assurance.

'Well, I should go and finish it,' she said then, and looked at her book again.

Her cuffs were turned back to reveal narrow wrists. A pin-prick of spaghetti sauce lay, like blood, on the pale grey wool of her sleeve. It discomfited me, as though I had seen something private. She was entirely unadorned, like a reserved child who had learnt to keep herself to herself. Her body was slight. Her hair was straight and cut to her shoulders, and she had the kind of face – pale-skinned, her nose a little larger than her features warranted – that I would probably have forgotten by the next time I saw her.

'I'm going to go now,' she said, and smiled directly into my eyes.

Lelia wound back around the tables, and somehow the girl had gone, disappearing somewhere in the other room. I glanced at her pasta, cooling in its bowl.

'Did you ring my mobile when I was in the loo?' said Lelia.

'No.'

'I thought not, but it didn't say what the number was. It's starting to melt.'

'Eat some,' I said, and put a glaring-pink spoonful of ice cream in her mouth. 'Here,' I said, and held my wine glass to her mouth. 'Mix red and pink.'

'What if I were up the duff?'

'*Are* you?' I said.

'How would I know, you berk? It's not my period for a couple of weeks. We haven't been very careful lately, though. Don't you keep track of it at all?'

'Oh yes, I forgot,' I said. 'Sorry.'

'You great loon. Walloon. You don't even know how often I have it, really, do you?'

'*Menses.*'

'Very clever.'

'When are you going to marry me?' I said.

'Now?'

'Good.' I pulled a stick-shaped packet of sugar from the bowl, emptied the contents, and attempted to tie the paper into a ring. It sprang back stiffly. I spat upon it, moulding it into shape, and pressed it on to her finger. It hesitated, then flopped on to the table in a pulpy mess. She laughed.

'I'll make you another one,' I said, emptying more sugar into the ashtray, spilling some on to the table. 'When shall we – you know—?'

'Are you asking me to marry you?'

'You know I am. Don't we ask each other all the time? Let's just do it next year. This coming year, I mean. What if you were pregnant? Would you then?'

'Not for that reason. I just want to be able to do it properly. But when are we *ever* going to be able to afford it, to have a big party?'

'Fuck knows,' I said. A stab of shame caught my throat: a glimpse of truth. 'Surely we'll make a wodge this coming year.'

'Will we? *Somehow?*' said Lelia, more tied to simple fact than I was.

'It's really irritating, isn't it?' I said moodily. 'They're all getting these huge thundering bloody houses suddenly. These are my *friends*. I want everyone to still eat pasta and live in studio flats. Much more comforting. It's got to the stage where you can't bring a bottle of Hardy's without it being hidden away. It's really pissing me off.'

'Shut up, Richard,' said Lelia. 'Shut up about it or move out of Bloomsbury to somewhere sensible. Or get rich.'

'Yes,' I said, and sighed. 'You're right. Anyway, I've got you. I'd live in a Wimpey bungalow with you.'

'I thought it was a garden shed!' said Lelia indignantly.

'That too. A kennel. A *drain*.'

'A sewer, you said. Would you *actually* live in a sewer?'

'To be with you, yes. A mews house in Hampstead on my own, or a dark dripping stinking sewer with you? Easy bloody peasy, sweetheart.'

'Good. But would you live with me in New Zealand?'

'Of course. As long as you behaved. Wales. Uzbekistan. *Guam.*'

'Good.'

I smiled at her.

She licked a last melting lump of ice cream with the tip of her tongue. 'That's as it should be.'

'I'll pay.'

'Right. I'll bring the car just outside. I'll hoot.'

'Be careful on that side street.'

On the way to the till, I glanced at the table where the mousy woman sat, and saw her writing, surrounded by precise, ordered things like a girl's: a small leather-covered address book, lined paper, a notebook. The light caught her clean-looking hair. I'd forgotten about her. I hadn't even remembered to tell Lelia that she was there.

'Bye,' I called. I struggled to remember her name. 'Nice to see you again.'

She turned.

'Yes,' she said. She looked at me. 'It was lovely to run into you,' she said. 'A surprise. I'd only just seen you.' She hesitated.

I paused. She looked up at me again. She appeared very solitary in her nest of books, like a neat but sequestered pigeon.

'Look, give us a call,' I said munificently, feeling for a card, and not really meaning to say what I had just said. 'We'll ask you over next time we have Ren for supper or something.'

She turned to me again. The car horn hooted.

'I can't find one. Sorry. Just come over with Ren sometime.'

She paused. 'Here's mine,' she said, and wrote down her number.

'Oh, you live near me,' I said, surprised, glancing at the small figures on the paper.

'Do I?'

'WC1?'

She nodded.

'See you,' I said.

Lelia pulled away, the car's faulty heating jerkily emitting warmth and then streaming cold.

'There was that girl in there,' I said. 'She was at MacDara's last night.'

'Was there?'

'That mousy-ish one. You know the one I mean? I couldn't really remember her.'

'I think so – the one next to Ren, you mean? There was someone kind of quiet but quite nice-seeming, but I didn't talk to her.'

'She told me her name. Look at that wanker doing a U-ey. Slightly French, I think.'

'I don't know. I wanted to say something to her, but I didn't. I felt like I should introduce her to people or something.'

'Yes, well she was in there.'

'I didn't see her at all.'

'I kind of vaguely said she could come round sometime with Ren.'

'Oh God, we don't want to go that far, do we? She seemed – a bit – um . . . dull? But I'm a bitch. You're much nicer. Sometimes.'

'Christmas largesse.'

'Yes, it's funny, isn't it? I go all sloppy at Christmas. It makes me want to cry, the idea of old people on their own. Is it just guilt?'

'I don't know. I think charities collect more at Christmas. You can give the *Big Issue* seller those manky clementines from Safeway's if you want.'

'You bastard,' said Lelia, and laughed.

'What I never know,' I said, 'is whether or not you're

supposed to say "Happy Christmas" when you pass a stranger on the street on actual Christmas Day. Do you, you know, just ignore each other as normal, or do you call out a cheery Dickensian greeting like you do to shopkeepers and telephone operators, or do they think you're a nutter if you even catch their eye?'

'Oh, Richard,' she said, smiling. 'Only you—'

'I know, I know,' I said. I leaned over and moved further and further up her thigh till she laughed and screamed at me to stop.

As we approached the flat, I remembered the email I had been sent. Through the windows of the houses strung with lights, their trees burning white, another dirty little message would wing its way here to sully my computer. That beardy wino, sitting in some sordid café in South London, dumping his strangeness on a stranger, or a madwoman in a bedsit distorting her youth. I knew it would be there; I was curious, but I decided to leave it untouched until after Christmas, as though preserving my life exactly as it was.

THREE

Richard

We lived in Bloomsbury, among the green shadows to the right of the city's heart, where no one but students and strange old ladies of forgotten Mitteleuropean origins lived: the transient and the dying beneath a crust of American tourism.

I insisted on staying in Bloomsbury out of some misplaced metropolitan imperative that was, beneath it all, a parochial terror of mud and small-town people. Then the country boy in me made a village of London WC1, so my daily life was strung between the limits of seven dog-marked squares, and newsagents beneath blue plaques, and strip-lit rip-off shops. For my office job, editing the book pages of a newspaper four days a week, while I attempted the increasingly nightmarish task of completing a biography on the fifth, I had to venture into adjacent Clerkenwell, a ten-minute walk, which seemed a different land; while Lelia, who worked at the university, could take a tiny stroll from our flat towards Russell Square. I lived in that central area for odd, stubborn reasons – Bloomsbury was not Bodmin Moor; the sheep could not come back to get me there – among those who were younger than me or older than me. I never expected Sylvie to live there too.

Our cramped, lovely flat was in Mecklenburgh Square, up three flights of stairs, overlooking the private garden on one side, with its improbable airy tumblings of green, and an Art Deco monstrosity on the other, with washing lines and crumbling metal balconies above the muted roar of traffic. The place changed when Lelia moved there. It was transformed from my untidy small flat with newspapers on the stairs to a crookedy home, up and down, like the tiniest house.

'A cottage!' she had exclaimed, and I began to think of it, after that, as one of those miniature sloping cottages by the sea. One bedroom and a boxroom beneath a low ship's ceiling of mahogany-coloured wood; skylight on to a minute section of roof, with Lelia's plant pots up there in the high gritty air; my tiny study and one big room downstairs in which we lived, its tall windows looking on to the world, its curtains brushing the old floorboards, the table always high with toppling piles of post and work, with candlesticks, plants shedding leaves, and glittery things bought by Lelia.

Such choices were more universal than I'd thought. Even the candlesticks, dusted with pollen, were probably categorisable, as was our very existence; but I, blundering male that I was, had failed to realise it. I was once aggrieved, when flat-searching, to find that everyone was the same. In Farringdon, in Camden, in Kentish Town and Chalk Farm, identical novels sat on shelves; the same CDs, evidence of exhibitions visited, plays seen, Taschen postcards propped against spines. The cross-referencing proliferated: familiar bowls from early-nineties Habitat, the same tiles behind sinks, poetry fridge magnets, those chipped orange cast-iron pans, and, inevitably, among the other horrible reminders of one's own limitations − always, always, on floor, sofa or table, *The Guide* from the *Guardian*. I felt irritated and claustrophobic, as though I had inadvertently been corralled into a club or a competition in which everyone imbibed identical cultural information for a surprise exam. We too could be categorised, then, along with everyone I had ever laughed at. But of course we could, said Lelia calmly in the face of my disgust. We had less money than those tossers, I pointed out. I grew up hundreds of miles away with fucking sheep; she was half-Indian, for God's sake.

'So?' said Lelia.

So. Perhaps our lives were ripe for disruption. My career was going well, even if it was badly paid, at that point, although it still filled me with a sense of inadequacy. I had, miraculously, found my love. Her discovery seemed to me like freakish fortune. I feared cancer, wheelchairs and MS as punishment for my luck, but perhaps my fears were merely an insurance policy, and beneath it all we were more complacent than we knew.

I drifted to my computer, my back clutching at the cold, the following morning. Christmas morning. She was still asleep, clasping the duvet. I eased myself out, protecting her sweet sleep. My hair stood on end. I had a piss. I looked at the street as I shaved. Windows lay dead across Gray's Inn Road. I turned on the computer, fearing she would hear the opening cluster of notes and think me a madman. The crackling as I went online sounded like a fire of static echoing through the flat. There it was. There was nothing else. I was mildly affronted. I had expected a couple of greetings from friends abroad who couldn't be bothered to send a card. I double-clicked on the indecipherable Hotmail address. The message had no title. It had been sent, I noticed, only minutes after I had arrived home the night before.

★

It occurred to me one morning that I had been born for suffering, just as other children were produced like small purses to sweep chimneys, or help with harvest, or pick pockets. I dreamt of orphanages, tantalising myself with a fortress in my head: a prison for little women who had committed the crime of being unlovable, because an un-lovable child was against nature. I knew what I was. I was a runt, saved from an institution because I performed a purpose. My task was to receive my mother's displeasure.

The weirdo was clearly sending me fragments of fiction. Someone who knew what I did for a living was trying to tempt me with sections of their short story or novel, so that I could discover their nascent genius. They probably also posted instalments on their website for three unemployed wasters to read between pub visits. What was I supposed to do? Reply, *You write like an angel*? Ring my best friend the publisher as a matter of urgency? Or simply have my curiosity piqued in private? I was perplexed. Grateful to be free of the curse of literary aspiration myself, and surrounded by novels jostling for attention, I was highly intolerant of friends-of-friends' out-pourings, saddened and guilty in the face of their immense effort. Reading the email, I felt once again as though I had touched a stranger, their particles of skin upon my fingers.

I went upstairs. I felt the warmth pockets, smelling of Lelia, that her body had made between the duvet and the sheet.

'Tea,' she moaned, sleep-rumpled.

I brought it to her, and she shifted herself against the wooden back of the bed.

'Good Lord, a stocking!' I said.

I pulled out miniature tiles from the British Museum shop.

'Thank you,' I said, kissing her lips. Her eyes widened against sleep.

I found pens, a Professor Calculus keyring, a 1960s children's sailing guide.

I was immensely moved by the care behind her choices. I put my arm round her and drew her to me. I pulled out a net of chocolate coins, and we started to eat their delicious, tasteless, powdery substance. She removed the tangerine from the sock's toe, and opened it.

'The Christmas smell,' she said. 'Tangerines and chocolate.' I felt the startlingly hot hollow at the top of her thigh.

Memory came spooling back. Her nightie, sweet, cottony, was suddenly scented with my mother. I wanted a child to be with us at Christmas.

We stumbled through the tree-lit flat barely dressed. We argued idly, for the sake of it, and sat on the floor watching Christmas films beneath an outspread dressing-gown. Lelia sat rapt and happy through girlhood chick flicks – *Little Women, National Velvet, The Railway Children* – sobbing amidst embarrassed laughter at returning fathers and precocious triumphs, before we entered the darkening day in search of late Chinese lunch, or coffee in cheap, steaming cafés. I knew then that I loved it, that seamless round of laziness scented with pine needles; yet a habitual tumour of anxiety located in my stomach spread its tendrils through me to prevent pure happiness, and I was aware that I wasn't enjoying it quite as much as I'd think I had later, when nostalgia imbued memory with less complicated loveliness. The acceptance of good fortune is an almost impossible feat for a standard neurotic like me.

At the end of December, we went to a private view of Ren's paintings.

Dear, clever Ren, the reserved workaholic whose expertise in computer technology gradually metamorphosed into this. His intricate paintings on glass: blips, beads, interconnected by a hair-thin network, resembled an open radio panel, the connections glowing as though electrified.

It was a shouting gathering, the guests carefree with Christmas inactivity. I saw the mouse girl standing there with someone, and I instinctively looked elsewhere to avoid having to talk to her before I found more interesting company.

Ren was mingling with the suits who now bought his work, his expression considerate and Ren-like as he talked. I looked at him and contemplated the dedication that lay as an invisible stratum beneath his success, and felt a spasm of guilt at my comparative laziness, an indolence that I could ill afford yet spasmodically, self-loathingly indulged.

Ren had studied Indian miniature painting with an expert he had tracked down in Southall. For some years, he immersed himself by day in computer technology, then drew the same line, fine as a scratch, over and over in the evening, disciplining his hand. The same whisper of a line. Nothing else. After half a decade of silent work, the computer connections in his mind flowered on glass. The large panels, fruits of many months of intense labour by steady-handed Ren, began to grace corporate lobbies. The idea of Ren – my old, unexpected friend, with three children to support – the idea of Ren as artist was so incongruous, it was exhilarating. Anyone could do anything. I'd always known it, but I realised it again with a lurch. I'd lost the urgency of my faith along the way.

'Come on,' I said to Lelia. 'Let's get a drink.'

'Well, should I be knocking it back?' she said. 'I could always be pregnant.'

'God,' I said. I kept forgetting. The idea was thrilling, and alien; it seemed impossible. 'Let's get you some dull fruit punch or something, then. I don't have to, like, "*support*" you, Lelia, and not drink or anything, do I?' I asked in Stoke Newington tones.

'Thanks so much,' said Lelia dryly. 'Look, there's Kathy! She looks bloody awful. I want to go and say hello.'

'Hypocrite,' I said. *Hypocrite lecteur*, I thought. What did that mean? I never knew. I could ask Lelia. Hypocritical reader? What was that? I felt indignant at my lack of comprehension, as I did with various titles – *The Fresh Prince of Bel-Air, Red Hot and Blue; Bo' Selecta* – whose meaning eluded, and therefore irritated, me. I looked for Ren, wondering whether I should go over and congratulate him a bit, but he was still talking to some suits, who meant business, and boredom. I had a sneaking suspicion that they patronised him when they spoke to him because he wasn't English.

'Hello,' said the mouse, speaking into a gap between people.

'Oh hello,' I replied. I scanned my memory. With a huge effort, attempting to dredge a weight out of murky substances, I failed to remember her name again. As I stopped trying, I got it. 'Sylvie,' I said. 'What does *hypocrite lecteur* mean, apart from – as it sounds?'

'– *Mon semblable – mon frère*,' she said. 'Baudelaire.'

'Right.' Beneath her quietness, I could hear an authentic French accent.

'It's from "Au Lecteur". *Les Fleurs du Mal*. He's teasingly accusing the reader of being an accomplice of the author – a sort of knowing hypocrite.'

'Good gracious, I should know that, shouldn't I? Thank you, miss.'

'It's one of the emblems of modernism.'

'Well, thanks for explaining to the ignoramus. Are you French?'

'No. A bit,' she said. 'My father was three-quarters.'

'Which makes you . . . my maths . . . a third. Ish?'

She said nothing. I glanced at her. She was as plain as a girl in a French film, with her clean-skinned frankness of face, the full sting of her mouth. Despite her pallor, her eyes were shadowed with faint bruisings of colour, as though she stood in an unlit room in the evening. She wore a plain little narrow frock thing, and her hair was a dark dull brown, and very straight. Her pale clear skin rendered every small detail of her face visible: a blue vein where her hair began, the shadows under her eyes, her unpainted lips.

'Where did you grow up, then?' I said.

'All over,' she said in her surprising, slightly gravelly little voice.

I waited. I found I was gazing at her mouth when she spoke, to have somewhere to look at.

'Basically,' she said. 'Where did you?'

'Cornwall.'

'Oh,' she said. 'That would be very beautiful.'

'Well, people always say it is. It is. I couldn't wait to scarper, though. Flee the cows.'

There was silence. I hesitated. She was impossible. I felt my teeth meet in frustration.

'Right.' I glanced to one side, calculating when I could escape.

'It's dull at these things, isn't it?' she murmured. 'You're bored.' She looked at me and a slight smile lifted the corners of her mouth. 'I think I was too. I was imagining all the other places I could be.' Faint animation lit her skin.

I paused. 'Where?'

She gazed at me for a moment, then glanced away. 'Any number of other places,' she said.

'Tell me,' I said, thrown by her silences. 'Tell me what you do.'

'Oh,' she said, looking to one side. She seemed to catch someone's eye. 'I – study. Literature. I'm finishing my PhD. And then I write. Academic publications. And you—'

'I—'

'Do you know how much I loved your book?' she said simply, interrupting me. 'I truly did. I thought at first I wasn't going to like it at all, but it crept up on me; you got the very essence of him. I started to know him. It was as though I lived with him, sailing all those seas – the Strait of Magellan; Tierra del Fuego; all those *names* – for the days I was reading it.' She moved her hands finely, precisely as she spoke, her fingertips grazing her neck. 'It's something remarkable to do that – conjure a world, pin down a person, a whole life.' She turned away, as though she had said too much. She glanced down at her shoes. I glanced at them too. Little narrow lace-ups, reminiscent of a young Edwardian woman's. I noticed that her ankles were narrow and finely cut. She caught her breath awkwardly.

'Thank you,' I said.

Automatic pleasure rose inside me – despite myself, despite the terrible dowdiness of my critic. Praise was the reward for innumerable hours alone in a study toiling at my ill-paid books, all two and a half of them so far, the equation so unbalanced that such shards of compensation contained a jolt of sweetness.

There was silence.

'Are you new to London?' I said, trying to be kinder.

'I've been here about a year.'

'And—' I said.

'Yes,' she said. 'About that.'

I wanted to break the silence; I felt driven to offer help in some unspecified way, despite her appearance of almost chilly self-sufficiency. Her mouth twitched with an expression of self-consciousness, as though she was embarrassed that I had detected the solitary nature of her existence.

'Give me a call at work,' I said, finding my card in my wallet, and feeling bountiful as I gave it to her. 'You might like to take away a few books from my office – people do. Clear my filthy landslide shelves for me. It's beginning to look like Iris Murdoch's house in there.'

She laughed, a full laugh that made her eyes crinkle.

She leaned closer to me. She smelled somehow of extreme cleanness. 'I once saw her, in North Oxford,' she said. 'She was sort of ugly, and sort of very beautiful. I was with someone I *shouldn't* have been with, and there was Iris Murdoch on the street, like a living ghost. The two became interconnected in my head. It was a good day.'

She smiled at me, and she walked away. I watched the back of her hair as she made her way through the room and disappeared.

FOUR

Lelia

I had finished talking to my old friend Kathy, and suddenly I knew that I was pregnant; or I thought that I knew. I felt different. I had conceived twice before, with another man – the first pregnancy an accident; the second a strange attempt of mine to prove to myself that I was fertile, that I wasn't always surrounded by death – and both times, the uneasy sense that I was not really pregnant at all had bothered me, and I had lost the baby weeks later in a mess of clotted blood and grief. The loss had faded, but it never disappeared. I felt guilty about those children, as though I had caused the briefness of their lives. I wanted to look after them, and honour what might be their ghosts. If I thought about them too much I always cried, so I tried very hard not to remember them.

Yet, in the face of this, I was suddenly filled with the confidence that my body worked and I had the power to bear a child. I felt a rush of hope.

I looked up to find Richard, to mouth at him, 'I'm pregnant.' He was tall; I located him easily, bending down to talk to someone and laughing. The baby that married our DNA was just beginning to form itself inside me. I looked at his mid-brown hair, his distinctive big eyes with creases beneath them, his imperfect nose that only a man could carry off, and joy curved inside me at the thought that our heights and skin tones would meet somewhere in the middle as our genes merged: I pictured the pigments of our eye colour as a striping swirl of my dark brown and the blue-green-grey that I thought of as Cornish, though his parents' origins lay elsewhere.

A surge of terrified love hit me as I watched him. He looked like a fisherman from a story to me, a seafaring creature who rarely actually dirtied his hands with oily rope, but seemed to belong to a windier place than the streets on which I saw him, his hair's springing waves hardly constrained by his short haircut, and his restless air more suited to wider spaces. I stared at him to catch his attention. He didn't turn round. A rod of tiredness seemed to press into my forehead, and I sat down. Ren's ghastly paintings glared at me. My inner eyelids prickled as I closed them, and I held them closed for some seconds, the dry tingling carrying on with a life of its own.

'Lelia,' came a voice that I didn't know.

I looked up. I saw someone I recognised. She seemed very familiar, and then less so. Blankness descended on my memory.

I realised who she was. My mouth opened slightly. It was the woman we had met at MacDara's house.

'Hello,' I said. I smiled at her. The addition of her name in response ran through my mind, but it sounded stagey. I murmured something, but she didn't respond.

'Hello,' I said again, instead. 'How are you?'

'Oh, I'm well, thank you. But you're not – you're quite pale.' Her hand touched my head for a moment. 'I think you need some water.' Her voice was sweet and foggy, its tone unexpected. 'Don't you?'

'Oh, I'm fine. Actually . . . I would, really. Where do you think—?' I looked around.

'I'll find you some,' she said.

The rod of tiredness seemed to bore through my skull, leaving me almost faint; then it receded.

She returned. I didn't hear her.

'Here.'

I took big gulps of fizzy water. I felt as though I were in a swimming pool. The water lapped, blue, against the sides of the cup, enclosing my mouth, nose, eyes.

'Thank you,' I said. 'I feel bad—'

'Do you?'

'No, I mean – Richard said you were at Marine Ices the other night – on Christmas Eve, wasn't it? – and I didn't realise. I would have said hello. I'm sorry, I just didn't see you there.'

'Well, you see, it seems that I can be invisible,' she said in that tranquil, faintly husky voice, the corners of her mouth tilting. 'I just can't – I can't really do the social thing. I don't know if I want to either. It's all right.'

'You should have come over.'

'No.' She looked evenly at me. 'You two were together.'

'So? We're not surgically joined. As you can see,' I said, stretching my neck, looking for Richard again. Too many bodies were in front of me. The party had become louder. Clothes brushed against my knees. She bent awkwardly to talk to me. 'Sit down,' I said. Someone knocked into her as she sat, and she reached out to steady herself on my shoulder. The pressure was nice. My back was tired; I longed for Richard to massage it.

She gazed coldly at the person who had unbalanced her.

'The proof,' she said. 'That I'm invisible.'

'Of course you're not!' I said, laughing a little.

But she was essentially accurate. She was not notice-able in a room. Yet despite her lack of ornamentation, there was something about her I had remembered. She could have been any age between her mid-twenties and early thirties, while appearing younger: it was hard to tell. She was slight and straight-haired, and her features combined plainness and near-beauty, so that she was almost *jolie-laide*, her nose quite prominent, the movements of her mouth, with its tilted curves, restrained in compari-son. Her skin, though it was fair and very fine, seemed to pull shadows to it that gathered under her eyes, beneath her dark eyebrows and at her temples. Her face was very even. Only her mouth was full: I could see what to do with that mouth.

She was as prosaically dressed as the dull people at school we had called the beige girls, though her clothes were probably more expensive than they looked. I could see exactly what needed to be done with her: cut her hair more sharply; disguise those shadows; paint that one obvi-ously good feature, so it was a show-off's mouth. Then dress her from scratch so that she concealed herself less. But she would never do it. Whenever the odd beige girl with aspirations rebelled for the first and last time at school, she would take the ethnic route, with drooping pink bags, and beige-on-maroon waistcoats with frogging, and self-aware earrings; or she would add cochineal streaks to dishwater hair.

'Do you work?' I said, for something to say.

I had once visited a pub in the small Cornish town close to where Richard had grown up, and we had talked to people he had once known, and there they all were, still sitting in the same pub they had frequented at school, and I realised I could never say to any of these people, 'What do you do?' They took courses; they drove vans; they were looking into film-making. And meeting them had made me more circumspect.

'Well,' said Sylvie. 'I'm finishing my doctorate, but I'm writing papers too. What do you do?'

'I teach at UCL. Comparative literature. French and German.'

'You're an academic!' she said. 'I should know that, shouldn't I, but I don't know your surname.'

'Oh, I never know. I'm always meeting people I assume are some kind of caretaker, and they're the Emeritus Professor of Byzantine History at Trinity.'

'Exactly. I walk *past* them, all the time. Some of the people drifting in and out of the Historical Institute on Russell Square look like the inmates of a Victorian asylum,' she said, then paused.

'Don't,' I said. 'I have to work with these people. I often think I'll catch nits from them.'

I looked up for Richard again, but he was invisible, lost to me in a babble. I was pregnant. The extreme weariness had lifted, but I felt certain, as I had never felt before, that I was pregnant. Losing it was too distressing to think about. I muttered a little prayer in my head for the baby to survive. I pressed my nails into the side of my seat.

'Where do you work?' I asked, idly inventing questions since I couldn't think of anything else to say.

'At home,' she said. 'My PhD's supervised at Edinburgh, but I've moved down here.'

'Is it OK working at home?'

She paused. 'I hate it,' she said with intensity.

'Why?'

'It drives me mad, to stay in one place, just working, working,' she said, in the same impassioned tones. 'I don't think life should be like that. It's a form of madness. I need *people*. I go out, I work in cafés, just to avoid it.'

I pictured Richard, on his Fridays at home, discovered by me at lunchtime still banging round the flat, wild and irritated in his dressing-gown, his hair dishevelled, or watching *Neighbours* with cereal propped on his knee in a frenzy of self-hatred, lamely inventing semi-lies about plumbers and computer crashes to obscure his inactivity, and then spending the whole evening catching up.

'But you could work in the library – it's fantastic to work in. Senate House, I mean.'

'How? I'm not a student there.'

'I'm sure I could give you a reference for a card.'

'Oh!' she said, and turned to me, her eyes resting on me as though I had handed her a large gift.

'I can just say you're one of my students.'

'What – oh, that would be so lovely. Thank you,' she said with passion.

There was silence. I tried to think of a comment or a question.

'Where did you grow up?' I said.

'Oh, all over the place.'

I waited. 'In France?'

'I went to school for a while in France.'

'Where?'

'It was an American school.'

'Right,' I said. 'And were you brought up here too?'

She shook her head. She smelled distinctive, I noticed as she turned, like expensive soap: that very pure almond and milk soap that lingers lightly on the skin and made me think of old houses.

'And – your family?' I asked, but instinctively I knew I was drifting into difficult territory and that I might hurt someone who was possibly solitary. I paused. 'Do you have family?' I said.

'No, not . . .' she said.

'Oh,' I said.

She was silent.

'You must come over to ours,' I said. 'I mean – it's not connected,' I finished awkwardly.

'I'd like that,' she said politely.

'Come next week. Can you do – let's see.' I found my diary. 'Friday's free. Could you do that?'

'I think so,' she said. Her knees were closed. Her hair hung very neatly, almost limply, below her chin. She looked like a reticent French schoolgirl. 'I'd love that. Thank you.'

'Come then, then. Good,' I said.

The sounds of people laughing and drinking rose in front of us.

'You're not very well, though,' she said. 'I feel worried about you.' Her voice was warm in my ear and comforted me.

'I'm just tired.'

'You look exhausted. I think I know what it is,' she said, and smiled.

I blushed. 'Do you?'

'I . . . think so!' she said playfully.

'Really?' My heart thumped uncomfortably.

'I can sometimes tell.'

'Well . . .' I said.

'You can tell me – next time I see you,' she said, and turned to me. Entirely unexpectedly, she kissed me before she rose, and I felt the desire to confide in her right then, to tell a stranger something that I wouldn't even tell my mother for a few weeks.

Her hand rested on my shoulder.

'I have to go,' she said.

I felt her kiss upon my cheek, the varying pressure of her palm against my shoulder. I placed my hand on my stomach and I searched for Richard, so that we could be together, so that he could take me home.

FIVE

Richard

Even if I was abused, dismissed, despised, I possessed the power of hatred, a gift as rare as the cleverness I had been given, and I would summon it when the time came to save myself. I had attempted to be good; I had toiled to make samplers, gifts, surprises; I had tried so hard not to be a trouble to my mother, and in the end, it had come to nothing.

Earlier that morning, I had caught a streak of something new in her: a faint glaze in her eyes, a careful folding of her body as she sat down, and I knew in that moment that my enemy had come. Mother's tightly laced waist would soon relax; the servants would hush themselves, and the monthly nurse would be engaged. I would be swept into the corner, and this time, the starvation would have to begin.

Oh, piss off, I thought. What is this creepy stuff? I clicked on *Reply*, and I wrote *Piss off.*

I hesitated over the *Send* icon. I clicked the button. My answer disappeared into the ether. I laughed slightly, my own rudeness still inspiring amusement in me, piqued by the age-old fear of reprimand. I was always, in childhood, the one who triumphed in games of Dares, pushing myself to greater heights of boldness, secretly terrified of the punishments that might befall me, my pleasure equally secretly enhanced. And even in adulthood, my superego was teacher-shaped, and haunted me with interesting threats.

The only one who never reined us in was my mother, who, in her kindness and tolerance, was wryly amused by our exploits as she raised five clamouring children with dramatically varying quantities of money in the middle of nowhere; and I loved her in return with an ardency undimmed by distance or time. She had been my one constant, my dear old friend. And now Lelia, who was somewhat less tolerant of my outbursts of silliness, was here beside me too. I felt blessed by them.

I stayed online for some minutes, waiting for a reply. There was nothing.

'Oh, goodness – shit,' said Lelia, her diary open on the table. 'I forgot. We've got Sylvie – you know, that girl – I asked her round on Friday.'

'*Why?*' I said.

'I just felt like it.'

'But why?'

'I *like* her. I think she's probably on her own, and we could be friendly, that's all.'

'Oh, Jesus. She's just one of your bluestockings. You're reverting to type, my love . . .'

'Oh, bugger off. Better than the total *lunatics* you used to know. And fancy.'

'Yes, yes,' I said in bored tones.

'I've never met such a tribe of madwomen in my life.'

'Look, darling. Just because you're the exciting one among your goody-good swot gang from school – the obvious shining star among a load of dullards. They don't deserve you.'

'But they're my old friends,' said Lelia, as she always did in this particular discussion. 'I actually *like* them.'

'Fine. But let's not *invite* a *new* twitching academic into our midst.'

'Oh, she's not like that. She's just a bit shy. Anyway, didn't you nearly invite her over too, you hypocrite?' she said, grabbing my shoulders and widening her eyes to bring them up close to mine. 'Didn't you?' We kissed, banging our lips together on purpose.

'Did I?' I said, frowning. 'Oh yes. I felt sorry for her. Yes, well, she can be as shy – boring – as she wants, because we've got other company on Friday.'

'What?'

'The Fearons. Da-der! They're all trolling up from home. All of them except Rachel.'

'Oh, my God.'

'Let's invite MacDara to disperse things a bit.'

'OK, but *please* don't get all upset by your family. I can't bear it.'

'Yes, yes. At least they'll save us all from crashing boredom, thanks.'

My slacker siblings operated as a squabbling gang. Only Rachel was absent: the less obviously loved, oldest girl, who had always perplexed my mother with her solemn, plodding ways, had escaped to Edinburgh, as driven as I was. I felt protective towards her, and empathetically hurt for her, and I had always kept in touch with her. Our parents had separated when I was in my late teens, and I always felt that my mother, having spent years balancing my self-employed architect father's wildly fluctuating income through the rural shambles that was our childhood, deserved an easy coast into old age. But now, touchingly, hopelessly maternal as she was, she had shouldered the responsibility of three lumbering adult offspring.

Those three arrived at Mecklenburgh Square in a van on Friday afternoon, never considering that I might have work to do, and were amazed and flustered by having to pay for a parking voucher. And I, as I had dully anticipated while restless in the night, was required to throw pound coins on to the pavement below because nobody possessed enough change.

'Fuckers,' I growled at Lelia.

By the time MacDara arrived to buffer me from irritation, while Lelia warded off ancient family wounds, the air was thick with Old Holborn, and tea bags sat in pools of tannin on the stove, and various urgent calls had been made, interspersed by indignant crises about the parking which I was supposed to solve, and trips to the van to fetch acceptable music, our own CDs rifled through, dismissed and restacked in a sliding topple. Finally, the combination of wine and falling light and the right Brazilian music had made them happy, and when Sylvie arrived, they were stretched out and mellow beside the Christmas tree, the girls laughing with their dirty cackles. Clodagh, Bethan and Dan. The three youngest Fearon siblings, drifting on the back of their exquisite misbehaviour into adulthood, shored up by various benefits and dodges. Alien creatures to me, some years younger, many times less responsible, yet familiar as my own breath, my own blood.

'Save me,' I muttered to Lelia, who was dressed in some brightly patterned skirt she said was new and the high heels in which I always fancied her. I made her giggle by pretending to grab her fanny while the others weren't looking.

Sylvie disappeared, re-emerged to help Lelia, and became invisible once more, or I forgot about her; MacDara took a long phone call from some American bank in my study, and I was left cooking for the Fearon slackers, and began to revel in their demanding company and my own age-old affection for them. What an uptight bastard I was, after all, with my mortgage and books and petty concerns. They, in contrast, had all the freedom in the world, living as they did in cheap outbuildings and barns near our family home; taking odd jobs, signing on, stinging our poor mother, who had to take in lodgers to support her own kindness, for funds. A louche, afternoon existence of dressing-gowns and Rizlas and smoked salmon despite poverty, and the meandering cordless phone calls of the depressive. A new world, a new language, of goats and blims, of pink diesel, festivals, barn roofs, bidis, CD burners, eBay purchases, bailiff avoidance and infra-red detection. They told me local gossip involving various monosyllabic farmers, the WI, inbred neighbours, and it was as though my childhood ran before me on a cinema screen. I drank wine and laughed at their excesses, goading them to reveal more. MacDara had joined in, putting on what he thought was a Cornish accent, interrupting and bellowing out indignant questions as he sat, his large bear's body crumpled into a cross-legged position beside the others on the floor. We lobbed tangerines across the room to one another. Sylvie was in the room, and I had introduced her, but she remained invisible, even quieter than before. I forgot about her, noticing her only in pauses between drinks and cartoon images of Bodmin Moor. Lelia, animated, sweetly included her, but otherwise she was silent.

I glanced at them together: flesh and air; a woman and a ghost.

Lelia talked, cutting bread, bending differently over the table because of her heels, and angling glances at me: the subtlest arrows, loaded with irony that only we understood; promises of hilarity later in bed about the ways of the slackers. When contentious subjects nudged into the air – money, mine and theirs; the inequalities of the Fearon household; ancient favouritisms – she caught my eye again, instantly prepared to do battle on my behalf. Though we squabbled frequently about my siblings, we were now united in the face of them. My everyday love welled up and filled me. I stretched the length of the table, its edge pressing into my ribs, and felt her hand. I loved her social ease; I loved her kindness.

'Chuck the bread, Dick,' called MacDara in an excruciating yokel's accent.

When I next noticed Sylvie, she was in the shadows, pretending to examine our books on shelves. My head slurped more drunkenness as I moved, and I looked at her narrow back, her dark V-neck, her nothing of a skirt over legs which, in shadow, seemed a good shape beneath thick black tights, as she skimmed books to hide her social reticence, and I wondered, does she ever shag anyone, that sketch of a woman? Has she ever been laid? It seemed unlikely – an unsavoury concept in such a strange and self-contained person, as though even thinking about it was an encroachment upon her cool primness – yet you could never tell. I recalled that a handful of the dullest girls in college – bespectacled grinds from the Midlands; timorous Barnet Catholics – were reported, via girls I knew, to enjoy frequent and even kinky bouts of love-making. The notion was as repulsive as it was oddly pleasing: one never knew, one couldn't guess. Life held its secrets.

My head banged with wine. I cleared the plates, and went to my study to search for a Carl Larsson book that Clodagh claimed I had stolen from her some two decades before and she was demanding back.

It was cooler in there, the leaf shadows from Mecklenburgh Square diffusing the street light. I stood by the window. I pressed my forehead against the glass. Sylvie wandered through from the hall, slight as a child in the gloom.

'Hello,' I said. We looked down on the street together. She had been silent; I was drunk: there was no need for conversation. Bethan's van was a dark hulk on the square, like a ship. Further along, the floodlit tennis courts on Brunswick Square formed a grotto of artificial brightness.

'How are you?' she said eventually.

'Pissed,' I said.

'Do your family drive you to that?'

'God, yes. Don't yours?'

'Oh. Families do,' she said in her quiet, cloudy voice. 'The source of true madness. I like yours, though.'

'Piss artists. Scroungers. I don't know. Con artists.'

She smiled. 'They're inspiring too. They know how to live—'

'Well, *that's* true.'

'I think you should relax too, then, instead of being jealous of them,' she said, surprisingly.

I paused. '*Jealous?* You think I'm uptight?' I said, sounding grumpy.

'Well, probably. Aren't we all — people like us — you, me and Lelia? I'm so tightly strung, I think, I sometimes exhaust myself. I can see that in you too.' She glanced at me.

41

'Yes,' I grunted. My half-sentences were truncated by wine so that I could hardly speak. I could tell that she hadn't been drinking. I leaned closer to the window so the glass cooled my forehead.

'It's like a green graveyard out there, isn't it?' she said. 'No one lives here – except us. Perhaps that's why I like it.'

'Why?'

'For those reasons.' Her voice was sweet, calm, low. Her hair hung loosely in a kind of bob, like a little Alice Liddell's, a scrappy Victorian girl's. That was what she looked like, I realised: a Victorian doll, but no plump-cheeked beauty; rather, a more earnest, susceptible creature, a small thing hidden in a cupboard instead of displayed on a shelf.

I felt united with her, watching the scene together from that enclosed space. Thoughts moved slowly; my brain wouldn't work properly.

'If you lived in Soho or Camden,' she said, 'wouldn't you feel as though there was a party going on to which you hadn't been invited? Here, it's all greenness, and silence. All those academics, completely cloistered. That's what I like, because then I can make my own life out of it, and find excitement in that.'

'No media pimps, running about with their elephantine great portfolios, you mean? I suppose all that stuff does make one feel pretty crap. It's like—' I threw open the window, wine warm and queasy inside me. 'Jesus,' I said, inhaling a breath of damp earth beyond the stain of traffic, 'I've never really said it, even to myself, but it's the same as – I hate the first fucking crocuses. I want to curl up and kill myself or something, dive back into winter.'

'Oh, so do I,' she said passionately. 'Just what you said. Just that. Even the snowdrops in late January make me want to freeze time there, so there are no sounds of summer, no radios in the street or children in playgrounds, and then I can stay indoors, and in my head. And read and read books. Sit by the fire. Lie in beds.'

'Beds?'

She said nothing.

'Plural?'

I turned and looked at her. I felt at ease, the mechanisms of my body fluent, as though they would enable me to do or say anything I desired.

She laughed a little into the cold night. She stood beside me, the window raised. A breeze shifted her dull-girl hair.

'Maybe,' she said finally.

Of course, I thought. This is a woman, not a plain child. I could suddenly detect the subtlest thread of sexual confidence beneath her reserve.

'I didn't always have – my own,' she said.

'Your own? Your own what?'

'Well – I—'

'Bed. Home, you mean.'

'Yes, well.'

'The kindness of strangers?' I said.

She smiled without looking at me, and her eyes were impenetrable behind their shadows in the night.

'You've been very kind,' she said.

'Have I?'

'Yes.'

'I'm afraid that I haven't.'

'You invited me here – twice.'

'Yes. I'm sorry. We haven't really talked, have we?'

'You ignored me, because you thought I wasn't interesting to you. Why should I be of any interest? I'm – well, I'm hopeless when I first meet people. You're quite the opposite.

Amazing. You're all life. You talk, and make people laugh, but it's not trivial small-talk. I feel when you talk to me as if I know you.'

'I—'

'Whereas I just go into my head if anyone ignores me. But we're talking now.'

'Yes. God, I'm so sorry. I'm such a rude prick. I forget sometimes. I get caught up in my own strange concerns. Lelia's so much better than me.'

She was silent. She looked thin, leaning out of the window, the angle dangerous, as though she might blow out, her legs slenderly awry as she balanced herself. She gazed at the trees, her eyes wandering to the rooftops. The sound of three Fearons laughing, talking and moving drifted in from next door, interspersed by barks of laughter from MacDara; and from time to time I heard Lelia's voice. And then, one day, a baby might live here, perpetuating the evidence of human life, adding to existing presences, visited by my parents and Lelia's mother and my siblings' future children. Whereas there was this girl, who lived alone in Bloomsbury, who seemed untethered to family or past and who seemed to observe the world with the clarity of an outsider. I wanted to cut through her pride and protect her, to put my arms around that slight body in its plain schoolgirl's jersey and share my fortune, while shielding her from any pain that her own might bring.

'Come to my office, then,' I said. 'You can choose some books. To read by a fire.'

'Thank you. When I have time,' she said, and I felt stung. 'That would be very lovely.'

'Whenever you want,' I said.

She turned from the window and smiled at me.

Spontaneously, I hugged her, and, briefly hesitating, she leaned against me as though I were her father, and when I brushed my hand against my chest later, I felt what must have been her tears there, wetting the wool.

SIX

Lelia

I woke just before the dustbin vans arrived. My heart was racing. The front of my nightie was damp against my chest, as though I had sweated off a fever. Richard was snoring beside me like a Cornish hog, and in the silence between his breaths, the clang of metal rang up from the street.

I jumped.

'Sweetheart,' he murmured, turning. His breath snagged in a final snort. We embraced. I was safe there, in a dark and sweaty hollow. At times like that I thought life was simple: that having a person of your own, holding you, was the very best thing in the world.

'What is it?' he said.

'It was a nightmare,' I said.

He grunted. He stroked my head.

'The one I've had before.'

'The Finals one? Oh, my bluestocking.'

'Not that. No,' I said.

The Finals dream – examination halls slipping from their known location; coursework neglected, its very existence forgotten about and recalled in panic – had, to my amazement, revealed itself to be a common curse that wormed its way through the nights of even long-retired academics. The other recurring dream appeared less frequently and was less definable.

It had to do with sex. I had dreamt it before and woken disturbed with fear, yet wet with desire. It had to do with when I was a child. The dream was about children, and the children were rubbing each other, mounting and murmuring and rustling in another room, far away from me. But sometimes the focus changed with a fish-eye swivel and the dream-screen came closer so that I was one of those children, and there was another child moving on top of me. The child took on a sexless appearance, like a doll with its nub of a plastic crotch, mechanically rubbing as the heat grew inside me. I knew who it was. I could barely think about it. I wanted to be safe. I wanted to be pregnant and safe from myself.

I tried to pull my nightie up, to feel for proof without Richard noticing it.

'Hands off!' he said, and snatched my fingers and smelled them, then kissed the tips. 'My territory.'

I pressed harder against him. The desire was heavy with guilt.

'Well, something's given you the hots. Come on. You're only allowed to be unfaithful in your dreams if you tell me. What did you think about in your lovely lunatic's head?'

'Nothing,' I said. 'Nothing.'

Because I couldn't tell him. That recurring nightmare was rooted in France, where I had started to understand desire, but its sexual edge was repulsive to me because the time was linked with death. My father had just died. I could never talk about him, even in adulthood. I loved him more than anything in my life. There were things I didn't want to remember because of him, because of the grief, but they came to me in the night, and now perhaps they were

47

returning to my life as well. I found, as the years went by, that I withheld as much from myself as I withheld from Richard or my mother, burrowing further from the truth in fear.

'Talk to me,' said Richard.

I buried my face in his neck, and my mouth opened against his skin, wet and hopeless.

'Cleopatra,' he said, urging me in his characteristically irreverent manner to talk. One of his favourite lumbering jokes was to call me Cleopatra, Queen of De Nile.

My childhood was uneventful until I went to France, or at least innocent, innocent of sex, of death, of knowledge beyond the North London suburbs and the hidden little-good-girl existence that I led out there. I must have been an exemplary daughter once, working hard to make my parents proud, and loving them with a ferocious love squeezed from the terror of their future deaths or divorce or dis-appointment in me, but I hadn't realised it. We were a unit, with me as their difficult and affectionate cement.

'I'll look after you,' said Richard. 'You know I will. Mad bad loveling.'

I winced. 'Am I bad?' I said into his neck.

Richard laughed. He pulled my head away and looked at me and kissed me. 'You're so *good*,' he said, seriously. 'So good I can never hope to match up to you.'

'I'm not.'

'You are, my love. Except when you fart and pretend it's not you.'

'You hypocrite.'

I had gone to France – French exchange, Easter, Clemenceau-sur-Loire – in a state of sorrow. It was two and a half weeks after my father had died. My mother shouldn't have let me go: she should have kept me at home and arranged bereavement counselling for me and noticed that her adolescent daughter was poisoned with grief, but she would never have done so, and would never have known.

I had scrubbed myself a little harder there: there were no Indian girls in the Loire Valley. Up in the metal tubby bath in the house on the edge of Clemenceau-sur-Loire, I rubbed my skin red with soap as I read Pagnol, Colette, Sagan, all those authors of adolescence, and smelled the bad plumbing, and watched my lust tangle with sorrow until it felt as though it would strangle me. There were not even quarter-Indians there: *quadroons*, I thought. There were pale women with spectacles; asses; prostitute-looking teenagers in market clothes; Algerian undesirables on the route to Paris. I could peer through the gaps in my curlicue shutters, and believe that with soap and loofah I could make myself a little paler by scratching yellow lines into my arms and chest and neck. Two children made love in a room close by at the top of the house.

He stretched, moving the duvet. The air chilled my nightie. 'Lelia.'

'I'll think about it when I wake,' I said, purposely yawning, burrowing into his stomach.

'OK, my darling.' He stroked my hair. 'But I have to get to work early,' he said in a low voice.

'I have to sleep,' I said, tiredness tugging me back already. 'My seminar's not till half-two.' I pulled my knees up, almost to my chin.

'Kiss me goodbye now,' he said.

I caught the edge of his chin with a kiss. I slept.

When I woke, he had gone. I hoped that he hadn't left imagining that I was in a mood: my supposed moodiness, which was only the unfortunate expression of my own anxiety, maddened him beyond anything else.

I took a pregnancy test out of the packet, though it was a day early, and peed on the stick. You had to wait for two minutes. Within seconds, a blue line had leapt into the second panel.

I sat on the loo with my head in my hands, and my future life spooled before me, just as they say the past spins by the dying.

I had a superstitious conviction that this pregnancy would last. Fear raced beneath the certainty, running black and fast, as though I stood on a bridge and glimpsed a dark mill-stream just below before I turned. My heart thumping, I phoned Richard at work. He was in conference. I left no message and sat still on the bed. My arm felt weak, still extended and holding the phone, a vein twitching under the skin. I stood on the mattress, stretching upwards to view my stomach in the mirror, and as I lowered my body again, a gurgle of a laugh escaped from me, a disturbed-sounding 'Yahey'. I had to tell someone. I was meant to be marking some essays, but I put on my new, much-loved dusty-rose coloured coat and I walked towards my doctor's on Great Russell Street, where I reported my pregnancy and the practice nurse offered her congratulations. I wanted my temperature to be taken by my kind Australian GP, who would offer brisk advice while understanding my own excitement, but she was busy. I walked up the stairs. I wished I could launch myself into Richard's arms. Coming out on to the street, I bumped into Sylvie.

'Oh!' I said.

'Oh, you!' she said. Her smile caught her eyes and made her radiant. 'You look beautiful today.'

I smiled back at her, as though she already knew my secret. Excitement pushed me. I tried to stop myself.

'I'm pregnant!' I said in a rush. My voice rose.

'I know,' she said. We laughed at each other nervously, almost embracing, then hesitating too long. Hug me, I thought. That's what you're supposed to do.

'A baby . . .' she said. 'Oh, congratulations!' She hugged me.

A bus boomed past.

'Thank you,' I said. Even among the traffic fumes, I absorbed her smell of expensive soap, of clean hair. 'But how do you know?'

'Because you were like a child, almost fainting with exhaustion.'

'Oh − yes.'

'It's that intense tiredness. I've noticed it before when women conceive. I can recognise it.'

I could hear Richard's voice in my head: 'Mumbo fucking jumbo, sweetheart.'

'There are tiny clues,' she said. 'Nothing more.' She glanced at my body.

I touched my neck. My breasts were sore, already slightly enlarged.

'What am I doing telling you?' I said, suddenly breathless. The sky was bright and rinsed above the museum. Christmas was very clearly past. 'I wasn't − I wasn't safe before. I was only going to tell my mother, and one friend. Only the doctor's nurse knows so far.'

'Not Richard?'

'Not even Richard!'

'Oh!' said Sylvie, and she sounded pleased. 'Let's go to a café. Let's celebrate.' She looked at her watch. Her nails were perfectly shaped ovals.

I thought of the empty flat; I pictured my attempts to read strained undergraduate arguments while new life bubbled inside me.

'OK,' I said.

'They're all for *tourists*,' she said, turning up her nose as we walked down Museum Street so that I laughed. The shopkeepers still washed the pavements. 'This one's OK-ish, though,' she said, guiding me into a café displaying Italian crockery. She wore a fitted white shirt with large lapels, and a dark grey skirt, and I suspected again that her dull, muted clothes were in fact expensive and carefully chosen after all, since every aspect of her was so ordered and precise. She reminded me of a little French nun on a day out.

'I'm pregnant!' I said in an amazed whisper as we sat down.

'Are you happy?' asked Sylvie.

'I'm happy at this very moment,' I said. I considered the surprising truth of this statement. The sun came into the room and landed on a yellow bowl. I saw the human brushstrokes on its glaze melt into sun fluid.

'Good,' she said, and smiled, and the sun caught her skin too, making it so pale and clear that she looked like a breathing spirit, the minute pigmentation of her skin flaring to life. Her eyes in that strong light were not the nondescript hazel I had half absorbed, but a kind of bright brown, almost golden, with aspects of green.

'Perhaps I'll even know contentment when I'm very pregnant and as dozy as a cow.'

She laughed slightly. 'I'd have loved a mother like you,' she said with her disconcerting directness.

'*Would* you?' I flinched, feeling myself blush.

'Oh yes,' she said, casting her eye down the menu so that her hair stroked her brow. 'You'll love that baby, won't you?'

'Yes,' I said. I do, I thought. I do already.

She traced a pattern on the paper tablecloth with her fingertip, that delicate oval skimming the surface. 'You'll

52

always love it. However much you think you love Richard, you'll love this even more. It'll be the great joy in your life.'

Her head was bent, following the pattern, and her hair fell forward, obscuring her face, though most of it was hooked behind her ears in the classic manner of square girls. She looked young and grave. I watched her ringless fingers tracing their pattern, the sunlight washing her naked skin, and again, I wanted to dress her. Not to make of her something that she wasn't, but to dress her as a mother dresses her child, to make her warm and pretty. I almost wanted to take her on to my lap, but the impulse was absurd, and made me quiver with unwanted strands of sexual quickening, as though remnants of my nightmare stayed with me. I felt the remembered pressure of a body, heavy on my pubic bone, and instantly wanted to wipe away the image.

'I will,' I said. 'But surely . . . any mother would. Someone has loved you too.'

She breathed through her nose with a small laugh of denial.

'But you must have been loved,' I said, embarrassed. 'A parent would have been proud of you,' I said. 'And seen all your sensitivity and intelligence, and—'

'No,' she said simply.

'Oh well, I—'

'It's all right,' she said, and she looked up at me then, her gaze catching mine, resting upon me intensely for a few moments so that I had to smile in the face of her focus, her chin still semi-inclined towards the table until the angle made her eyes large and tilted. I knew who it was she reminded me of. I remembered *The Lover*. I thought of the photograph used on the cover – that bewitching little doll photograph, eyes bruise-shadowed through fading sepia, mouth impassive. A face that said *hit me, worship me*. The young Marguerite

53

Duras. I used to read her all the time when I was a girl. I always thought that reading her work early had made me want to study French literature, and later, the *nouveau roman*.

'It's strange,' I said, 'I think you might look like Marguerite Duras. It makes you look familiar to me.'

'*Le Ravissement de Lol V. Stein*,' she said in a rapid French accent. '*L'Amant*. "I have a face laid to waste." I read *L'Amant de la Chine du Nord* recently.'

I smiled.

'You know me through French literature, then,' she said. 'A face on a book. I know you more than that.' She glanced at the table, her face, so marble and even, now faintly colouring under the scrutiny of the winter sunlight. Her mouth was quite beautiful. 'Don't you think?'

Heat hit my face. I hesitated. 'Do you?' I said.

'I think so.'

I said nothing. My heartbeat began to speed. I wanted to break the awkwardness of the pause.

'I feel – I feel as though you *know* me and I know you,' she said.

She was silent.

'I knew you were pregnant, didn't I?'

'I suppose so. My – boyfriend didn't seem to realise, though. I want to *tell* him.'

'Let's go now then,' she said decisively, and out on the street, she held my arm, or I held hers, as though I was already eight months pregnant, and we walked, her arm crooked slenderly in mine, all the way home.

As I looked up at the bedroom window, where the glass blankly reflected the light, I remembered the old nightmare. A sharp shudder went through me. I started feeling breathless, the recollection of a choking, rubbing sensation merging with a suspicion that I might imminently vomit. Yet beneath the panic, that nightmare thread of sexual arousal stirred again. The juxtaposition sickened me. I began to feel light-headed. I wanted to get away from her.

'Goodbye,' I said to her in a rush as saliva filled my mouth, and I ran upstairs and vomited before I could reach the sink.

SEVEN

Richard

MacDara rang me at work.

'Something's happened,' he said.

'What?' I said.

He began to rap out instructions to someone in his office, as he tended to do, a different MacDara from the one I knew; I could picture him there a mile or so to the east of me, stubbled or sporting shaving nicks, his tie loosened. Bulls and bears, I thought, imagining MacDara in his high glass building in the City. MacDara was both, I thought: a bullish bear, growling and messing around.

'Can we meet after work?' he said.

'Yes,' I said. 'A quick one.'

'Yeah, whatever.'

'What have you done, you berk?'

'Nothing.'

'Really?'

'I'm in an open fucking plan office, Fearon.'

'Get off the bloody blower,' I said. 'I'll see you about seven.'

I put down the phone and looked at my diary. I glanced at the clock on my computer. The mousy girl was a little late for lunch. I was surprised. I didn't really want to go out. We were having too much fun in the office that day, emailing round a developing pornographic story starring our much-loathed deputy features editor. Suppressed sniggers could be heard intermittently emerging from behind monitors. My best features friend Sophie and I were privately sending each other our own more obscene additions, and I had a whole special American issue to plan with my editor.

The receptionist rang to say that Sylvie had arrived. I reluctantly left my desk.

Where had this woman come from, I wondered, catching sight of the back of her coat? I didn't really know. Ren? I thought of him and smiled. Trust Ren to cultivate a black sheep. Of course, Ren and his wife Vicky would want to help her, the way they embraced any number of oddities and strays – Albanian students, impoverished artists of a vaguely dissident nature, friends of distant cousins studying in London, and, quite frankly, terrible bores. Out of the kindness of his heart, a lack of social snobbery, and a sense of gratitude to a country in which he had found marriage, employment and happiness, dear Ren, the champion of the underdog, threw dinner parties featuring much broken English and smiling formality. Sylvie would have come in on the back of some outsider, some flatmate or foreign language student, and been unquestioningly accepted by Ren and his wife.

She had been waylaid, and had had tea with someone, Sylvie said. I was mildly put out. We went to the predictable gastro pub round the corner, everything char-grilled and seared under a tent of noise.

She had never been so reticent. She seemed like a naïve girl, restrained by her own pride. She was private, chilly and entirely diffident. She hardly ate; she rarely talked; I could barely hear her voice. I tried to get her to share my wine to loosen her up, but she took a couple of sips and left it.

I glanced at the clock. Very nearly an hour had passed. All goodwill was finally subsumed by irritation. 'OK,' I said. 'Sorry, but I'd better scarper. I've got a meeting.'

She turned to me. She paused.

'Nice to see you. Sorry it's so short, but I've really got to go.'

'The office,' she said.

'Sorry?'

'I mean . . . I think you've forgotten why we were going to meet. I was going to take away some books, wasn't I?'

'Books. Yes. Books. Those things. Shit! I forgot.'

'I'd much rather have books than lunch.'

'You were going to clear some of the toppling piles, weren't you? God, I'm really sorry. Today's almost impossible—'

I glanced at her. She said nothing.

I paused.

'Yes,' I said. 'I'm so sorry. Come quickly. Let's go now, if you can rifle through them before my meeting.'

'Yes,' she said. 'Of course.'

I spoke to a publicist while she knelt on the office floor and sifted through the piles of hardbacks as though she were a long-experienced secretary, checking the press releases, rejecting titles at a glance.

'Take all those,' I said, glancing at her modest selection. I put the phone down. 'That one, though. What's the publication date?'

She paused. 'February the sixteenth,' she said.

'There's still time to do it. Oh, but fuck it. Take it. I don't need to review the old biddy anyway.'

'Oh, but she's − extraordinary,' said Sylvie.

'Is she? No one reads her.'

'I do.'

'Do you?'

'All of her. Every single one. From the fifties onwards. The essays too.'

'Really?' I said, frowning. 'How surprising. Take it, anyway. Hang on. Is she really that good? I've only read – what? – a bit of the famous stuff.'

'Exceptional,' she said quietly.

'Do me a short review while you're at it, then,' I said in a cavalier fashion. I heard myself, and stopped. My stupid words rang in my ears. I tried to backtrack. 'Well, maybe that's pushing it—'

There was silence. I glanced at her; she knelt there, her lips slightly parted. There was further silence.

'Do me a tiny review,' I said then, to fill the aching pause. 'Just – three hundred words or so.'

The faintest smile seemed to illuminate her face.

'Could I?' she said.

'Of course you could,' I said, because there was nothing else to say.

After work, I met MacDara in the gastro pub, now full of shouting people propping themselves up to drink Salice Salentino and dramatise the events of their working day. I had a headache. I wanted to go home, but MacDara was like a remnant of my old life, bearing arrows of freedom, little feathery tokens of liberation, and it seemed as though, when our conversations reached a certain burbling, over-lapping pitch, we could throw everything down and go off white-water rafting, or propel ourselves from some mountain, cinema ad style, trailing plumes of snow as we span through a saturated blue sky. Lelia's spirit was more home-bound.

'Something stupid's happening,' he shouted into my ear, as we sat at a rickety table in the corner and bolted down salted almonds.

'What is it?' I said.

'Get me a drink,' he said. 'I need a drink. It's so bloody noisy in here.'

Obediently, I queued for drinks. Colleagues drifted up to the bar, and we leaned over for snatched conversations. It was interesting catching up with the news desk. The impression of Sylvie, sitting in this very room mere hours before, had disappeared: it seemed impossible that even her ghost presence had been here before it melted. Solid MacDara, successful yet rebellious son of Italian-Scottish café workers, sat in her place, as substantial as she was subtle.

'Here,' I said. 'Tell me, then.'

'You need a megaphone in this place to impart a bloody secret,' he bellowed.

'Shut up. Shout into my ear.'

'I think I'm about to have an affair.'

'No!' I said. Horror, amazement and unexpected beads of delight bubbled through me in staggered sequence.

He said nothing. He looked slightly grim, his stubble-shadowed jaw set, as though he were a disappointed parent. I thought of Catrin sitting at their home, self-contained and womanly, with her smooth fair skin and her unruffled love for boisterous MacDara.

'You're not!'

'I really think so,' he said. 'I don't know how . . .'

'Yes?'

'How I can't. Can not, I mean.'

'God.'

He said nothing.

'MacDara.'

'Yes, I know.'

'Who is it? It's that – whatdyamacallit. That glammy old bitch you work with, isn't it?'

'Hell, no. That's just a silly flirting thing. Nothing.'

'And this one isn't? Who is it, then?'

'No one.'

'Right. Thin air. No one. Who?'

He began to shake his head.

'No one I know, you mean?'

He nodded.

'How did you meet her?'

'Oh Jesus, usual way, friend of a friend of a friend or something. Don't ask me about her. If I don't tell you, then you can't accidentally tell Catrin.'

'Like I fucking would! "Oh, Catrin, yes, yes, fine, thank you. MacDara's having an affair with this woman. Dark, curvy, name of – blah."'

'Don't,' he groaned.

I pictured Catrin's reaction. She had already suffered a tangle with alcoholism and a broken marriage, yet she seemed calm, almost motherly in her composure. She was one of those Celtic chicks whose colouring always got to me a bit, with her white skin and her contrasting dark hair so long it reached her bum. Somehow, I could imagine infidelity tipping her back into her former, less tranquil ways.

'Have you never, in all this time?' I said. 'I can't remember now. You did though, you rutting old goat.'

'*Once*,' he hissed. 'One fuck, once. Never saw her again. Eight *years*, and that's it. I don't want to do this. Complete bloody madness.'

'So what are you going to do?'

'Try not to.'

'But you will, won't you? You randy bastard.'

He shook his head. Wine stuck to the stubble on his upper lip.

'How do you manage to see her?' I said.

'I don't, very much. It's all quite recent. You know – we talk. Phone calls and stuff. She's got me by the bloody balls. I swear, I swear. I want to stop it right now.'

'Well, perhaps,' I said, and a cough stuck in my throat, 'you'd better.'

'I can't,' he said, shaking his head. 'Make me,' he begged, turning to me, his eyes drooping like an ageing dog's.

I laughed. 'I'll try,' I said. I took a gulp of wine. 'But it would be so much more interesting for *me* if you did. I could hear all about it, and stay smug and safe. I'd like daily instalments.'

'You complete prick,' he said.

'Look, we'll do a twelve-step programme, then,' I said. 'One day at a time. Don't contact her tomorrow, and report to me by the end of the day with your progress. I'll go all draconian on you. That should turn you on enough, since you're a bit of a perv, and then you can maintain your conscience, marriage, social standing, etc., etc.'

He smiled slightly. He stopped. 'I – it's really serious. I don't know what to do,' he said, his mouth slack. 'I know I'm going to – whatever. Fall. Fuck. *Yes!* Oh Christ. And I shouldn't. You know, apart from Catrin I mean, she's got responsibilities—'

'Children?'

MacDara put his head in his hands and didn't look at me.

'MacDara?' I said.

He said nothing.

'She's married, isn't she?'

He nodded almost imperceptibly. 'She's got me by the balls,' he said in a muffled voice.

'Sounds bad,' I said, and began to laugh, unable to stop myself.

'It's monstrous,' he said, and started to laugh as well.

'Report to me tomorrow. What will her name be, then? Madame X?'

He gazed into the distance. He nudged an almond across the table. 'No. Not that,' he said.

'Mystery Woman, then,' I said. 'She can be MW. You look like a bloodhound.'

He smiled. 'OK,' he said. 'But office email only – both of us. For God's sake.'

'Oh, I'd thought Globals, to be sent to Catrin, Lelia, your boss, your sister, your neighbours, etc. Calm down, MacDara. First report tomorrow.'

I cut through Laystall Street and along Mount Pleasant, the Art Deco gleam of the post office floating in the cold. The day had been furred with sun; now, in the eight o'clock darkness, the cold rang and tightened and smelled of iron, my breath steaming all around me, and I was excited. I was gripped, as though by a soap opera. Pity for Catrin was uncharitably submerged by pleasure in drama. I didn't even envy MacDara, as I once would have done; I felt sorry for him, and amused, and unhealthily engaged by his predicament. Lights burned in windows along Gray's Inn Road. I walked faster, perversely inspired by MacDara's unwise dilemma so that I had a sense of life being good, of events about to happen.

I ran up the stairs at Mecklenburgh Square, my lungs hurting with crystals of air, and I hugged Lelia in an enve-lope of coat-trapped coldness like a blast of snow. We fell on the sofa together, and I jerked her further up my legs so that she was sitting on my lap, and she nuzzled my cheek from above. Her neck smelled of bath oil and deeper tones of warmth and skin: the Lelia smell. I breathed it in.

'I'm pregnant,' she said.

I fell from a high wall, tumbling through trees, tearing leaves, sky, snapshots of my life.

'Are you sure?' I said sharply. I heard it as I said it: my automatic and inappropriate response. 'I mean—'

It was too late. A film of tears sprang to her eyes and she turned away from me.

'Yes. *I'm sure,*' she said with horrible slowness.

There was nothing I could do when she used that voice. 'Oh, Lelia!' I said. I kissed her, all over her neck, over her cheek, feeling like a slobbering hound as she sat there stiffly, refusing to turn to me. 'Oh, darling,' I said. 'Oh, that's – oh, well done, you're so clever, you're so beautiful. Our baby!'

I wanted the moment to stop. I wanted to shake time and jolt myself back several minutes in my life. Surely it was possible? Laughably simple, even? To return to the navy frozen air and the traffic rumbling past, and me, speeding back with cigarette smoke in my hair and the taste of Salice Salentino somewhere in my mouth, and my great friend on the verge of an interesting mistake, and a book to write, and a girlfriend to love. Me and her. The flat in Bloomsbury. The last remnants of our youth. Was this it, then?

Rapids, I thought uselessly. The *rapids.* I had never been white-water rafting. As a boy who had sailed, I had always, always wondered what it would feel like to raft over tumbling white rapids. Just as, when the seasons changed in Mecklenburgh Square, the smell of earth and leaves made me want to flee, eat earth, mount a tree, do anything but sit in London and watch my life dribble away.

'I thought you'd be pleased,' she said. She sat, an unmoving weight on my lap.

'I am!' I said, but my words emerged sounding stiff and stretched. I tried again. I stopped. My voice wouldn't work properly.

'I was longing – I was longing to phone you. But then I put it off, because I wasn't quite sure. I had this horrible feeling. This horrible – feeling you wouldn't be pleased after all.'

'Oh but I am, I am!' I said desperately. 'I love you. Please, darling, look at me.'

I imagined myself. A dad in a jersey. A messy, stooping old fool making an idiot out of himself for comic effect and sent off to mend the broken bicycles while his wife phoned her friends about the PTA. I felt sick. I was angry, at myself or the world. I still felt as though we'd all only just finished our A levels, and were playing at having our own homes and might, with time, become fabulously successful. Another part of me felt weary and worldly-wise.

Lelia kept her head turned away from me. I tried to stroke her cheek, to pull her face around, but the attempt felt brutal as I pushed against her stiffness. I stopped. She turned her head. Tears had spread over her cheeks.

'Oh, darling!' I said. I was shocked. I pulled her face down towards mine and kissed the side of her mouth, her ear, and nuzzled her, her wet skin coating my hair and creating new friction there. 'Darling, please! I love you. Well done, well done. What can I say? I'm so pleased.'

'You're not,' she said.

'I'm just, I'm just taken aback. And – what happened to you before.'

'This feels different. Let's just hope.'

'I wasn't expecting it, that's all. I didn't realise.'

'I told you. I warned you.'

'Yes, I know, but I didn't really think. I didn't quite

believe, I suppose. How are you feeling? Are you – are you thrilled?'

'Yes,' she said in a little voice, and I pulled her to me, and as she bent her head against my neck, I felt the strange, unaccustomed feeling of tears in my own eyes. I dropped my coat on the floor, and we went and lay in bed, and talked and held each other very hard until we both fell asleep at nine o'clock. In the night, we woke, and extravagantly ordered Chinese takeaway that didn't arrive till almost one, and ate it in bed.

'I'm sorry, I'm sorry,' I said, our conversation eased by darkness and forgiveness now seeping into the bed. 'Of course I'm pleased. I just – oh, Lelia, I can hardly imagine it. A baby of ours!'

'*You* and *me*,' she said. 'If it – if it happens. It's us. Us whisked together, and then someone else again. I love you. Look after me.'

'Of course I will,' I said, pity plummeting through me. I put my arms around her shoulders. I stroked her stomach.

'Don't,' she said.

I bit back annoyance. I kissed her head instead. 'I'm sorry,' I said again. 'I'm so sorry this wasn't – how you expected. I'd do bloody anything for love of you.'

We fell asleep in a sticky, sweaty mess. Later, a snort jolted through me and woke me as I shifted, mid-snore. The moon was large, and I could see Lelia quite easily lying there, her nightdress glowing under the transparent dark blue of the sky. She lay very still, a little twisted in her light cotton, breathing peacefully, and I gazed at her with both a sense of awe and a secret thread of distaste that flickered through me as I realised that she was the repository of a new life. A life composed of us. New limbs. New webby, yolky sacs and weavings, new beatings and flutterings as the creature calmly created its underwater life. It could have freak limb stumps, or an animal body: there was a little alien, lying inside my bride Lelia. A police helicopter thrummed across the sky. Go away, go away, I thought. Don't wake her. And I knew even then that I would protect her and the little thing she carried inside her with my life. She murmured in her sleep. I leaned forward and breathed in her breath, already warm and human with night saliva.

I barely slept, and woke later with the granular hangover of extreme tiredness. She – they – were already up.

I knew, I knew with all certainty that my mother was with child before the servants did. I knew it before my father was told. After the stillbirths and infant deaths that had followed my coming and granted me a merciful gap of some years, she was filled once more with a child. Where there was once a grille in front of her eyes when she looked at me, there was now a prison door.

There was a sole companion: a friend. Emilia. I clung to her ever harder. But the next threat that came then made me weep. It nearly unravelled me. A new friend of Emilia's was visiting her house: a little Hindoo, freshly orphaned, neat as a stuffed squirrel in her alpaca petticoats, yet wild.

'Oh, for God's sake,' I said. I couldn't even finish the email. I pressed the *Delete* button and grabbed more coffee before I went to work. I had a headache. I didn't want any more talk of pregnancy, and I didn't want more weird gobbets of fiction. I wished the nutter would dump it on someone else. I addressed an email to MacDara, and wrote, *Well?*

Office computer only, he wrote back instantly.

It's only me who uses this address, I replied.

She called, he wrote.

'Richard!' Lelia shouted.

I deleted MacDara's message and went offline. 'Sweetheart! I thought you'd gone,' I called.

'My first student's cancelled. Not till eleven.'

'How are you feeling?' I said. I went into the main room and put my arm around her.

'OK,' she said, looking up at me with a flicker of a glance. 'Are you?'

'I'm sorry. I – I was just feeling super-sensitive last night. You know how – mad I get.'

'God, no. *I'm* sorry. It all came out wrong.'

'Did it?'

'*Yes*. You know when you can't, just can't say what you're feeling. It was impossible. I'm like a blundering beast. I'll kill myself if you want. I love you. You're pregnant! How are you?'

'Oh, Richard!' she said.

'Are you OK?'

'I'm OK. I feel fine. I don't feel sick or anything.'

'Good. I'd better make you – some posset or something, though.'

'No! You madman.'

'Come on. Curdled – curds?'

'Oh, Richard, *please*. I will start feeling sick in a minute.'

'Hot milk grated with nutmeg and honey? Good baby food. Freshly squeezed, er, Seville orange juice?'

'Tea.'

'I'll get you tea.'

Dumped Christmas trees lay on pavement corners on the way to the office. Most people were in by the time I got there. I felt drained, as though we had spent the night drinking. The first trolley was already going round. I grabbed coffee, a muffin: things other people bought that I usually spurned. The reassurance of colleagues talking on the phone and an interview to commission made me feel normal again. The absurdities of office life entertained me immensely: an unwanted, seven-foot, inflatable purple palm tree sent by a PR had been propped up by a photocopier since the summer, inspiring jokers from the travel desk to place its accompanying pink coconuts on editors' chairs. I loved my job with a grudging and inconsistent passion, despite my complaints about restricted writing time. I sometimes made myself perceive with a sense of amazement that I, the scruffy boy from Cornwall with his half-baked bohemian upbringing and state schooling, was sitting in the offices of a national newspaper. The rest of the time, I cheerfully grumbled along with everyone else and suffered from the inevitable terrifying pressures and crass editorial decisions.

There were several messages from MacDara. I grinned. *Where are you?* he said. I opened his subsequent messages. *I'm resisting. Call me back. Where are you, you fucker? Stop press: MW's suddenly coming on strong.* I laughed, immensely cheered, and suddenly less tired. MacDara's imminent affair, the tone of his messages, all seemed childish and somehow vastly amusing, reminding me of notes passed on torn-off pieces of jotter at school.

Get a life, I emailed back.

Fuck you, he answered.

I punched through some other messages. There was an address I didn't recognise. It was an email from Sylvie, containing her review.

'*Shit*,' I muttered. I had forgotten all about it. I reflected momentarily on what I had done. I had never in my life seen fit to commission a review from an amateur. It was only tiny, I reminded myself hastily. I could simply spike it, blame it on space, apologise, and pay her a kill fee. I delayed looking at it. It bothered me. I winced, and opened the attachment.

Several hundred words appeared on my screen. I emitted a muttered groan. I read the first two sentences. They were good. It occurred to me that she had got someone else to write the review. I snorted. While meaning to stop, I read further. The prose was animated, persuasive and eloquent, qualities almost entirely lacking in its putative creator. The piece was untamed, its elegance edged with excess, but it was compelling, and almost affrontingly erudite in its references. Some old hag who had passed me by was presented as a major rediscovery whose tenets chimed thrillingly with the zeitgeist. A passing reference to Iris Murdoch made me smile: I read it again, and saw that it had been designed to make me smile. I hesitated. Was my own judgement slipping? I checked my schedule. I could get it cut by a couple of hundred words, tidy it up, and run it in mid-February. I made a note.

I turned to a more recent paperback round-up. My mind drifted back to Sylvie's review. I pulled down her email. *Sylvie Lavigne*, it said. The name somehow suited her. I replied to her with a tone of cautious encouragement. Another thought struck me. She must have written her review yesterday afternoon, or during the night. She was a faster worker than I was. *PS*, I wrote, somewhat rudely, *I'd never have guessed this was written by you. Do you employ a ghost writer?*

I called Lelia. I always rang her a couple of times a day from the office anyway. It was only as the phone was ringing that I remembered I had to ask her about the baby, and I swallowed a stab of panic, followed by guilt. My own blankness surprised me. I had considered myself an over-emotional type: a hormone-ridden male, prag-matic, yet given to bouts of tortuous analysis and regret. Perhaps there was a monster in me after all, a hard and inhuman beast that I had merely suppressed. The phone rang a few more times. She answered. I softened at her voice. 'I was having a bath,' she said.

An email appeared in my inbox. It was from Sylvie Lavigne.

A message from MacDara appeared while I was reading. *I haven't contacted her all day*, he wrote. *It's fucking killing me. Tell me what to do. Give me some bribe. An alternative.*

A prostitute? I wrote.

But she's fucking with my mind, replied MacDara. *Find me a solution to that. She's* married – *as good as. Find me a solution to that.*

One day at a time, MacD, I wrote. *Cold turkey today. Might allow one phone call tomorrow. Report to me first thing in the morning.*

I smiled. My heartbeat speeded momentarily as once again I experienced a sadistic surge of interest in MacDara's predicament.

I pressed *Reply* on Sylvie's message. *On the contrary*, I wrote. *Thank you.*

Lelia rang. I saw the number on my phone screen. 'Love line,' I answered.

Her voice thickened with a return smile. 'I want to go to John Lewis,' she said. 'It's late-night opening.'

'Do you? Is it?'

'Yes.'

'There's nothing I'd like less,' I said cheerfully.

'Oh no, I know,' she said, half laughing. 'I know. It's going to bore you stupid. But I'm going mad here. I want to have a scan, or tell everyone, but I can't. Oh, Richard, I really, really want to go and just *buy* something, just a tiny token that's not tempting fate too much. Come with me. Or shall I go on my own?'

'Of course I'll come,' I said, my evening already written off. A couple of big bound proofs had come in I really needed to read. I found I was gazing at the duck-egg coloured partition that separated me from the film editor. Over in the smoking room, where the best conversations always took place, a lively discussion was under way, the volume so raised that it was audible across the desks.

Sylvie Lavigne's name came up again in my inbox.

Oxford Street was woven with the breath of evening shoppers in the dark blue air. I put my hand lightly on Lelia's back, guiding her through the crowds as though protecting a glass vessel that contained a child. She looked elegant and somehow interestingly dressed. The store was strip-lit with a flat glare: it felt as though we were in a warehouse, or a shop from another era: Marks & Spencer in the late fifties. By the time we had taken several escalators to reach the baby department, we were in a different land: glaucous and queasy, an echoing hall of devices and disturbing ointments that made me feel as though I had been herded into a dairy farm. Even Lelia seemed temporarily taken aback. I wondered whether she was remembering her miscarriages. I put my hand on her arm.

I looked around with something approaching revulsion. Breast pumps and other inexplicable gadgets that looked vaguely designed for physical torture sat on shelves below an array of objects with straps and checked torsos, hanging butcherishly from hooks. After the cold of the street, the heat in there was overwhelming, our coats already like felty encumbrances.

'Oh!' said Lelia. 'Look at all this *stuff*.'

'But this is a place of horror,' I burst out.

'But – oh, Richard. For God's sake! That's worthy of MacDara. If you don't like it, go and sit in the café, you great wimp.'

'Sorry,' I said. 'Well, look at it though.'

'Should I buy things yet?' said Lelia.

'Er,' I said, surfacing. 'Yes.'

I thought about my mother. When Rachel and I were five and four, she had given birth to a baby followed by two others in quick succession. I had vague and unpleasant memories of nappies and shit in buckets of disinfectant, of boring sibling supervisory tasks, and ceaseless baby screeching. Somehow she had coped, despite my father's lengthy absences in his studio or in the outhouse where he made the complex wooden boxes which later became his passion but rarely sold.

By the time Clodagh, the youngest, was a toddler, we could drag one another as a warring gang through our unstructured days, free-range but maternally adored. We were packed into a series of old cars, wedged on laps and stuffed into the luggage space with neighbours' children, and driven to a haphazard collection of outlying schools where Rachel and I, self-motivated as we were, and then encouraged by our reasonably erudite father, took to our books, while the others drank snakebites and learned new guitar chords. Rachel and I left home the moment we finished school, our mud-splattered souls aching for urban excitements and broader horizons. Both enchanted and dispirited by the life I found in London, I felt happy to have escaped the rabble, though I stayed in constant contact with my mother. Babies had never since impinged on my consciousness: even recently, even now, with a broody girlfriend and a lackadaisical approach towards contraception. Fool that I was.

★

I looked around the department. Women with fascinatingly vast bumps sailed past me with the oblivion and authority of sea-going ships. Others carried their babies on their stomachs in those same cloth torsos. The infants, fairly uniform, pudgy-cheeked creatures with a scrawl of geriatric hair, were mostly asleep. A few squalled unpleasantly. I watched a mother looking down at her offspring with an expression of glazed pride. She appeared stupefied, and somehow she was repugnant in her own subjective world, so stunned and focused, it was as though I had caught her masturbating. I realised suddenly that every single mother here considered their own child was the *best*. As simple as that. The very *best*. On whatever warped and hormonal scale they measured the brats' unguessable qualifications, they were all under the blissful illusion that their little sack of breathing life was superior.

Prams, apparently called 'buggies', sat in a bewildering array. I simply could not imagine how I would summon even a show of the required interest. The concept made me feel weary. Lelia was kneeling down and fingering some clothes with pastel edging, hesitating. I grabbed the packet from her and tossed it into her basket.

'Get them,' I said.

I saw the back of a head – dark brown hair cut to the shoulders, a slight back, a familiar posture – and I had the strange sensation that I was in a dream, or that danger was imminent. It can't be her, it can't be that woman again, I thought, but I knew that it was. She was there with another woman. I said nothing. I was embarrassed that I had been in contact with her after teasing Lelia about her square friends; I was even more embarrassed that I had somehow commissioned a review from her. I looked away. I felt nervous in the face of my odd, unnecessary subterfuge. I began to

74

think about how I could tell Lelia right now that I had seen her and commissioned her.

'I – what else?' I said.

'Well . . .' said Lelia. 'We shouldn't get too much.'

'Why not?' I said vaguely, staring in shock at a box of objects called nipple guards, and some vast vats of nappy cream. Were these things really necessary, or there to fool defenceless mothers into spending money? I felt queasy again.

'Superstition. I must just *look* at the buggies,' said Lelia.

'You go and look,' I said. 'I'll just look at these – um, baby baths. We need one probably, don't we?'

'I think you can just bath them in the washing-up bowl. But I don't really know. Maybe you should check out the muslins. See you in a minute.'

'What's a muslin?' I murmured.

I wandered, dazed, around the corner. I considered having a quick read of the newspaper, but I feared she might catch me and be cross; or, worse still in the case of Lelia, hurt. I couldn't stand the idea of her irritating wounded expression.

Sylvie stood with her back to me for a few more seconds talking to her friend, then the friend walked away and she turned around.

'Are you following me?' I said.

There was silence.

'I was going to ask the same of you,' she said calmly.

I paused, indignant and then amazed. But she was right. I could equally have been following her.

'We both live in Bloomsbury,' I said, shrugging.

'This isn't Bloomsbury. But I'm glad to see you.'

I noticed her mouth. Her top lip seemed to move delicately, curving as she spoke, as though its movements were independently choreographed. She was wearing a ridiculously English tweed coat, severe and old-fashioned, but I could see the French in her clearly for the first time. Her eyes were quite ordinary. Her mouth, uncoloured though it was, was noticeable. Her features seemed to have rearranged themselves so that she was not simply plain, but a mixture of things.

'Your review was brilliant,' I said for something to say, though the choice of adjective was stronger than I had intended.

'"*Brilliant*"?' she said. 'I don't think so.'

'It was good.'

'I just read as much as I could,' she said, speaking clearly in that husky little voice, like sun and fog together. 'All night. I kept finding more references that seemed relevant. It occurred to me, somehow, that you might be up too.' She flicked back a strand of her hair. 'By the time it was dawn, and those strange seagulls were wheeling about – why are they so far from the sea? – I'd finished. It felt as though I'd been sailing through the night. I was worried that it was thin.'

'Not at all,' I said. 'Better than the stuff of half my crass hacks, or the crusty old experts I call in. It needs a bit of fiddling with, that's all.'

She smiled.

There was silence.

I tried to prevent myself from filling it. I almost heard what I was about to say before I said it, and tried to stop myself: 'You can do something else for me if you'd like—' I said into the silence. I halted abruptly.

'Something else?' she said, her lips parting. Her grave, pale face remained quite still, as though she were a sculpture. Then she smiled, her full top lip curving.

'Why are you here?' I said abruptly to change the subject, her intensity bothering me.

'Oh,' she said, and gazed into the distance. 'I have to buy a baby present for someone. Where's your—'

'Lelia.'

'That's her name. Of course. It's a beautiful name.'

'She was named after someone,' I said, halting myself. 'I—'

'What?' she said simultaneously.

'Oh, I—'

'Never mind,' she said.

'The Duchess of Westminster,' I said. I stopped. I glanced up to where Lelia had turned the corner to look at prams. The origin of her name, and the parental aspirations it revealed, were a source of unreasonable embarrassment to her. My throat felt hot: I had betrayed her.

Sylvie glanced to one side.

'I'm going to go now,' she said.

'Why?' I said. 'Where?' I suddenly wanted to look at her unadorned face, to hear what she would say next in her cloudy voice.

'I don't know,' she said. 'There's someone I need to meet. But you can always find me.' She turned. 'Bye,' she said in a murmur, and as she left, Lelia arrived. Lelia could have seen the back of her head if she had looked towards her, but she was smiling straight at me, holding something in a packet.

'I just—' I said. I stopped, struggling for the phrases with which to express my explanation; but I hesitated for too long, and the moment passed, and then I didn't tell her because she would tease me, or be mildly amazed or annoyed.

Lelia's face was still pale, like pale gold, pale straw. She held her stomach. A flicker of anxiety crossed her face. 'We're going to have a baby!' she said.

★

77

The quickening, it is called. The movement happens when the infant is half-grown, a flawlessly formed miniature turning in its watery sac. Yet I imagined the offspring of my mother not as the perfect wax-plump doll of a boy it would be, but as a hen. A monstrosity preserved in brine: a waterlogged clump of spines and scratchings, its feathers yolk swollen, its beak a nib of orange. A hen of a child. Would the creature live to its full maturity?

EIGHT

Lelia

By seven weeks, this little life with folded limb buds has a heart hardly bigger than a poppy seed and a tongue of its own. There in its liquid world, it can open its mouth. That fact alone filled me with a rush of love. I pictured the foetus shaped like a baby dinosaur with a hinged square head, the mouth serrated with tiny triangular teeth as it opened and closed. I went into the miniature boxroom at the back of the flat where the baby would sleep if it survived. But it would. Some instinct in me, or a desperate optimism, knew that it would.

'Someone was hanging round for you,' came a voice from below as I rested against the window.

There on the pavement stood Lucy, the daughter of the people next door. Richard claimed that Lucy was alarming, clever and sly, referred to her as a meddlesome little tart, called her Lucille to her face and Lucifer to me. She saw me at the window, and waved. Though it was cold, she wore a skimpy top over jeans with clumpy boots. She motioned to me to open the window, and her top rose, revealing inches of bare stomach.

'When? Who?' I said.

She shrugged. 'Some little creep waiting around to see

you,' she said, her lip curling up. 'Don't know her.' She shrugged, beginning to rock on her feet impatiently.

'What did she look like?' I asked. Cold air streamed into my face.

'Like nothing,' said Lucy, turning away and beginning to walk. 'Crap clothes. She had a parcel for you or something.'

'Did she leave it?' I called.

'Dunno,' said Lucy's disappearing back.

I knew. Of course I knew. Sylvie had come to give me something for the baby.

I had signed a library form granting her access to Senate House the day before, a simple task. I found the phone and rang the number she had given me.

'I've signed for your ticket. You can pick it up from the library reception,' I said.

'*Thank* you,' she said, elation merging with the faint huskiness of her voice in a warm, dense rush of air in my ear.

'Your fantasy is a carrel,' I teased her. Bright white clouds blew over Mecklenburgh Square from the north.

'My fantasy granted,' she said.

This, I thought, running my finger along the window's base, is where my baby will be safe – in a wooden cabin with her parents reading and cooking and working, keeping out strangers. I thought of my baby, from the beginning, as a girl.

'I got you something for the baby,' she said.

'That's so nice of you,' I said. 'Thank you.'

The clouds blew, fierce and white, tearing into strands. A draught seeped in through the old frames.

'It's very exciting.'

'Yes.' I said, exhilaration soaring inside me. 'Richard's not excited, though.' I paused. As I spoke, I realised that it was true. I hesitated again. The truth hurt me, my heart suddenly a sinking, sore thing.

'But I am,' she said. 'He's a man. How could *he* understand? You need looking after now—'

There was a noise in the background. 'Oh,' she said. 'There.'

'Who's that?' I said.

'Oh, nothing,' she said. She hesitated.

The sound of objects being placed on a hard surface continued and then stopped.

'Is someone there?'

'It's just Charlie,' she said.

'Who's Charlie?'

'Oh, my – room-mate.'

'Right!' I said. I was surprised. I felt unreasonably affronted whenever anyone blew apart my impression of them. Everything about her had suggested a private exist-ence. I had assumed for her, without conscious thought, a life of books and self-sufficient solitude. But here was the previously unmentioned Charlie who shared the practi-calities of her daily existence. A sense of relief was tinged with disappointment as I abandoned my vague sense of responsibility for her: for her library ticket, for her social life, for her sensitive disposition.

'I've never heard you mention anyone there,' I said.

'Well,' she said. 'But, well, no. We share a flat, but we don't see each other for days at a time.'

I looked down at the square, the clouds spinning past me as I moved, and I held the window ledge.

'But you,' she said. 'I really want to give you your baby's present.'

Your baby. *My* baby. The use of the possessive filled me with pleasure. It made me feel important, normal. In an astonishing move, I could bear a baby. I realised I had been feeling lonely.

'Come round,' I said, desperate for distraction, calculating the amount of time I had left before I saw my research student, and in that moment I succumbed to my obsession and mentally allowed myself a few days' grace, despite proliferating committees and taxing doctorate supervision.

I turned on my computer and went online. While I suspected that Richard spent whole mornings looking up obscure personal references on Google, I hardly used the net, wandering down false routes when I tried. Still remembering the flavour of my nightmare, I typed in 'Sophie-Hélène', the name of my French exchange partner. I couldn't remember the family's surname. Five hundred and forty-five references were listed. I wrote 'France'. Up sprang details of Marie Antoinette's fourth child and information about the Tour de France. 'Loire,' I wrote, only to find the genealogy of the Princes Biron and yet more cycling news. Richard, the internet time-waster, would no doubt be very happy to help.

I tried a little further, but I was sadder now, caught by a sense of melancholy. Richard wasn't excited, I remembered. He pretended. I wondered whether all men regressed in the end, and whether even Richard, who seemed to me to be a different creature from the man who had most hurt me, was selfish and boorish after all, and not the flawed exception I generally believed him to be.

There was very little I couldn't tell him. I revealed dark humiliations to him, and cried snottily, howlingly, if I felt like it, legs unshaven, reading glasses on, hair in a chopstick, because with him it made no difference.

But there was an old source of fear that I could hardly define in my head, let alone bring to light, like madness glimpsed inside me. If I had somehow been responsible for the deaths of two foetuses and a father, what else was my subconscious mind capable of doing? Who else's death could I cause? I feared myself. Only by digging my nails hard into my wrist could I become calm again.

I had begun to understand why an image of France haunted me. The baby exacerbated it. It was as though there was a valve, below which lay nausea.

My parents believed that I was a good daughter – I gobbled pony stories as a break from Latin; I realised from a precocious age that education was my ticket to somewhere more fulfilling – but my mind was wilder than they knew. I had guilt about being half-white when my father was Indian, and guilt about my secret attitude towards being seen as Indian, and guilt about all the family expectations upon me. I think my father, who had worked for years to support himself through his medical studies until he qualified in his thirties, wanted me to be a doctor. I chose to study French instead: French because, later in my life, there somehow seemed no choice. He died of a heart attack when he was forty-three and I was fourteen. The night he died, I promised myself in a pact with God that I would never let anyone down again, because I'd failed my father at his time of need.

I went to France a mad girl. My French family were kind to me: without mentioning my grief, they gave me affection and whispered sympathy among themselves, easily understood. Sophie-Hélène, my penfriend and exchange partner, was seemingly my perfectly matched companion. An only child, she lived in an odd little cottage off the tiny main street of Clemenceau, with beamed low ceilings and an extension sprawling behind a stream that plunged through the garden, the washing dancing over the water. They put me in a double bed in the spare room slung above a garage at the back, like a room in a bed and breakfast, the wallpaper a texture never previously seen. A teenage cousin's motorcycle was housed in the garage below.

Sophie-Hélène and I read and whispered about books and then boys in the times of numbness between bouts of grief. The local schoolboys, zitty and surly and long-haired, equipped with cigarettes and mopeds, were indistinguishable from the farm hands and garage workers to me. I attended school with Sophie-Hélène for the final week of term. We walked together arm-in-arm like two French girls through a world of squared paper and Orangina and I felt as though I was trailing the blood of my father.

And then the Easter holidays started: so elaborate, so devout, their *Pâques*, and her neighbour, a grave, strange and sweet-natured boy, returned home from his boarding school, and everything changed. I lost my penfriend. She was round at the big shuttered doctor's house by the junction where he lived. They were white-gloved, page-boyed Catholics, exploring each other's bodies in a dressing room, and I was a *sans-papiers*, a muddy heathen dribbling my sadness into the water.

The memory of a baby smell still preyed on me now. The Clemenceau cottage had been scented with a French supermarket smell: ironing-board covers and ready-make cakes rather than baby. I tried to think. I felt sick. I stopped. I halted myself, keeping suspicions away by leaving them wrapped. Richard would call me Cleopatra.

The doorbell rang. She had been so fast. Of course, she

only lived two or three squares away, up there among the mansion blocks and Georgian terraces.

'Hello!' she said. She was out of breath, her laughter rapid and husky at the top of the stairs. She looked about twenty.

She smiled. 'Here,' she said, holding out her present. I unwrapped it, and a pile of soft cotton fell on the table: doll-sized vests bright white, and a little violet body suit, and some bibs, with different shades of piping at the edges. I pressed them to my face, inhaling the shoppish clean scent of them.

'Thank you,' I murmured through a vest. I kissed her, still a bit shy of her. 'That's my first present.'

'Not your mother?'

'No one else knows. Let me make you tea.'

'I'll make it for you,' she said.

She filled the kettle and fetched cups, and then pressed herself against the radiator. She must be cold, I thought, looking at her, her ankles in thin tights, slender and goose-pimpled as she sat down. It was January. She wore a thin pale top with a dark jumper slung over her shoulders. Her hair was hooked behind one ear, the other side falling dark on her face beside her full scrubbed mouth.

I knocked the computer mouse as I passed it, and the screen saver cleared, revealing my Google search. She turned, and looked at the monitor.

'"Sophie-Hélène + Clemenceau",' she read in her calm, distinctive voice. She glanced at me and looked away. The sound of the name pronounced in a seemingly perfect French accent made me jump, as though Sophie-Hélène herself had come back to me. Sylvie looked straight at me with her brown-green eyes.

'Is there a French Friends Reunited?' I asked

'What's Friends Reunited?'

85

'Well you might ask,' I said, as I thought of Richard, entrapped by the website when I came across him in the evenings, cackling in pleasure or shouting with scornful laughter as he read a new entry. He cut and pasted information and emailed it to his old schoolfriends, or turned sulky and paranoid when he found an unexpected success story. His large body looked wrong bent over a computer, as addicted to a screen as he'd once been to seas and sailing boats.

Even his clothes seemed to belong somewhere else: he threw on his father's old navy-blue Guernseys, like the richer, older girls at my school had worn on field trips, and his shirts were soft, much-washed cotton, surprisingly well ironed by him. He wore jeans and faded tops, and however long he'd lived in London, there was something rural or nautical about him. I had bought him stripy tops over the years, knowing that he would like them, and I had tried to replace his holey socks. I bought him black shirts and the odd openly trendy man gift, but he rarely wore them, and I was somehow glad, because he was surrounded by media workers in black shirts. He was entirely lacking in vanity, I had realised early on: he never noticed when he needed a haircut until I instructed him to have one, but he had the confidence that came from being tall, and from having been a loved child who was allowed to run wild by the sea, with hot meals and stories to return to. I had only once, ever, seen him sail a boat, through a bat-laden dusk in Cornwall; he had glided, his back to me, out of the estuary, and in those moments I had the strange realisation that I could lose him one day.

Sylvie pulled her knees up to her chin in one movement, revealing the noticeably good legs that she hardly ever showed;

she looked very young, but there was something subtly polished or exact about her that gave her a more womanly air, so that her appearance was not like some nubile teen's, but like a child-woman's. Her appeal to men, if she had any, would be of a slightly worrying kind.

'You look very lovely now,' she said, her gaze fixed on me again. 'I think the glow hormones have kicked in.'

'I've just bunged on some lipstick,' I said.

'Well, I like it. But you're always well dressed and—'

'I'll put some on you!' I said.

She hesitated.

'OK then,' she said.

I leaned over her. I tried a couple of shades and I painted her mouth. She opened her eyes and glanced at me.

'Now,' I said. 'Whoever you like – if there's someone you like – they should see you now.'

'Really?' she said, and with that full curving mouth as a focus, she looked more knowing. The effect was a little alarming, as though an innocent had become a courtesan.

'Yes!' I said. 'Is there—?' I began, but I halted in the face of her privacy. To enquire was to invade.

'Someone?' she said.

'Yes . . .' I said into the silence.

'There's someone I – like,' she said. 'Understand.'

'And does he understand you?'

'I hope so. A little. I think so. As far as anyone ever can.'

'Are you – seeing him?' I asked, attempting to perpetuate her minor flurry of confession.

'I wait to hear from him.'

'Oh,' I said.

I got up and took her cup. She half-circled my wrist as I passed. 'And you,' she said in a murmur. 'Have you – loved someone, anyone? Much? Many times?'

'Yes,' I said. 'Oh yes.'

'How many times?'

'Three. Two and a half, really.'

'Really?' she said. She moved her hand from my wrist and touched my palm, then dropped her hand. 'Richard.'

'Oh yes. Richard. The most. By far the most. But my first proper boyfriend – what a little bastard, really – I thought I was earth-shatteringly in love with him at the time. And then there was an older man later, and – just horrible things happened, but I was totally caught up with him. *Fixated!* It was somehow obviously linked with my father, who had died when I was younger. A horribly Freudian cliché. Then lots of things. Then Richard.'

'Love and death,' she said, her full red lips mesmerising. '*Liebestod*. There's often a connection.'

'Is there?' I said. 'Have you had – had a death happening to you?'

'A long time ago,' she said.

'Oh, I'm sorry,' I said.

'Let's talk about something else,' she said. 'Please—'

'I'm sorry,' I said again, and touched her arm.

I wanted Richard to come back. But even when he did return – smelling of offices, his hair unkempt, energetically making me tea even though he felt tired – he would pretend a little. He'd ask me how I was with a short list of questions he'd prepared on the stairs, anxious about my well-being but detached from that smear of a baby inside me. I suddenly felt, for the first time since I had met him, that I was on my own.

'You look pale,' said Sylvie. 'Sit down again. Come on, you have to sit. Are you warm enough?'

'Yes.'

'Then sit there. Lie on the sofa, and I'll read to you from

– this,' she said, reaching out and selecting a novel randomly from the bookcase. It was *Angel* by Elizabeth Taylor. She found some lime cordial and made me a glass of it, then sat beside me holding my arm and read to me in her hoarse-sweet voice, and I drifted, lulled by the words, and I almost slept, until I was in a different time and a different place, and I was fourteen again.

NINE

Richard

She won't leave my mind alone, wrote MacDara.

I snorted. *Never realised your mind was connected to your dick*, I wrote.

Ha, he wrote.

You're only allowed a limited amount of contact today, and then there's a ban for two days, I wrote, enjoying the sensation of wielding power over MacDara.

How much?

One brief phone call/send one email and receive two max. What's MW got to say that's so fascinating anyway?

Don't know, don't know, she's just got me. I want to talk *to her all night – yes, Fearon! – if I can't fuck her all night.*

And haven't you?

No no no no. She's stalling. She's stoking me up to this bloody great fever. I hardly see her. How can I ever concentrate again? Nothing's *happened yet.*

Nothing?

Well, almost. I'm left high and dry like a fucking teenager. If I'm not checking my voicemail, I'm 1471-ing.

I laughed. *To your desk, MacD*, I wrote. *I have a living to make.*

★

I was addicted to emails. There were other messages waiting for me: a dozen or so from my freelance writers, and two from Sylvie Lavigne. Somehow, we had got into the habit of emailing each other every day, Sylvie Lavigne and I. I hadn't seen her for a few weeks, and I had stopped bumping into her since our meeting in John Lewis, but I felt I could hear her voice enunciating the words that leapt to the screen.

That evening, I walked over to Marchmont Street to buy some hooks, and I saw the back of a head. Brown. Brown hair falling to the shoulders. A slender little back in a mac. She walked swiftly through the orange-lit gloom. My heart began to thump. My breath left me momentarily, making me falter before I called out. A taxi passed, obscuring her from me.

'Sylvie!' I called. She hesitated. She half-turned, then walked on.

'Sylvie!' I called again, more loudly, but she continued as though she hadn't heard me, and turned the corner. I tore towards her. I stopped. What was I doing? I took a few more steps, my feet flapping on the pavement. I stopped again. My heartbeat was ragged. *What are you doing, you fool, you fucker?* my own voice muttered in my head. I stood, tense, outside the dry cleaner's. I saw myself in the window: a frowning madman, half-poised for flight, feet flailing cartoonishly. What on earth was I doing? I walked, breaking into a run, speeding and gulping air until I reached Mecklenburgh Square.

The door was closed with only one lock, yet there was silence in the flat. I realised Lelia was asleep. I tried to catch my breath, still feeling like a lunatic. I shut out thoughts of Sylvie Lavigne. I blanked them, like cloud cover obscuring the sky, and I caught my breath and looked around. The radiator ticked. Little packages sat by the kettle, their tops closed with plastic clips, Lelia fashion: crystallised ginger, ginger nuts, ginger tea, Rich Tea biscuits. Each packet opened and resealed, bought by Lelia to ward off her sickness. She had gone, alone, to a shop and bought the things she needed for her condition. Alone – and, I realised with a surge of sorrow, lonely. I should have bought those things for her, or accompanied her on her poor search. It had never even occurred to me. I was a pig, a snuffling, selfish pig who couldn't remember the sensation of nausea unless my head was down a lavatory.

But then I remembered the look she'd started to shoot at me from the moment she'd found out about her pregnancy. I thought of it as her Madonna of the Rocks face – holy, hurt and fantastically guilt-inspiring, an expression that repelled me even as it sent me scurrying round for drinks and useless cushions. Her reaction to her pregnancy secretly annoyed me. *So what?* I wanted to bark out in less charitable moments when I'd just crashed in from work and felt an obligation to do everything. *Get over it.* Hadn't any other woman in the history of the world been pregnant? Her tiredness, inexplicably combined as it was with a new interest in sex, was hard to read accurately, and so a small and nasty part of me failed to believe in it.

I looked around again. I saw the food clips. Guilt fingered me. A deep sadness came in its wake. A pregnancy book lay open on the table. Another one sat on the sofa arm. I had never looked at them; they were invisible, indeed repugnant, to me. I picked up one of the packets of ginger and smelled it, and decided that, bastard as I was, I would make a huge effort to improve.

I crept up the stairs, the wood creaking under my clumsy feet, and I found her asleep in the bed, calmly rosy as a cartoon heroine, her breath soft and steady between parted lips, her eyelashes long against her cheeks, so beautiful, and gold and raspberry and sleep-flushed, and I leaned over her to smell her and breathe her in, tense in case I should wake her and shock her. I contemplated her every feature, the tiny hairs on her face, the rhythm of her breath. Was I dismissive at some dreadful and deeply hidden level because she was clearly half-Indian? Because she was female? Because I nurtured some vague class superiority? Was I in fact a racist, sexist bigot? I suddenly snorted with laughter. I tried to force myself to examine my thoughts, my head spinning, and found no answers.

Then slowly I stroked her hair until she woke with a small jump. I curved my body round her and took her into my arms. Sylvie Lavigne briefly flickered through my mind. I got rid of her.

Later in the night, Lelia woke. 'I was dreaming . . .' she said.

She stroked my back. It was comfortable. I grunted. I stirred, leaning towards her. A small gurgle of laughter came from under my armpit. Her teeth clamped on to my nipple. I woke, and stroked her hair and kissed her. She quivered under my arms. Her skin felt hot. Beneath the duvet, I caught a faint scent of her.

'Come here,' she said, feeling for me.

'Lelia!' I said, and she put her hand against me.

'I want you in me now,' she murmured.

'*What?*' I whispered.

I tried. I skimmed my hand across her breast. 'Lelia, I can't,' I murmured, and laughed.

She laughed too, pressing her pubic bone against me. 'Are you too sleepy?' she said, her tones curving in my ear as she tickled her fingers against the back of my neck.

'Yes,' I said. The smell of her rose in hotter waves. I was tempted. I didn't move. 'I have to sleep,' I said.

'Oh, darling!' she said, laughter in her voice. 'But I'm so . . .'

My fingers drifted further down. 'Yes, yes,' she said, lifting her hips impatiently against my hand.

'What's got into you?' I said. 'Have you had a randy little dream? Have you got a crush?'

She laughed. 'Press me, touch me. Hard, hard,' she said.

'Well?'

'A crush on you,' she said between uneven breaths.

She pushed my hand away, and she made herself come with rapid movements, juddering and crying out.

'Sweetheart!' I said.

'Mmm,' she said, and turned, hot and damp, into my arms and fell asleep.

There was a frost in the morning. I rose earlier than her, and cranked up the radiators, and found one of my old fishing jerseys from Cornwall to keep me warm. I shivered as I shaved, and nicked myself and swore. It was a cold February. I glanced at my computer, twitching a little in my impatience to get to my work emails, and decided to go online before I left for the office, though I had a stack of copy to edit. The Hotmail address was there. I grunted, and read the message half-reluctantly.

I spied Mama once from behind the curtains when her maid was dressing her, and I saw a swelling as pale and bulbous as a mushroom. She had become the casing for a perfect fat baby, as though her body were trying to correct the mistake it had made with me. I found a deeper place inside me – tucked away, beneath the entrails – in which to bury myself.

If *I* had given birth to the runt that was me, I would

have loved it and nurtured it, and gazed into its ugly puggy face while I fed it milk through a reed and kissed and kissed its silver-veined skin. I would have poured my spirit into it as it quivered with the effort of life. I would dress it in a bonnet. I would hold it close to me and never let go of its poor bald body. But my mother had not wanted the under-sized thing that had once grown inside her. For who would want a plain girl? Hair the colour of the servants' tub water. Small sharp triangle of a face, eyes hungry despite the effort to dull them. Who would want her? No one. Except one. The only friend, Emilia. And Emilia and I drew closer, until our bodies and souls were almost one.

'Yeah, yeah, yeah,' I muttered. I paused momentarily, then deleted the file.

Lelia wandered into my study, rumpled and sleep-cross. Her breasts were larger.

'I really hate computers,' she said in a croaking morning voice, glancing at my screen. 'How do I "refine my search", or whatever it's called?'

I laughed at her intense expression.

'Everything leads me to complete rubbish and repetition,' she said indignantly. She yawned. 'Why are you online?'

'I'm looking for a Ladyboys and Chicks with Dicks website.'

'Richard, you talk like this,' said Lelia, flicking my shoulder. 'But where are you when I want you?'

'Listen, you,' I said, 'if you suddenly want to get jiggy in the middle of the night, my love, you can't guarantee that I'm on standby like a crazed bull.'

'Can't I?' said Lelia, raising one eyebrow.

'Well. Not always,' I said, smacking her buttock in passing. 'Women always do that!' I was suddenly indignant. 'They go on and on about how men – the beasts! – don't want foreplay – we're not even supposed to use that word, are we? – and write great long diatribes about it for magazines, and then they want you straight in there, rearing like a bloody Italian stallion without a moment's notice.'

She hesitated. 'Shut up,' she said lazily, and put her arm around me. I tweaked her nipple.

'Ow,' she said. 'I'm pregnant. Be careful.'

'Yes,' I said, having forgotten again. I was amazed at my own capacity for amnesia. 'How are you feeling?'

She glanced at me. Her Blessed Virgin expression. 'Fine. A bit sick.'

'Listen,' I said, getting up and walking into the big room. 'Let me get you something. Ginger tea?' I scooped some gunk out of the sink and winced.

'Tea, please. Tea tea.'

'Yes, none of this lesbian herby bollocks. Some good tannin for you, my girl, then it's back to bed with you.'

I walked to the office, the pain of the cold already ringing through my feet as they hit the pavement. I pulled my coat collar up, cheerful in the face of minor adversity. I arrived impressively early, and therefore made my presence felt by offering drinks on my way to the machine. A cup of tea safely in hand, I sat down at my computer. I had five reviews to pull into shape and a loathsome contributor with whom to wage battle, but I went straight to my emails. There was nothing from Sylvie Lavigne. I was somewhat amazed. I hit *Read messages* again and scanned my list of incoming addresses. There was nothing. Not a single one of her strange mind-reader's emails. There was no text from her either. I didn't want to think about it. I needed distraction. I got straight on to the phone to MacDara, who had been at work for three hours already, earning five times my salary.

'Mac,' I said. 'I'm bored. Today's instalment?'

'Nothing. She can't always talk.' The sound of ringing phones and shouting traders filled the receiver.

'It's still early in the morning for normal people, MacDara.' I waved at my friend Jim from the arts desk as he arrived. A stray smoker wandered past the door of the smoking room: I longed to leap up and talk to her. Anything, anything but sit here and fiddle with work.

'She can't talk a lot of the time because of *him*.'

'Oh yes,' I said.

'The git. The bastard,' he said.

'But you've got a girlfriend, you fool,' I said. I laughed.

'Yes,' said MacDara in sullen tones.

I suddenly found his situation marginally less amusing. He would probably lose the essentially decent Catrin, wish he hadn't been such a fuckwit, alarm old married Mystery Woman by being single, then go through a bit of a sorry-for-himself alkie phase, break apart our group, end up with someone we didn't like, and live in regret. The whole predictable process struck me as futile.

'Who's the husband?'

'I don't know – I don't want to ask too much. She doesn't talk about Catrin. We've got a tacit agreement, I suppose.'

'What's this chick actually *look* like? You never tell me.'

'Oh, like—' He made an appreciative moaning sound. 'Well, no. But – yes. Skinny, though.'

'Articulate as ever.' A sub slapped a proof down in front of me.

'She's not – she's not my usual type, even. Not at all. But – what a bitch. She's got me by the mind, balls, stomach, I don't know.'

'Where's this going to go?' I said, maniacally see-sawing a pen above my desk. The furniture the subs had added to my page was execrable.

'Fuck only knows,' he said in a mutter, and coughed. I could hear him drawing on a new cigarette. 'You think I'm just an idiot, don't you, Fearon?' he said grumpily. He paused. 'I am. But – she's gorgeous. No, she's not gorgeous at all. Well, she is. She's hot. She's cold. She's—'

'A married woman who blows hot and cold. It's not exactly *unique*, is it, MacD? No contact today,' I snapped, my new power so easily wielded.

'Bastard.'

I laughed as I put the phone down. Three new messages had appeared for me. I scanned them quickly. Ren, and a couple of hopefuls suggesting themselves for work.

I had an image of myself: a man poised ready to run, agitated and indecisive on a late-afternoon street, heart inexplicably thumping.

When you go through the streets / no one recognises you . . . no one looks at the carpet of red gold / that you tread as you pass, I thought, a poem half-known coming back to me.

A message came up. I tapped on it. It wasn't from her.

I began to write to her. I stopped myself and edited half a review. Impulsively, I started again. *Where are you?* I wrote.

By midday, there was no reply. A few weeks before, I had bumped into this woman with tiresome regularity. She had then sent me further suggestions for reviews, having clearly called in all the book catalogues and scoured them in standard hack fashion, a method surprising in a reserved academic; until gradually our emails had become regular and frequent.

There was still silence. I waited. What was the matter with me? Perhaps I didn't have enough work. Yet proofs were piling up, writers were beginning to bother me tentatively for a response to their reviews, and I had barely begun to edit the week's pages. I felt as though I was going slightly mad. A message came up. It bore her name. I clicked on it.

Oh! Your voice just came to me on screen. I dreamt of you, you might be amused to hear, last night. It was as though I'd seen you somewhere in the day. I dreamt I'd caught sight of you, but when I looked, you weren't there. Where were you?

I'm all disorientated — I've been working on something, and I just emerged, haven't dressed, haven't eaten — it seems to be afternoon . . . I hope you're very well. I've been thinking about you. With love, Sylvie.

The foggy voice with its slight formality and faint, indefinable accent ran through me. I wanted to hear the catch in that voice, to see the plain, pale face. I felt a sudden urgent desire to meet her again, and yet I really didn't know why.

Laughter emerged from the desk further along, followed by cheering. My phone rang. I let my voicemail take it.

I looked up her number and rapidly tapped it into the phone. I gazed, distracted, at the pile of letters and press releases that had come with today's post, and I couldn't imagine working through the afternoon without seeing her first, as if to satisfy some unknown imperative akin to deep curiosity. I held the receiver rigidly, each ring bleeding electronically into my ear followed by an echoing pause that lasted minutes. I could put the phone down at any time, I reminded myself.

She picked it up.

'Hello, it's Richard Fearon. Hello. Come to lunch,' I said in a gabble. I coughed. I sounded like a lunatic.

She paused.

'Isn't it a little late for lunch?' she said.

'I haven't had any. You said you haven't eaten. If you came now, we could still get something.'

'I can't,' she said.

'Why?'

'I shouldn't. There's someone—'

'Why not?'

She paused.

'I never speak to you,' I said. 'We email all the time. It's getting ridiculous.'

'Is it?' she said lightly.

'I think so.'

'Well,' she said, 'I could come, very quickly. I have work to do.'

'Reviewing?' I said.

'Well, I don't – yes,' she murmured.

'Who for?' I said in amazement. 'Not someone else?'

'Well—'

'The bastards.'

She laughed.

'They can't. Do more for me.'

'I'm quite busy,' she said.

'*Busy!*' I roared. 'I discovered you, girl! Loyalty. How long will it take you to get over here?' I barked. 'Fifteen minutes?'

'Twenty,' she said.

Twenty minutes. I glanced at the clock on my computer. It was already quarter to two. I had done virtually no work. I ripped through some post with alarming efficiency.

I met her at the same gastro pub along the street, where no one would even look at her. She sat there, pressed among others, serene but almost invisible. I had forgotten the essence of her; or the surface of her. I hesitated slightly. Her hair was pulled back into a strict, sleek ponytail. It made her straight nose dominant. It made her mouth stand out. A sexy mouth, I thought suddenly. I had never consciously noticed. She didn't colour it, like other women did. What a perfect little blow job of a mouth she had, its pale raspberry curves picked out in the light.

'I thought of – I remembered – a poem by Neruda today,' I said. '*When you go through the streets / no one—*'

'*. . . te reconoce,*' she said. '*Nadie ve tu corona de cristal . . .*'

'Bloody hell,' I said.

She gazed at the people milling past.

The pub was crowded and smoky, even then. We sat beside each other on the only seat available, an old church pew, and others sat at their own spindly tables along the same long bench. Her arm touched someone else's jacket; she was intermittently pushed closer to me, and through the smoke and wine and char-grilling I could smell her own scent.

Talk to me, I thought, recalling all the words that she sent me, casual yet formal at once, as though she were half-lodged in a different era.

The man next to her gestured, pushing her, and her shoulder pressed against my upper arm. A sudden ripple went through me. She was closer now, and I could smell the scent which seemed to rise from her neck and I floated on her voice, and I wanted her to touch my arm again. Touch it, I thought, to my own amazement. The man moved, and so did she, and my skin rippled in response.

'I don't know how to be with these people,' she said calmly.

'Don't you?' I said.

'Their haircuts. Their language – their intonation, even. Their very way of life is beyond – anything I know.'

'Tossers,' I said.

'*You* know how to deal with them. With anyone.'

I sat there, and warmth gradually suffused me, as though red wine were trickling into my senses, yet I had drunk nothing. She never seemed to drink. We talked. I felt as though all my day-to-day movements were choreographed in water, and I could free-associate and say anything that occurred to me, so perfectly would I be understood.

'But do they cry at night?' she said. 'When I meet someone whose life seems so much more sorted out than mine, I wonder – *but do they cry at night?*'

It was as though my arm swam, encased in bubbles. A feeling of exquisite arousal rose through my body.

'Do you cry?' I said.

She smiled. I smiled at her.

I did nothing. We sat and we talked, interrupting each other. I waited, and then my nerve endings twitched in sequence, the electric ripple travelling to my shoulder and across my chest. I tilted my face towards her hair to smell her, because I liked her smell. Subtly, through the smoke, I breathed it in.

The man next to her half-turned to call over a waiter, and his movement pushed her, unbalancing her momentarily so that her hand jolted against my thigh. My skin leapt to life. She snatched her hand away. An unreadable expression flitted over her face. The same poem came back to me. *There are lovelier than you, lovelier . . . And when you appear all the rivers sound in my body*. It was twenty-five past four. I had to make myself leave. We said nothing. I stumbled a little as I rose to return to work. We said goodbye briefly, and she disappeared down Clerkenwell Road, as expressionless as a little white statue.

Our flat was glowing in the dark when I got home. Lelia had cleared up, she said, and there was the smell of something hot and floury in the oven, which was unusual, since she rarely cooked. It was luxuriously warm, as though she had kept the heating high all afternoon, and the lamps were on, every bright little lamp casting a bright circle on the wood. It was as though we lived in a crooked treehouse swaying in the sky above Mecklenburgh Square, I thought: too small for us, yet breathing with wood. She sat curved on the floor among cushions, clicking her thumbnail between her teeth in front of her computer screen. Her hair was tethered with a pencil, yet she was as beautiful as I had ever seen her. I looked at her in the lamplight and was struck anew, as I was every few weeks, by her face; by the particular rightness, to me, of her obviously good looks.

She smiled at me, her Madonna of the Rocks expression absent.

A curl of raindrops blew against the window; something metal fell with a bang outside. Recent weak sunshine had retreated back into winter. I glanced at the mobile blue-black air outside. I felt glad. Someone else had understood the sentiment recently. Who? A starburst of rain hit the glass. Sylvie. The long curtains gathered a little fringe of dust.

I wanted to howl, suddenly, with emotion for Lelia. I wanted to shout out, *Never leave me, I'm your one, marry me*.

'Marry me,' I said. My voice broke up with a sort of gulp as I said it. It sounded abrupt in the silence between wind gusts. Did I mean it? I stood there, momentarily panicking. Did I mean it?

'Really?' she said. She turned to me. Her eyes – those long big eyes – swallowed me. I soaked myself in their brown substance.

'Yes,' I said.

'You mean it, don't you?' One side of her lip twitched nervously. She seemed to hesitate.

'Of course, of course. I always mean it. Every time we say it. But I want to do it *now*. What on this earth are we fannying around for? Let's get married now.'

'Now?'

'Absolutely.'

'Don't you have to book? Anyway – drag witnesses off the street, you mean? I don't want to do it like that. I want it to be Mum who's with us.'

'OK, OK. Next week, then. Tomorrow.'

'I will, I will, but why do we have to rush? Oh, not – not because of this? Surely not?'

'No, no,' I said impatiently, following her hand as she stroked her stomach. The air gushed and turned outside, curling in cold breakers into the room. 'I just want to. Enough is enough. I feel this urgent great *need* to do some-thing about my love for you, Lelia Guha.' I sat down and took her shoulders, quite roughly. 'We're never going to have a spare fifteen grand just knocking around, and I bloody well want to marry you. Give me a date, then. Just give me a date.'

She hesitated again. I frowned, affronted.

'June the twenty-sixth,' she said.

'Why? It's a long time.'

'It was – don't you know?'

My thoughts revolved; I set them speeding. One of Lelia's impossible tests that always caught me short and needled me. 'Um,' I said.

'Dad's birthday,' she said.

'Of course it was,' I said. Her mouth had set a little. She glanced to one side. Any moment now, Madonna of the Rocks would appear. I swallowed the thought. 'Do you want to do it then?'

'Yes, I'd like to.'

'We will, we will. Will you marry me on June the twenty-sixth?'

'Yes.'

I waited, raising my eyebrow at her.

'Will you marry *me*?' she said.

'Yes,' I said. I pulled her to me, and kissed her.

We ate the ciabatta that she had put in the oven, and searched around in the fridge to find pieces of cheese and hummus two days past its sell-by date and some horrible vegetarian sausages, then we went to bed early, running from the cold bathroom and piling the bed with dressing-gowns.

'I keep thinking,' she said.

'What, my love?' I said vaguely, trying to blow billows of warm breath on to us under the duvet.

She pressed herself into my arms.

'An image keeps coming into my mind.' She was murmuring into the duvet, so I only half-heard her.

A seagull wheeled and cried its mournful cry. Who had mentioned the seagulls in Bloomsbury? I remembered. I dismissed the thought. I stroked Lelia's thigh. She quivered, and unexpectedly, she turned towards me. I had thought her settled for sleep in my arms. I stroked her back through her nightdress. 'Against my skin,' she said.

I put my hand under the cotton and felt her shoulder blade. It was hot. I ran my hand down her back. She shifted on her hip towards me.

'This image,' she said, moving closer to me so that her breasts were pressed against my chest. 'Two bodies, rubbing together.'

I closed my lips against her ear lobe. 'Hmmm . . .' I said.

Her breath heated my neck. 'Well . . .' she said. She flicked my nipple.

'Tell me, then,' I said. I kissed her breast. Her breathing began to change.

'I think of bodies together,' she said. 'Not ours.' I pulled her to me and pressed my mouth on her neck. 'Mine, perhaps, but so much younger.'

'Faithless,' I murmured.

'Two – almost children. They're together.'

'Huh?'

'Richard,' she said, and I heard the click of separating saliva as her mouth opened. Her breathing changed again. She lay on her back, inviting me. 'Press me.' She moaned lightly as my fingers inched downwards. She murmured in uneven tones as I stroked her more rapidly, more lightly.

'You're a secret goer, Lelia Guha.'

She laughed. She buried a groan in my neck. She was alive, scented, hot. Her very enthusiasm perversely subdued me.

'What's the *rudest* thing you've ever done?' she said, her bright tones a laughing curve in my ear. 'Apart from everything you've told me.'

'Oh God,' I said. She flexed her fingers against my buttock. I was barely stirring. 'I don't know. Threesome?'

'I'm sure there's more,' she said.

I lay there on my stomach. A memory of a pale, proud wraith pressing against my arm flashed through me and leapt to my groin. I grunted involuntarily and shifted against Lelia's hip. I threw away the image. It came back to me, shooting ripples. I lingered upon it for long seconds before I obliterated it again, then I opened my eyes and looked at Lelia with her tilted dark eyes, and shut out the ghost.

'*That's* better,' she murmured, and moved her thigh against me. 'Harder,' she said. I sucked her skin until she cried out. 'My shoulder hurts,' she said, her voice rich, encouraging me.

'I've never known you quite like this,' I said.

She smiled into the darkness. She murmured, her words barely audible.

I ground against her with my thigh.

'Yes,' she said, her breath emerging in a small explosion like a hiccup.

I licked her shoulder where I had bitten it. She exhaled sharply. The spectre glimmered.

She moved her hips, and mine met hers, and she gasped and we ground into each other, racing, crying out, and I circled there, and for the first time in our lives, we came together.

In the morning, there was an email containing a section of novel on my computer. I had begun to expect it.

We had our own corner of the house. There was a small yard by the cellar where moss lived and snails sucked and where we grubbed among the ferns that glared pale green above the soot. We played and planned there. It was inside, in the dressing room, that we merged and became one.

I tried very hard to be good. I tried to temper myself like metal, but the wrongness in me came back, and I made myself thinner, until the roar of hunger in my head frightened me.

As the new child grew inside the womb like a tumour, I knew that the time had come to enact the plans that were stirring so brightly in my mind. One afternoon in the dressing room, we considered the dimensions of a baby's chest.

I think I had realised for some time who was sending me these emails. I had known without wanting to, and in my wilful ignorance I skimmed them, unsettled and feeling faintly stalked, before deleting them from my computer and, to a lesser extent, my mind. But the more I thought about Sylvie, the more I was drawn to read her strange fiction. I read and then erased the latest instalment. It was quarter to nine.

I took a detour through the little garden hidden at the back of Mecklenburgh Square on my way to the office. I was early, as I often was now, and as I wandered through that secretive serpentine garden with its glasshouses and graves, I realised that I was not about to walk straight to work. I meandered towards the far gate, kicking at the frost tussocks, propelled by unspoken purpose. I had last seen her on Marchmont Street turning the corner towards Tavistock Square, yet I didn't know exactly where she lived. The editorial assistant would have her address on file, but I couldn't remember ever having asked her, and in any case, I could hardly loiter on her street. I could walk instead among the frost and delivery vans for no apparent reason, and satisfy some terrible, unformed compulsion.

Marchmont Street was dead. Only the newsagent, narrow and sagging-ceilinged as a cardboard-box home, glared yellow light. I went in and bought some chewing gum. The sky was bruising, and I wondered if it was going to snow. Of course she wasn't there, a shadow in a dull mac coming to buy a newspaper. Tentatively, I turned towards Tavistock Square. Taxis coasted past. The windows on the square were largely dark.

I had to stop myself. I had to stop myself right now. I turned, my heart racing, and sped back, jogging down Gray's Inn Road until I arrived at work, my lungs stretched sore with frozen air.

'MacDara.' I grabbed the phone. 'Tell me, tell me about what's happening,' I said hopelessly.

'You sound like a heavy breather,' he said.

'What's happening?' I said, attempting to control my breathing. 'With you?'

'You mean – you know I can't talk,' he said in a low voice.

'I – I,' I said, and then I had nothing to say.

I had to see her again, once more, to kill it. It had to be today. I worked in a fitful fashion, fiddling with my flatplan, then paced around the office, then phoned a few of my journalists instead of emailing them, to waste time I didn't have. I was under pressure from the deputy editor to find a more famous author for the interview slot, and I had to put in some calls.

At twelve twenty-five I suddenly knew that if I left for lunch now, right now, and walked west towards Bloomsbury, I would bump into her. The knowledge came to me as a gift of premonition. I rose, a feeling of madness sifting like sand through my head as I grabbed my keys and wallet, and forgot about my coat. I hesitated, knocking my chair so that it rolled into my desk.

I stood there hopelessly.

'Got a writer to meet,' I said to the books page assistant, who nodded. 'Has to be early,' I said. He looked up at me. Heat constricted my torso.

The rush of air outside calmed me. The temperature cut straight through my jacket, and I plunged my hands in my pockets, aware that I couldn't skulk back in like an idiot for my coat. I lolloped along Theobald's Road in a cloud of breath, the air sawing at my lungs, and headed west until I hit Brunswick Square. People wandered about, sharply delineated in the cold. I was in Bloomsbury, and I hadn't yet seen her. I looked around wildly.

I stormed across the street and legged it, three steps at

a time, up the stairs of the Brunswick Centre. Would she be loitering in the cinema foyer? I could hustle her into the steaming warmth – oh, warmth – of the Chinese opposite, whose hot salted scents were twisting my stomach, and we could talk to each other. Where was Lelia? What if she had decided to do a shop at Safeway's? Had we got any food at home? I tried to rack my brain, swinging from foot to foot, but my mind was numbed, and I could only picture an empty fridge with a crust in it, like some symbolic image from a children's film. Oh, Lelia. Oh, fuck.

My newly sprouted psychic radar appeared to detect waves that then faltered, and I felt seasick as another conviction gripped me: she would be on Marchmont Street. I ran, hobbling, my feet needled with ice; the street was busy and hooting and litter-strewn, and she wasn't there. I ran back and burst into a café, where the warmth began to settle on the frozen surface of my jacket, my lungs still fiery with ice. Fuck this, I thought. I had known I would bump into Sylvie Lavigne if I left the office at that precise moment. And I hadn't. Yet I had *known*. A new verb was required, I thought crossly, and pictured a committee of etymologists, the name 'C. T. Onions' springing into my mind as it did whenever I thought of a dictionary, the editor of the old hulking *Shorter Oxford* I had frowned over during my schooldays forever linked with the word: one of the tiny irritations that lodged in my mind and buzzed there, baring currents of insanity.

I felt indignant and fantastically foolish, standing in a haven of cheap pine and stainless-steel tea pots, fiddling for my mobile. Yet I had to do this. I had to kill it.

I pulled an icy sliver of metal out of my pocket and found the number I had kept when she first texted me.

'Hello,' I said when she answered, and as I heard her voice, I smiled. 'Can we meet?'

'OK,' she said.

I stood there in the warmth. I had forgotten about Safeway's. I cowered in case I was spotted, a shivering wreck in a nasty café. I waited.

Sylvie arrived wearing a scarf, her mac tied around the waist, and she looked more European, like a slender little Frenchwoman in the war with her shadowed eyes and pale skin.

'Let's walk,' I said, and I caught her arm in mine, and we walked silently towards Brunswick Square, where the great horse chestnuts canopied winter twigs and the ground was stubby with cigarettes on bald earth, and the new mothers perambulated serenely among the men drinking Special Brew.

'Jane Austen thought that the air was superior here,' she said.

'In Brunswick Square?'

An aeroplane flew overhead, its lights flashing, and the image was always scored in my mind afterwards: that plane passing by, choosing that moment to fly low in a thickening grey sky.

'It's going to snow, isn't it?' she said. We stood in the pathway near the horse chestnut.

'Yes,' I said, looking all around me. 'I think so.'

The horse chestnut roiled above me as I leaned down, so cold I felt I was moving through ice – I was in the Arctic; I was stiffened by ice; I had died – and my lips met hers with a shock of cold-warm flesh. Time halted and frag-mented into distinct split seconds. Her mouth moved minutely with a small, stiff twitch, then she pulled her head away from me. Humiliation rushed through me. The skin on my neck flooded with childish wounded pride.

'I—' came a voice from behind me.

I turned around and gazed at Catrin, standing beside us on the path. In my confusion, I recalled with a jolt that she worked in King's Cross. Her expression bore the terrible studied blankness of knowledge.

'I—' she said again, the beginning of fire just visible in her cheek as she turned her head from us and walked away. My bowels tightened; I felt sick. This was followed by the strange sensation that I felt nothing at all.

TEN

Richard

I crashed in there. I ran two, three steps at a time up the stairs to our flat, and rammed at the keys so that the locks shot open. My mind was blank. She wasn't there. I made myself some coffee. If I rushed; if I turned the taps on so that the water gushed into the kettle, making the metal vibrate and sending harsh spray over me; if I acted mechanically and *fast*, then my life was normal. I ripped open an envelope. It cut my finger. The brief moment of pain felt reassuring. I took out an onion and pressed a knife against the skin at its end; it wobbled dangerously beneath the blade. Dumbly, I chopped. The sky was a glowing dark blue outside the window. It was an ordinary day. A sense of relief suffused me: the significance of what I had done subsided behind a screen of normality. And the humdrum seemed sublime. Whatever had been wrong with my life before? Nothing. Yet I hadn't known it.

'Hello!' she called. Click of lock, echo of door. A baby inside her. I felt a slap of shock.

'What's the matter?' she asked, her smile switching off.

How could I? How could I? I was frozen, trapped within that moment in a chamber of static, interference, snow. *No no no*, I wanted to bellow. The sensation of seeing her was

113

much worse than I had anticipated. I had tarnished it. The perfect thing had been violated, as it had in nightmares, when I had woken excited yet relieved from dreams of infidelity, with her always there on the pillow beside my waking body: me faithful, her faithful, our own nest of cotton and night sweat. And she was pregnant.

I never knew what home meant to me until that day. The word 'home'. It had once been a house in Cornwall, that chalk-white, grubby-fingered rose-twined bedroom wallpaper against cream wood, and particular corners of flagstone and wainscot and slope, old walls, and a river, and some snail-wet grass, and at the end of a pilgrimage of gritted toes and stinging nettles and pines, the sea. And now, at this moment, it meant this. Lelia in a doorway in a wooden room with me.

I coughed. I smiled, and the smile stopped beneath my eyes, impossible to complete.

'What's the matter?' she asked again, coming towards me.

I hugged her, my nose filled with the movement of her hair, and I betrayed her even by touching her.

The memory of Sylvie flickered against my eyelids.

But I hadn't kissed her. My lips had only met hers for a twitching fraction of a second. Did that count? Perhaps not. Oh God, perhaps not after all. Familiar Lelia smell was rising up to me like ether, blanking out the guilt. Perhaps, on the scale that God and normal people agreed upon, it amounted to a glitch so minor it could be discounted.

But there was Catrin.

I went and sat on the loo, queasy. And then I remembered that this was what Lelia had to suffer every day. 'Sweetheart,' I muttered into my skin, my face pressed into my hands.

★

In the night, the phone rang. My heart expanded and contracted with a wallop that made me fear a coronary attack. I leapt up, disorientated, and virtually skied down the staircase in my clumsy haste.

'Sorry it's a bit late,' said MacDara.

'You cunt!' I hissed, relief and irritation tangled together.

'What?' said MacDara.

'You woke me up.'

'Sorry.'

'Where are you?' I asked, sleep-muddled.

'At home. Downstairs,' he whispered.

Home, I thought. MacDara. Catrin. My heart slammed into my chest cavity again. I wanted to bang the receiver down before he confronted me.

There was silence.

'She's disappeared. Bloody *gone*,' muttered MacDara into the receiver.

'What?' I said, my sleep-logged thought processes tugged in different directions. 'Who?' I said feebly. 'Oh, you mean—'

'Three days. She's fucked off. I've rung and emailed several times, and nothing.'

'You weren't supposed to,' I said vaguely, my heart just beginning to calm itself.

'Yes, whatever. Anyway, she's ignoring me. It's never been anything like this.'

'Three days, MacDara.'

'You know how it is.'

'Go to bed,' I said. I pictured him padding up his thick carpeted stairs – that show-off's carpeting he had bought – to bed, where Catrin lay like a monster in her lair rolling my future about.

'Another thing,' he said.

My heart pincered.

'There was a kind of unspoken agreement we were going to do it,' said MacDara. 'The full thing. We were building up to it.'

'Really?'

'I was getting horny as hell. I was having to go to the showers at work. And now she's buggered off.'

'Go to bed,' I said quietly. 'Don't worry. Let's talk tomorrow.'

He put the phone down. I thought of standing in the hall, waiting for him to call me back once he'd heard the news.

I went to bed and lay down with a sense that the night was already buoyed by dawn, and sleep was an impossibility. The hours that followed were fragmented with frantic calculations. Calm assessments of probability were ambushed obliquely by terrifying scenarios involving a combination of Lelia, Sylvie, MacDara and Catrin, chance meetings, phone calls and miscarriage.

I had been unfaithful to a small number of my previous girlfriends, the resulting guilt varying from the troubling to the non-existent, accompanied by occasional pathetic spurts of pride at my own behaviour. With Lelia, it was different. The aim was lifelong monogamy. We had always stared mock-solemnly into each other's eyes and quizzed each other about fidelity, one trying to trip the other up with deceptively casually delivered statements designed to mask lumbering traps:

'That time you went out with Joe – the time you snogged him—'

'I did not!'

'*Didn't* you? Really?'

'No! Honestly. I promise.'

'But it was near the beginning. I'm sure you said you were tempted, or something.'

'*No!*'

We imagined that by staring into each other's eyes we would be able to read the signs of infidelity in each other, but our attempts always ended in laughter and renewed rituals of loyalty. There were rules: snogging counted. Future crushes of a temporary nature were to be half expected, mentally indulged, and then overcome. Any more prolonged or significant desires were to be confessed to the other in an attempt to ward off developments.

A brush on the lips could possibly be dismissed; but, unaccountably, I had tried to kiss Sylvie Lavigne properly, and with intention came culpability. I shuddered. Embarrassment trailed guilt and whipped me in the face with its sting whenever I remembered that I had betrayed my inexplicable feelings to that mouse, only to meet rejection.

I breathed in Lelia's breath. Hot, thick, drowsy. I gazed at her peaceful face and caught the taste of nightmare.

Catrin. If Catrin hadn't seen me, I could have got away with it. I could have buried it guiltily and used it as a warning to myself, like an electric cow prod. But Catrin had seen me, coatless beneath a laden sky, bending over a woman to press my mouth to hers. Fuck. Shit. Bloody Catrin. The former alcoholic with her gentle Welsh tones and her pale face and steelier soul who now held the key to despair. I had always liked her. I hated her name. *Catrin.* What kind of a pig-ugly thumping anachronism was that? I hated her name, and now I hated her.

I must have fallen into a brief, heavy sleep, because my pillow was dark with a dribble circle, and a dull stream of light filled the room. I jolted up with a shock: Lelia had already risen.

'Lelia!' I called in a panic, but there she was at the foot of the stairs.

'Have you had a bad night?' she said, and I nodded, and she held her arms out to me.

My study seemed hushed as though waiting for something. I paced around, distracted. I had to escape to the office. Lelia was preparing course work from home for the morning, and Catrin could call at any time in the next few hours. Worse still, Lelia had a couple of days of industrial action coming up. I was hoping she'd spend her time in Top Shop and the library, but nothing could be guaranteed. I wanted to stay hovering by the phone like a guard dog; I eyed it in misery, wondering whether I could somehow dismantle it without her noticing, and picturing myself ripping it from the wall so vividly that my arms tensed.

In the office, I sat in a strip-lit void and worked, and no one contacted me: Sylvie Lavigne was silent, as I, in awful humiliation, had anticipated. Catrin had apparently not yet called to wreak havoc. Lelia didn't ring. MacDara was still wittering on by email about his absent woman. I ignored him until, with MacDara-esque persistence, he sent me a new email in an oversized font demanding an answer, to which I replied in the guarded and sombre manner of the secret sinner who fears imminent blame.

The day was white and grey, and I sat and waited, suspended in its blankness.

I called Lelia, my bowels suddenly light and unstable, and she was simply Lelia, and funny, and tiresomely strict about the cupboard I hadn't yet painted. I doodled on some paper as I tried to devise a way to tell her about my attempt to kiss Sylvie before Catrin did, but every explanation seemed trite and impossible. The day continued uneventfully. I had to put several pages to bed, but even a deadline barely penetrated my thoughts, despite growing pressure from above. In my disbelief that all evidence against me had failed to materialise, I began to revel in the blankness, praying for its perpetuation.

I remembered Sylvie walking through Brunswick Square, and a worm of desire stirred. I groaned in my head and rested my chin on my hands. I made myself recall her dull persona, her dull face, and yet she wasn't dull to me any longer.

The snow had not fallen. The sky was still hushed and weighted when I returned home, and colder the following morning. Again, nothing happened. Lelia went to the university, and I worked at home. Lust came to me fleetingly, unbidden, and I forcibly distracted myself.

That weekend, I opened the books pages of the *Sunday Times*, and there beneath a short review of a paperback were the initials 'SL'. My eyes darted to the bottom of the page to check the contributors' names. *Sylvie Lavigne*, it said. A small sound escaped from me. Lelia looked up from her paper and said nothing. *Sylvie Lavigne*. How dare she? How the fuck dare they? She had virtually told me as much, but I had expected her to write for minor academic publications rather than a national broadsheet. She was *my* discovery, my inexperienced nonentity cleverly plucked from the bloody slush-pile of life. What would she have to show other than work she had done for my pages? The idea made me want to roar. Sylvie Lavigne, who'd never been to a publishing party in her life, and wouldn't spot a contact if it was trying to shag her, had somehow wormed her way into a paper other than mine. I'd given that reticent neophyte one inordinate great leg-up, and then managed to humiliate myself and frighten her off in the process.

'What?' said Lelia.

'What?' I said.

'Your breathing's funny.' She looked back down at her paper.

A headache hovered by my temples and then began drilling into my forehead. The snow still hadn't arrived. It was about to fall. I could see that it was ready. 'It's going to snow, isn't it?' the mouse had murmured in her husky voice, three days before. The snow had hesitated for three days, like pre-storm silence. Like the silence of Catrin whatever-her-Welsh-name-was. I wanted it to come. I wanted Catrin to call, and get it over with; or to have a lobotomy and continue to hide behind blankness for the rest of my life.

'Are you ever going to do that cupboard?' said Lelia, raising one eyebrow and not moving from her work as I opened the sports section.

I sighed, suppressing it, immensely irritated. I slapped my hand on the table. '*Yes*,' I said.

'Well, you don't have to,' said Lelia. 'Just do it or don't. But then don't go on about it.'

'I thought it was you who went on about it,' I said, feeling anger rising inside me.

'Don't do it, then,' she said. 'Let's have an infested cupboard that gives our floorboards woodworm, covered in flaking maroon paint.'

'Right,' I snapped. I stood up. I made a face at her. She pulled one back at me. The tension subsided. I gathered a couple of old newspapers from the table to protect the floor, and glanced at a sliding pile of post and receipts beneath them. On the back of an envelope Lelia had scribbled 'Catrin'.

I froze and checked again. It definitely said Catrin. I half-glanced at Lelia. I turned and walked out of the room, towards the study. I appraised the stupid junk-shop cupboard, but I felt sick. I had to get it over with. I returned to the main room, and pretended to look for more newspaper.

'Catrin,' I said, and picked up the envelope, my mock-casual tones so strained I had to clear my throat.

She said nothing.

I stood there.

'Mmm,' she said.

'What does she want?' I said into the thin air between us.

'Oh, I don't know,' said Lelia.

I paused minutely. 'Why?'

'*What?*' said Lelia, frowning and looking up from her marking. 'Oh, I don't know. She left me a message. But she's away.'

'How do you know?'

'What?'

'Well, that she's away.'

'Because her voicemail says so. Why?'

'Nothing.'

Lelia read.

'Wonder if MacDara's away too, then?' I said feebly.

'I don't know.'

'How long for?'

'What?'

'How long's she away for?'

'I haven't a clue.'

'I just wondered. I – could, you know, meet up with MacDara. Nothing. Where's that old paintbrush?'

I looked out of the window at the black swollen twigs huddling together. The sky was so weighted and still and grey, I wanted to kick it to puncture it and release the snow. I slapped poisonous chemicals on wood in a careless fashion, half-hoping to splash my skin for distraction and tension relief, and gulped cold air from the open window. I went online the moment I had finished.

My mother was ridiculous with child. Her belly was the rump of a market animal. I wanted it to start: I wanted her cow-sick with love for the thing inside her, so that what I dreaded would come true.

We were left alone in the house with only the nurse-maid downstairs to watch us, so Emilia and I went to the little room with cream walls to practise. What we did, I can hardly say. We practised, for marriage. I was the gentleman who had come to take her away, and she a maiden, pretty as I was plain.

I knew what it was to be small, and invisible, but she made the fire come to my cheek, a pink dusting rising from my chest to my neck. I rode a sore red wave that carried me to such pleasure I sobbed. There was no air up there where I took her. We flew together, like gulls through arcs of blue. The rustling of calico was loud in my ears. My petticoats peeled from me like skin. When I could no longer breathe and the blood was black in front of my eyes, my body understood ecstasy and I cried out.

The Hindoo, spying upon us, overheard us.

In the morning, the bedroom was filled with glaring stillness. I felt a child-like swoop of exhilaration. The world had turned white. Branches were intricately stacked with snow, and cars bore rugs. My study was a cold, light cell that seemed quite altered.

'Oh God, how beautiful,' said Lelia, and vomited into the loo.

She wiped her mouth with paper, and smiled. 'That feels so much better,' she said.

I kissed her, breathing in the smell of sick but not caring. I steadied her and took her to the kitchen. Something from the night before was flickering through the edges of my mind. I remembered what it was. 'The Hindoo'. The term bothered me. I wondered whether she had chosen it as an obscure racist insult towards my girlfriend. I felt momentarily uncomfortable, ferociously protective towards Lelia. I put my arm around her and stroked her shoulders.

We drifted with ease through such bright, calm air. A neighbour stood in his shirt sleeves, drinking from a mug as he watched the square. A single bird crossed the sky. I had never seen such snow in central London. Lelia had been working on the flat – her 'nesting instinct', she said – and the floorboards were glowing mellow slabs of age, and there were new curtains. We put the espresso maker on the stove and the air smelled of coffee and snow and warm wood, and I was reminded of being in the forests of New England in winter, and she brought out checked napkins – 'gingham', she, the inveterate clothes shopper, said – and I wanted to nestle back in bed with her and watch the brilliant iced day on our ceiling and have time to think.

She was calm and milky, her hair roughly pulled back into a chopstick, her newly larger breasts visible at the opening of her dressing-gown. I hoped we wouldn't have to talk about the baby. She washed an apple and threw it haphazardly at me for my journey to work, opening her mouth in mock surprise as I caught it, and I thought, perversely, how pleasing it would be after all to have our child, kicking, smiling, grizzling in this warm place that we had made.

I stepped out into the cold morning. The air penetrated my clothes, and amorphous sex thoughts stirred inside me. The crystalline light hurt my eyes. Lelia tapped on the glass when I had taken a few steps, and I turned, and we waved at each other.

Where was Sylvie Lavigne? I didn't care. Her smaller footprints could be here on the snow, but I wasn't interested. People on the street half-smiled at one another in passing. A man leaned out of his window on Guilford Street, smoking and hammily singing. I walked slowly to work. People were laughing in the office, as though Christmas had returned, a simple change in the weather infecting the day with new significance. I wanted to ring people, merely to talk about the weather. At lunchtime a snowball fight began on the flat roof above our Sunday paper's offices, adults becoming hysterical and aggressive as they ducked and doubled up with laughter, their hacking coughs sounding through the cold air. Cigarette smoke drifted into the sky. The prissy old education editor's glasses were dripping with melted snow; secretaries and senior staff pelted one another in a licensed outpouring of grievance or desire, and we yelled and laughed with growing exhaustion. The cars hooted on a stretch of black below; the dome of St Paul's ghosted through the sky.

As snow smashed into my teeth, I felt happy for the first time for several days. Catrin and Sylvie couldn't get me up here. Disaster couldn't happen in the face of such boisterous mania.

We trailed back down, catching our breath, my hair wet and my forehead still prickling with snow, and there across the office was a slender figure with brown hair, talking behind a glass partition to the Sunday's literary editor.

My breathing stopped. *What?* I thought.

I watched in disbelief. I felt like punching the wall. What in hell's name was she doing talking to Peter Stronson? How dare she; how bloody dare she?

The others tramped down, still out of breath, leaving ridges of snow on the carpet and talking loudly. I waited as they piled into the lift or went to the staircase. I didn't know what to do. Sylvie Lavigne. I wanted to staunch my humiliation. I wanted to collar her in indignation. I wanted to hear her voice again. I waited until the last lift was filled, and she began to walk in my direction, still talking, gazing into the middle distance as she spoke. She said goodbye briefly to Peter Stronson, and walked along the passage towards me.

She looked delicate, the shadows below her eyes somehow appealing in a faintly consumptive way. Her brown-green irises were vivid, almost amber-flecked in the snow-light from the window, and contrasted with her pale skin. She caught my eye and gave me a radiant smile. Elation soared through me. I felt humble, grateful, inordinately pleased. Instinctively, I moved towards her, and we hugged, and kissed each other on the cheek in a normal social fashion, as though she were a normal social being.

'Where are you going?' she said.

'Out with you,' I replied automatically. I was both impressed and alarmed by my own boldness.

She dropped her gaze. 'Oh, I—' she said. She swung her arm, and her fingers brushed the back of my hand. The feeling of her skin on mine shocked me.

'Come on,' I said, and grabbed her arm. 'It's beautiful. We can walk – where? Through Gray's Inn Gardens . . .'

We got into the lift. I guided her along our floor, steering her away from my desk along a route obscured by a passage of cloth-covered partitions, and out past reception.

'Won't you get into trouble?' she said. I could hear amusement in her voice.

'Probably.'

I led her along Clerkenwell Road where we opened our months to catch the flakes that fell silently from a white sky, and into the great smooth expanse of Gray's Inn, where the scars of lunchtime footprints were already filling with new snow, and black-clothed lawyers walked past Georgian terraces rising from the whiteness, and we could have landed in any century.

I loved Lelia. I had a different woman on my arm. Insanity had found me and taken me, and yet I floated, obstinately and criminally unthinking, as if the magic that protected me from Catrin would shelter me once more. To my relief, I was reminded again of Sylvie's reserved demeanour and muted appearance. I knew that other men would never even notice her, though I occasionally wondered whether someone else – some amorphous, perceptive rival – might, after all, see what I saw. I promised myself that I would do nothing with her, and was comforted by my resolve. We would merely walk. And I would explain myself to her, and then consider the problem of Catrin.

She was silent.

'What is this novel you're writing?' I wanted to ask her, but I didn't dare, in case I alienated her by enquiring and she left me.

She seemed calm and self-contained, taking small steps through the snow and looking all about her. I glanced at her. I wanted her to do something: to desire me, or to tell me never to kiss her again, but she did neither. She ignored me, her features clean-cut in profile, never turning to me or seeking response. I found myself inventing comments to amuse her, or to interest that clever mind. Her mouth was composed, her lips slightly parted in relaxation. A snowflake lay on the faint gleam where her upper lip met her skin. I wanted to lick it. I wanted to shake her into a display of emotion.

Do something, I thought. Turn to me. Please me. Chide me. Say something. She didn't. Her lips moved faintly into a smile: at nothing, at the air, but she ignored me still. Her simple refusal to respond goaded me. I wanted to push her into the snow and delve through all those layers of clothes and take her, there and then. A deep moan formed in my mind.

'*When a woman falls from purity there is no return for her – as well may one attempt to wash the stain from the sullied snow,*' she said in her sweet, catching tones. 'That was written in the 1860s, but I think there's still truth in it now. Don't you?'

I turned to her, taken aback, but she carried on talking as though she had merely commented on the weather. The amplified compression of snow beneath our feet rang in the silences between her words.

I wondered what it would be like. The small body, the sudden neat flare of hair. The idea, so inappropriate, made me quiver. I imagined rocking against those narrow hips, her chaste self-containment worryingly novel. It would resemble a different season, a different world.

The barristers drifted like ravens across the snow to their chambers. Our breath merged.

She was delectable, I thought. She was not plain. I let the realisation take hold. She was fine-boned and subtle and scented; she held secrets. She possessed her own slender perfection, with her smooth white skin, her slanting dark eyebrows, her small private chest. She smelled of almonds and milk. Her shapes fitted together once you looked: her delicate hands, her wrists, her ankles, her movements.

Lights came on in the windows. The hiss of a bus beyond the railings. Nothing. Nothing else. Just us and trees, and berries gleaming through the snow.

She talked on in her enthralling, surprising voice.

My crotch tightened.

'My hands are cold,' she said.

'No gloves. Cold little paws,' I said, feeling a terrible, fleeting stab of treachery. 'Put this one in my pocket.'

I glanced at her again. She looked ahead. She was spiky, unimpeachable. The idea of being close to that alabaster skin was almost impossible, yet here she was, calmly referring to illicit sex in the lulling tones she might employ to tell a child a bedtime story.

She put her hand in the deep pocket of my coat. She moved about, resetting her fingers, the cloth whispering against my hip bone. She was motionless again. I wondered if our gait had caused the movement. Then I felt the faint drift of her hand, as though she stretched her fingers out into a star, and drew them back. Her fingers moved across me in firm, small patterns, seemingly incidental. The nerves at the top of my thigh sprang to life.

'A bench,' I said, nodding. We sat on snow below trees in a white cave, our merging breath forming another wall in front of us. We were alone. I pulled her small body towards me in one movement and tried to kiss her again. This time she responded. Blood rushed to my head. As if in a dream, we kissed hotly, deeply, for time-warped moments, then she pulled away.

She pulled away, yet her hand was still inside my pocket, and moving, making rings of my own blood. My head felt light. She stopped, arching one eyebrow. My mouth opened. I made myself still again. She inched towards the corner of my pocket, her fingers stretching out and whispering patterns, her nails dragging against the cloth until my skin goose-pimpled and I almost cried out. I tightened my grip, pulling her further towards me so that her head settled against my neck. She stopped the movement of her hand. 'Be still,' she murmured.

'No,' I said.

She bit me on the back of the neck. I gasped. The small pale ghost of a girl sucked my skin in one shocking stab of pain. I was indignant; I cried out; she bit harder, keeping her mouth attached to me until the pain was sharp and numbed, and distinct pleasure rose to mingle with its after-waves.

Snow fell on to us, sliding on to our clothes from the trees. She ran her finger through it and pressed it into my neck, murmuring laughter as its needles shot coldness into my skin. I turned to her. I could not stay still. Every instinct in me made me want to take control. But if I moved, she stopped. She gazed at me steadily, her bruise-shadowed eyes disconcerting but lovely in the winter light. She said nothing, her full mouth composed as she traced whorls on my thigh that made my breathing turn shallow. It was impossible. I turned to her and embraced her. She laid her head delicately against my neck and suspended the movements of her hand.

'Please,' I whispered, the end of the word emerging as a bullish croak.

'Next time,' she murmured into my neck.

The snow had stopped, and the afternoon had become a luminous blue. I turned once and watched her back disappearing and emerging again as she walked along the street towards home. She had gone. At that moment, I felt like fucking a prostitute. The desire had previously hit me only as the most hypothetical and tawdry fantasy. Now I wanted to disappear into one of the prim Georgian houses that lined my path and fuck out my orgasm with someone bodily and garlicky and unsubtle, before returning in a cleansed and tranquil state to contemplate Sylvie again in the snow. The thought made me laugh, just as it made me shudder.

I strode into the office, explaining nothing, and dealt with the pile-up of messages that had accumulated in my absence. I had to put my pages to bed the following day, and I was ridiculously behind. Six o'clock arrived. I emailed MacDara. I was unable to contemplate what I'd done, my thought processes a dislocated sequence of exhilaration and terror that couldn't yet be put into language. I had to delay seeing Lelia.

I chose a loud and grotty Italian a few streets away where MacDara and I could speak at a normal level and get drunk in a corner. We both grinned when he walked in, delighting in each other's company, and began to talk before he had sat down.

'I've turned into a fucking teenager,' he said, slapping his briefcase on the table.

'Wet dreams and foul moods?' I said. 'Att-*wactive*, MacD.'

'Worse,' he muttered, rearranging himself in a sliding pile of newspaper, snowy gloves and mobile.

'Are you a surly egomaniac with only your dick for a friend?'

He sniggered. 'Basically, yes.'

'A monomaniac. How is she?'

'How should *I* know? Ask her manly consort.'

'Haven't you seen her?'

'Nope.'

'Why not?'

'How should I know? I'm not *allowed* to, I suppose – I might get above myself. She must keep me on my toes at all times. Anyway, good little wifey has to stay at home and suck off hubby.'

'What does he do?'

He shrugged. 'Shovel shit?'

'So has she come back?' I said, gingerly picking up an oil-smeared plastic-covered menu. 'Been in touch, I mean?'

'Why do you like greasy spoons so much?' said MacDara grumpily, scanning the Specials board with its clumsy gothic writing. He was stubbled, as ever, his hair disordered with snow that had melted and dried it into short spikes.

I laughed. 'You look like Dennis the Menace,' I said.

'Thanks.'

'So what's happened?'

'Yeah, well, she's condescended to phone me. The bitch. I'm *meeting* her tomorrow. Fuck. It makes my insides go just to think about it.'

'Have you shagged her yet?'

He shook his head miserably, like the bear that he re-sembled. 'Everything but. We were going to. She slipped away. Don't know what's happened. My knob's just about . . .'

An image came unbidden. A spasm of arousal shot through me as I remembered the lapping heat in my thigh, the insis-tent pain at the back of my neck as it mounted to pleasure. I wanted to tell him. I wanted to shock him, surprise him, impress him. I took a vast gulp of rough red wine, then another. Its warmth travelled up my spinal cord to my head, and tempting plans began to bloom. Wouldn't marriage, enhanced by the most subtle, clandestine affair – all silent, urgent meet-ings in flats, tucked into slips in time – coat each day with a delectable sensation of *aliveness*? It would be like a passionate hobby, each day adding a jewel to the collection.

'Tell me,' I said, grinning, playing for time to prevent myself from rashly blurting out a confession when Catrin was holding fire.

'. . . coming off,' he said. 'Worn away.'

'I see.'

'I've never been like this,' MacDara roared, thumping the table so that the salt cellar jumped. I laughed. 'I'm doing everything I stopped doing at nineteen. Our communications era is a fucking *nightmare*, Richard. If I'm not 1471-ing, I'm checking the frigging call-waiting, fax, mobile − voicemail and texts − emails.'

'I told you to cut down contact,' I said in as strict a voice as I could be bothered to muster. 'Does she email a lot?'

'Emails − yes. Proper, normal human contact − no.'

'Right,' I said. 'Tell me more.'

'I can't − I can't *sleep*. When have you known me not to sleep?'

'Never,' I said. 'You're a snoring warthog with narcolepsy.'

'Exactly.'

The crowds began to fill the booths, smoke rising as we ate superior pasta and tasteless buttery fish. I ordered more wine.

'Catrin,' I said tentatively, my heartbeat accelerating. 'Has she said anything? I mean—' I said, hearing myself.

'No,' said MacDara blankly.

'Right . . .' I said.

I laughed. I goaded him into further confession, guessing at the most sordid of his new habits, teasing him viciously as I invented new perversions for him and drank more wine. Snow lined the sills outside. People arrived, breathing loudly and stamping their feet. Stern, overworked waitresses wove through crowded tables of shouting people, and the air was festive. I was in a kamikaze good mood. I had a few days' grace, though my crimes had now proliferated and I was intoxicated with lust. But beyond simple lust, I was buoyed up by the astonishment of desire reciprocated by a strange Victorian virgin. A stream of exhilaration, laced with alcohol, ran like poison through my blood. I felt the soreness at the back of my neck.

'How many emails tomorrow, then, slave driver?'

'Two,' I replied, distracted. 'When are you meeting her?'

'Afternoon,' said MacDara. He opened his diary. 'Three o'clock.' He laughed. 'She wrote in it.'

I pulled his diary towards me. *If we do meet again, why we shall smile*, I read. The handwriting was small, unremarkable.

'A quote!' I said. 'For a philistine like you. Does this woman *read*?' I asked, my mind drifting to Sylvie and her bookish ways and her mouth and that mouth on my neck. 'How do you cope, MacD?' I teased him.

'Shut up,' said MacDara. He paused and looked disconcerted. 'Give it back.'

'You'd better read a book.'

'Shut it, Fearon,' said MacDara, pouring me more wine. 'Tell me something else,' he said, pulling the diary back and closing it. 'What's new in the world of hacking?'

The wine descended through my head in languorous spirals. I checked my watch. I would have to go home soon, or Lelia would be worried and angry and we'd have a ghastly row about it, but I couldn't. I did not want to go home. The guiltier I felt, the more tetchy I was with her, and then the guilt itself worsened. I drank more. My mouth was loose with alcohol. I felt haggard. I sat there, and what was happening finally hit me. I had found the life, the woman, the love I had wanted after so many disasters, and then I had begun to destroy it. It was as though the police were tailing me, calmly following my car, and even though I drove a steady course, I knew that my alcohol levels were over the limit, and that when they stopped me, I would be arrested. There was nowhere to hide. And what I didn't know was whether we would drive and drive down interminable side streets, warding off inevitability, or whether they would pull me over at any moment.

ELEVEN

Lelia

As the nausea rose, I pressed my fingers together, watching the colour change beneath my nails. It sometimes amazed me that I had blood, like other people, flowing invisibly, and now revealing its flush of red to me. Inadequate, or strange, or unwittingly harmful as I might be, my body behaved like other humans', something that touched me and surprised me when I felt despairing about myself.

I hung my head over the loo, and sickness rolled inside me, my mouth filling with saliva. I heard the phone ring as I pulled the flush; it was too late to pick it up. There was another message from Catrin to call her, but I couldn't have a conversation when all I wanted was to vomit. I could do nothing. Was this what happened? Did sickness drive women into their own sealed-off world of obsession and memory, a place of nightmares and scrappy images from the past?

My body was changing. A dark line scored my stomach like rind. Veins glowed blue on my breasts.

I couldn't concentrate. For the first time in my life, hard work was a torment. I badly needed to complete an article for my RAE submission, but I had hardly begun, and my head of department was bothering me for it. I lowered my head over the sink and a couple of dry heaves followed. I was due to give a tutorial in half an hour to a somewhat sharp-tongued post-grad who was writing about the *nouveaux romanciers'* involvement with cinema. There was a Butor reference I needed to find, and some passages from Robbe-Grillet that needed checking over.

Lucy from along the street looked up. Stubble burn was pink around her mouth.

'Shit weather,' she said.

I looked across the gardens. The sky was muffled and expectant, as though it held more snow.

'I love it,' I said. 'How are you?'

She shrugged. She turned on her heel and faced the street. 'I see loads of stuff happening round here,' she said.

'I'm sure you do, Lucy,' I said somewhat wearily, and breathed in more air to calm my nausea. Richard's descriptions of Lucy as a teenage evil force returned to me. My throat contracted. 'Bye,' I said rapidly, and fetched myself a bowl.

I was so very tired, my head seemed weighted, as though it nodded from side to side. I fell asleep. When I woke, it was lunchtime and my student would have given up long ago. My shock at myself was buoyed by a kind of internal smile at my own new carelessness. Whenever the sickness wore off in the afternoon, my senses sprang to life. I drifted up to our bed.

Bespectacled virgin that I was, the first time I really thought about sex was in France. My penfriend Sophie-Hélène, with her thick black plait, her affronting tufts of underarm hair and blood-stained underwear, was more mature than I was. When I couldn't stand the pain of mourning any more, I talked about sex with this girl who knew, because sex seemed to be grief's opposite, the most fantastically exciting idea. We sat on the flimsy concrete bridge that curved over the garden's stream, where she whispered oblique hints of what it was she did, yet even with the limitations of my French, I understood.

But when Easter came with its prayer books and stilled mopeds, and Sophie-Hélène all but deserted me, I realised I had been just a substitute until her friend's arrival. He was called Mazarine, like the cardinal. A small, guarded and epicene boy with dull-brown hair and a vocabulary that defeated me, he warned me off even as he addressed me with the most formal good manners.

There was nothing for me to do. Sophie-Hélène's mother opened her door on to the street every day for the sweeping-out of invisible dust before a play-group invaded her house, when my own room was required for toddler naps. I couldn't bear to be in the way; I couldn't stand to be tolerated, so I followed Mazarine and Sophie-Hélène instead and hid myself there, on my own, killing the hours.

He was the doctor's son. The doctor ran her surgery in her own house, following small-town French custom, the patients filing in through a side door to a waiting-room converted from a conservatory. The emerging smells filled me with guilt-battered horror: medicinal wafts, edges of disinfectant; the scent of a heart attack, the ambulance coming to take my father away on a stretcher. The doctor, Madame Bellière, though heavily pregnant, worked well into the evening, frowning through her fifties spectacles and choppy, thick boy's fringe. She was an unsmiling dromedary of a woman, shirted and androgynous behind her pebble glasses. She left her son to his own devices; in fact, as I soon came to realise, she neglected him. It was painful to watch.

Mazarine's father, clearly absent, was never mentioned; his mother was pregnant by another man, and the child was able to spend the day – nine or ten hours at a time, each one noted as a ritual by me – whispering in a yard behind the kitchen door, or ensconced with Sophie-Hélène in their private room at the top of the house, unheard and un-observed by the mother. If I wandered down and happened to pass Madame Bellière in the hallway between patients, she would address comments to me in her formal manner, enquiring after my happiness, stiffly praising me for my French or my appearance as though she felt sorry for me, and in her pity for the fatherless dark girl, there was a glimmer of empathy that rarely emerged in her dealings with her own child.

Rival though Mazarine was, his efforts to please his mother nearly broke my heart. He tried so hard to be good. Whatever happened to him, he tried. He hushed his companion if the solemn-faced doctor came into the house, his face a pale triangle of anxiety; he prepared little gifts and surprises for her in a way that I'd never seen a boy do. He had no real concept of play.

I explored alone when they were in their room, climbing high through that shuttered miniature château of a house heavy with antiques – fading wool curtains strung across antique spears; chamber pots hidden in scrolly armoires – past books belonging to the boy that intimidated me, until one day, on a floor above the modern showers, I found a bath. An old bathroom, barely used, with dusty floorboards and closed shutters. I lay there for most of the day, and listened to silence and muffled conversation and sex, and praised a god that was my father.

He was there in patterns on the ceiling (I searched in a guilty panic as I lay down in the belching yellow water each morning until I found the particular stain that was him); his substance ran to me with the water; I heard him speak to me, and then the room was empty. There was his own island of chipped enamel in the archipelago that freckled the head of the bath, and the more I hit that particular spot with my forehead, the more I appeased the wrathful god attached to my father who blamed me for the ignorance and wilfulness that had allowed his death. However much I prayed, I knew that I had killed him. I had written of a father's death in an English essay only a week and a half before – tears pricking at the death-bed scene; glory in the martyrdom of the narrator's orphanhood – and then he had died. Through my dangerous powers I had managed to let him die. *A thankless child.*

I pressed my fingertips into splinters that fringed the floor as I tested myself mechanically on French vocabulary. From a room on the other side of the house, on that same attic level, came the muted moans and writhings of two children. We were fourteen. The boy, I thought, must be younger; he was slight, his voice unbroken, his skin pale-smooth. He had begun to fascinate me. I was deeply shocked that they were giving each other such pleasure. I could barely imagine him, earnest and undersized, entangled with Sophie-Hélène. And yet, somehow, I could.

Then the tenor of the house changed. The doctor was soon to have her child, a source of some scandal in the town. The day her son overheard his mother talking about giving birth by caesarean section at the end of the week, I listened to him vomit.

I lay in bed in our flat on Mecklenburgh Square and missed Richard. I wanted to feel his weight and disappear into forgetful darkness beneath his body. But Richard with his passionate, intense, exhausting ways had drifted from me and my baby. Part of me, sealed in my own world, was secure; but beneath the self-protection I was terrified, and wanted to beg him not to abandon me as I had always secretly feared he would do when he finally saw through me and found me lacking. And if he explored further, he would find worse in me, because there was something that I suspected about myself that I couldn't make myself tell him. There was a worm at the core of me.

That winter, he wanted to be with MacDara, or drinking, or pretending to himself that he was about to swap his urban existence for a life of rugged adventure. He did not want to be with someone who was pregnant.

'Let's go and live on a boat,' he always said.

'But it would be awful,' I'd reply, having visited friends in damp and rocking nightmares full of cold bunks on the Thames.

'I really think we should live on a boat,' he had announced more recently.

'Yes, we will sometime,' I had learnt to say for convenience, and my simple assent kept him satisfied.

As it grew darker, I went to bed once more. He hadn't returned. '*Richard*,' I murmured, and willed him to come home to me.

I lay back and opened my legs, and I thought once more of the little incubus, and I rose to the easy numb orgasms of masturbation. It was ten o'clock. I had a baby I was growing on my own. I had a love who was slowly abandoning me.

TWELVE

Richard

I had, perhaps, a few days left. Even without the intervention of the awful Catrin, I would have been toppled by my own guilt or by some nasty fate-ridden surprise. Yet I had only snogged a woman. Sense spoke to me, mixing caution and relief, and reminding me that I could salvage what I still had, scarred though it would be by the terrible weight of Lelia's angry disappointment. But every time I recalled a hot little ghost in the snow – like a film, like a film watched long ago – I wanted to see her again.

She didn't call. Catrin, it would seem, hadn't rung again. Lelia was my Lelia; we were both busy, I barely caught her eye in the rush between appointments and winter darkness and late bedtimes, and two days of eternity managed to pass. I escaped early in the morning along frozen pavements to the office, where there were no emails from Sylvie to break the silence, the air outside too cold for snow to fall again. I looked out at the street and contemplated confessing to Lelia; or simply waiting, as blindly and merrily as a half-wit, for my doom. At the back of my neck, as yet undiscovered by her, a patch of skin was tender if I pressed it.

Another day passed. I am dying, Egypt, dying, I thought

hammily, dementedly, my own internal voice a nervy ticker-tape of non sequiturs.

'I'm passing by,' said Sylvie Lavigne, her voice a shock on my office phone. 'We could meet very briefly if you want to.'

'Yes,' I said, stupid and husky. Where? I thought. *When?*

'There's that café beside your building. I'll pass it in about ten minutes.'

'Ten minutes?' I said dumbly, the nerves in my scalp leaping.

She was silent. I felt myself grow hot in the space between words.

'I'll see you there,' I said.

The café was a homey choke after the crystalline air outside. She smiled at me from the gloom of a corner at the back, where she sat upright behind a table in a beret and a coat. The beret lent a curve of life to her hair. She looked prim again, like an immaculately polished convent girl, all soaped and clean but unadorned. In today's prudish guise, she would inevitably appear in my night-time fantasy.

I moved towards her through a cloud of espresso steam, as if to kiss her, but her posture remained unchanged, and I merely touched her cheek with the side of my mouth and sat down, rebuffed. I caught fragments of her skin smell through the smoke and bacon fat; dislodged snow melted in glittering ovals on her beret; her mouth was a pale series of swoops.

'Hello,' I said. I smiled.

She turned to me and smiled back, her eyes creasing and catching mine.

'Oh, it's lovely to see you,' I said spontaneously.

'You too,' she said. 'Very.'

'Where're you going?' I said.

'I've got someone to see,' she said. I glanced down and noticed that she wore a ring made of three interlinked gold hoops on her little finger.

'Who?' I said in mild alarm, as it occurred to me again that of course she had a life outside her flat and her writing and her meetings with me. The idea made me immensely uncomfortable. 'Who?' I said again in disgruntled tones.

'It shouldn't matter to you,' she said.

'Well,' I said, taken aback, 'it does.'

'Then you have no right,' she said.

I pulled her to me and hugged her, aware of her fine-boned body, the delicate lines beneath her understated clothes.

'You know that we shouldn't even do that.'

'No,' I said, my heart plunging.

She was silent.

'Well, it is somewhat ill-advised, I suppose,' I said in a cavalier manner.

A thought suddenly hit me: what if Catrin saw us again? What if – as was just as likely – Lelia saw us? I looked at my watch.

I glimpsed someone from the news desk passing on the street outside; I lowered my head, and I understood with a twinge of self-disgust that if I was about to be unfaithful, I was doing nothing new. I remembered Wharton's Newland Archer experiencing the very same realisation, that this was a tired path he trod, littered with subterfuge and deceit.

I could think of nothing to say. Monologuing cabbies outdroned local women in tracksuits.

'What were you doing with Peter?' I said suddenly, turning to her.

'Who?'

'Peter Stronson. The literary editor.'

'Oh. Talking.'

'About work?'

'Yes.'

'Well, don't.'

'Why not?'

'It pisses me off,' I said.

'Why would it do that?'

'I'm jealous of other bastards printing you. And very jealous of him talking to you.'

'Other people talk to *you*,' she said. 'Other people *have* you.'

'Yes,' I said. Our arms touched.

A small hand found mine under the table. Unreasonable delight rose through me. I was a simple creature, a mere receptacle for her whims. I held the hand and pressed it, and moved my fingertips over her palm.

'You're married—'

'As good as,' I said, bowing my head as if courageously acknowledging the undeniable.

'And she's lovely. I like her. Tell me her name again. Lee . . .'

'– lia.'

'Yes.'

There was silence.

'I've been thinking about you, madam,' I said. 'A lot.'

She withdrew her hand from mine. 'So have I,' she said, looking straight in front of her. 'I do think of you, and I ought not to.'

'Oughtn't you? Shouldn't you?' I said dully.

'You know the answer to that,' she said.

'Yes, well—'

'But it's difficult. You know, when you find that understanding; when you seem to recognise each other—'

Do we have that? I wanted to say. Or do I just imagine the beginning of it? Do you feel it like I do?

'Do you remember, that evening I met you?' she said.

'I was drunk,' I said. 'I remember you—' I frowned. 'I think I remember you in the hall. It's really not good enough, is it?'

'I remember you,' she said. 'So very well. I thought you were funny. You talked a lot. I thought you were handsome.'

'I find you – beautiful,' I said, and as I said it, I knew that it was true. She seemed unmoved, as though used to the description.

I put my arm around her, and she leaned towards me hesitantly, without passion. She sat there, straight-backed with my hand on her waist, as though she had never been touched by me but was willing to tolerate the sensation. Her habitual alternation between intimacy and cool self-containment predictably hooked me as it maddened me. And yet I thought that there was an ache in her, a sorrow to her that moved me further.

She talked. She looked in front of her and talked in the way that she wrote, ornately and easily, until her throaty-sweet voice filled my ears; but still she didn't move. Eventually, pretending that I required sugar, which I then didn't take out of obstinate pride, I removed my arm.

She turned away from the window.

'What?' I said.

'There's someone I don't want to see.'

'Who?'

'Oh,' she said, a flicker of distaste on her face. 'He follows me.'

'What? *Who?*' I said.

'Oh, just an – ex.'

'An *ex*!' I said.

'Don't even talk about him,' she said, her full top lip curling.

'Well, I *want* to,' I said forcefully.

'Oh, Richard.'

Next time, she had said. I remembered, like a shot in the air, those two words murmured into the skin of my neck. Here we were; and next time was now.

'But,' she said, continuing her conversation of before, 'we don't really know each other. I don't know you, but in my head, somehow it's you I turn to – by instinct – to share a thought. I wake sometimes in the night, with the oddest things occurring to me, and I feel as though I hear your voice. I do obscure things, madnesses—'

I waited. The opinions of taxi drivers merged around me.

'What?' I said. I could barely think. She had bitten the back of my neck and traced delicate patterns upon my thigh. I glanced at her fingers. Small, delicate, still.

'What?' she said. 'Thinking the words for days of the week have colours. Favouring certain apples in a bowl and feeling sorry for others. My heart aching for a second if one's left uneaten and has to be thrown away, wrinkly. Why that one? That poor one?'

An image of a Victorian child, a neglected child, came to me then, her voice winding around my ear, buzzing warmly in its various chambers so that I hardly heard what she said.

'Over-identification with inanimate objects,' I murmured. 'I do it too, Sylvie.' I recalled her fingers pattering over my thigh.

'Oh, hush, you!' she said, nudging me. Pathetically, my nerves sprang to life.

'No, I do. Synaesthesia. And games in my head, self-rewarding games.'

'And so do you do this? It's when I didn't quite catch

something someone said, or can't be bothered to re-read something that's slightly confused me, and I wonder for a moment whether I'll be frustrated by not knowing for the rest of my life. Will I regret it for ever, when I could easily say, "Sorry?" now, or re-read the section; but I let it pass, still fixated on it?'

'Me too. Was that a Great Dane or some vast kind of wolf thing that just trotted past on Hampstead Heath? Can I be bothered to crane my head round? If not, will I always wonder?'

'Let's go to Hampstead Heath one day,' she said.

'Yes, let's fucking go.'

'Or fuck,' she said.

I froze. A vast clattering of crockery – heaven, suspended there in the steam; surely it will break, all that white vitrified ware they hurl together? – and a cacophony of glottal stops.

I coughed. 'Or fuck,' I said.

The espresso machine whined.

I turned slowly to the young woman beside me: pale skin, bruised eyes, dark schoolgirl V-neck. It was the subtlety that I wanted to taste, the tiniest markings visible against that pale skin, the miniature perfection of her. She was still composed, now opening a menu with slender fingers. The faintest suggestion of a smile was detectable on her mouth. I took her shoulders, the width of them together so surprisingly small, in both my hands.

'I think about you all the time,' she said, her tone unchanging.

'And so do I,' I said. 'I'll meet you at Pryors Field. Do you know that place? It's not one of the obvious ones. And we'll – walk.'

'I do know it,' she said. She glanced up. The espresso machine's steam-engine shriek filled the room.

'You have to go,' I said, to pre-empt her, because I couldn't bear the tension any more. She nodded. For the first time, she turned to me. She swept her eyes up at mine, as though scanning me. We kissed. Replaying it, replaying it all afternoon with a queasy punch in my stomach, I didn't know who moved towards whom. Despite all those people at the tables, despite the proprietors and the waitress and the possible proximity of colleagues, we kissed, my breath caught and flailing. I felt the spinning of oxygen deprivation in my head when I sat up again.

'Now I've let you in,' she said.

I nuzzled her ear and her neck, breathing in the skin. We kissed again and murmured, secretive, half-laughing.

She leaned towards me, and her voice was hot yet lulling in my ear. 'If you take me,' she whispered. 'If I take you. If – if one day – I want it to be wild.'

I let out a tiny, involuntary groan. I murmured assent through my nose. 'Yes,' I said.

She stood up, holding my hand, and I saw her to the door; we brushed each other's sleeves with our fingers, and I sank back down in the same seat, staring across the room.

Hampstead. I fantasised about it that night A wild heath, so tangled and brackened and howling, high and boar-ridden in the blue transparency of winter afternoon. I went to bed early to postpone guilt and think about Hampstead Heath. Why had I chosen a place where gay men met? Why had I chosen the tufty exposed slab of land that was Pryors Field? There were better places: divings of bush below Parliament Hill; gnarled old oak clusters, a delightful dairy. It didn't matter. The heath wailed at me: *The Hound of the Baskervilles, The Wolves of Willoughby Chase, The Return of the Native.* There I would take her. Lelia lay beside me. She had come to bed early.

'No – read,' I said to her.

'No, no,' she said. 'I want to be with you.'

My own stream of thought continued as she murmured, found her book, murmured again.

She cuddled up to me. For pleasurable seconds, I incorporated the whispering passing of cloth against skin into my fantasy. She bit my shoulder. She gave a pretend bray: one of the animal noises that we found ourselves making in bed for no remembered reason.

I luxuriated. I lay back with my legs lying casually open and loose at the hips like a frog's. Every time I pictured that slender pale thing meeting me on the heath, a hot metallic spasm seemed to seize me, as though I were a teenager and could barely control my desires. What day would it happen? Tomorrow? Tomorrow was too soon, too terrifying. I needed to delay it and savour it, but not for too long. Wednesday? My diary lay open in my mind, blank and ready. Any day, any day I would meet her there as dusk began to hide us: I had no work, no life, that would stop me. I lay in bed calculating the logistics of escaping to Pryors Field on press day.

Lelia wanted sex. I couldn't; I simply could not. I stayed pinned to the moment, her hand moving across my chest as I pictured the outer grounds of Kenwood, the ponds in ice, the hilly dive near South End Green.

Experimentally, I touched Lelia, my hand sinking into the hot folds of her nightdress. She wore billowy nightclothes, as though she were vast with child already. Even that fact seemed tiresome to me. Her breasts were ripe. She was vivid where Sylvie was subtle. I couldn't do it. Sylvie appeared from the hedgy shadows on Pryors Field. Lelia's lips opened. Her dark hair on the pillow.

We hugged. She brought her mouth to mine. The pleasing

scent of her pheromones was all about her breath, her tongue.

An urchin girl, dodgy as a photograph by Lewis Carroll, shadowed Pryors Field just as I had thought she had failed to turn up, and became more womanly and refined the closer I came to her. Lelia's thigh pressed between my legs. I couldn't marry the two. I couldn't offer Lelia Sylvie Lavigne's erection.

She was pulling me on top of her. My erection subsided. Desperately, I summoned images of loose women, sailor boys, raddled old screen goddesses; anything that would keep me hard. A ghost wandered through Hampstead Heath. I would not chase it.

The monthly nurse had been engaged. I seemed to hear a baby's cry, but it was in my head only, or it had flown ahead of time from its briny home to taunt me. The boy-to-be had placed a glow-smile on its mother's mouth like a kiss.

I tried every day to be better, by creeping and learning and disciplining myself. I sewed samplers for her. I hid and stitched in the day nursery. If I met her eye, I caught glances in return like speckled fish, darting distaste beneath the mud. I tried to remove myself from her as much as I was able. I thought that if I laced myself in so that I was as small as my body would let me be and made myself invisible and studied harder and more harshly until my mind was half-maddened with learning, then one day I could find a corner of the world that was mine.

Emilia and I practised. When I dressed as a gentleman, and we became married, then I could make her cry out and sigh.

It was dark in the early mornings. I got up, checked my computer and read Sylvie's anonymous emails, perversely hooked in my fascination with their sender. At other times, I skimmed their opening lines before deleting them, unwilling to allow my mental picture of her to be ruffled for the day by this disturbing aspect of her psyche. Although it was hard to fathom what she was on about, those creepy little segments of melodrama bothered me; yet I would never probe, just as I avoided a number of subjects for fear of frightening her off.

I waited, in frustration, for Hampstead Heath, but Sylvie Lavigne was as elusive as I was careful by necessity. The weather was still icy, tiny remnants of children's clumps of snow preserved in the shadows. I propped notes on the table and left for work when Lelia was half-asleep: poor Lelia, trying to ward off the moment when she must face her nausea because the child of both of us grew inside her. I clenched my fingers in horror at my own behaviour. Soon this would stop, I thought. I would make myself stop it, because it was wrong and unfair; it was despicable. It would stop, and everything would be normal, and I would attempt to be a good husband.

I frequently took detours, almost without noticing I was doing so, yet pleasurably nurturing some vague, talismanic notion that I might see her as I walked among postmen and street cleaners and early vibrating buses. I knew now where her block of flats was, and I edged towards Endsleigh Street, skimming the south end of Tavistock Square before turning back. I went past Gray's Inn Gardens, the magical land now muddy and ice-spiked. By mid-morning, I had usually contacted her.

We drank terracotta tea in a roar of taxi drivers many times during those winter days. Smoky boltholes full of grease and bursting sausages that seemed safe from colleagues and passing friends and Catrin, though I kept a perpetual nervous eye upon the street. With a stab of sorrow, I was reminded that Lelia liked greasy spoons as much as I did, understanding their glories, grabbing their stained tabloids and revelling in their cuisine as MacDara and no doubt Sylvie never would.

As we perused smeared menus over the steam of tea, we murmured about books and people and obscure notions, and she spilled fragments of her life: surprising splinters of revelation among all that was private and withheld. There were indications of another world she inhabited, another past, a life that I wanted to penetrate and possess that featured friends and exes and shadowy unwanted suitors and conversations with Peter Stronson, but much as I tried, I could never pin it down. Different locations were mentioned, then rarely referred to again. I caught echoes of her lunatic's novel in her fleeting descriptions of her childhood: her mother, a source of unexplained grief, appeared to be as absent as her father and sister. Her apparent alienation from her family bothered me, but I swallowed my sense of disquiet, just as I was forced to accept her evasions and refusals. She clearly had some kind of minimal private income that sustained her through her academic work, and money appeared to be a source of anxiety, but even that she wouldn't explain to me. Yet in her presence, I was blessed; I was understood; *we* understood each other, she said. 'You are like me,' she said. '"I *am* Heathcliff",' I said, teasing her. '". . . a very respectable man, though his name was Richard",' she said, teasing me back.

She asked me about my life, and my childhood, and all the moments that had made me before I had met Lelia. And then, sometimes, she would tell me more − a thought she had had, a certain aspect of her girlhood, a notion about writing − and I would listen through the scream of bus brakes, enthralled, as though I were being read a novel, the Italian dialect that she partly understood all around us, the catch in her voice near my ear. I luxuriated in her atmosphere and her tones and the smell of her hair, each clean strand of scent as subtly different as varying shades of colour.

She would look at me levelly and say things I did or didn't want to hear, as if viewing our insular land with an outsider's objectivity, and I was discomfited, and invigorated. 'Your gay boss,' she'd casually begin a sentence.

'*What?*' I said, a barely conscious suspicion flaring into life. 'Is he gay?'

'Of course.'

'How do you know?'

'But of course he is,' she'd say, then continue her theme, quite unemotionally, with a discussion about my own hypothetical homosexual existence. 'If you were a poof, you'd fancy MacDara,' she said.

'I would *not!*' I said, shouting with laughter at the idea.

'Yes you would. He'd drive you to acts of violence, but you'd be eternally, grudgingly wedded.'

'Bollocks, Sylvie!' I said.

'He'd be your kind of man,' she said, raising one eyebrow. 'Always warring. It's probably because you half-hate your father.'

'*Do* I?' I said wonderingly.

Or she would ask, in matter-of-fact tones, 'Why are you so fixated with your siblings' finances?', or tell me that I was kinder than I knew, or brusquer, and then suggest that my sailing obsession, charming though she found it, was an excuse not to engage fully in the desk-bound occupation I had chosen for myself. 'I think that you're very clever but you pretend not to be,' she said. 'You celebrate the lowbrow.'

'Do I?' was all I could say, somewhat stunned.

'Yes. Who are you protecting with it?'

At night, the choking dive or plain little bakery with tables in which I had felt her skin against mine that day returned to me. Hampstead Heath came to me as a promise once made, rearing above me like some precipitous, craggy terrain still held evasively, maddeningly, at one remove; and then I tried to sleep to drown guilt and marital sex.

'The French girl, Sylvie,' said Lelia one Monday morning in March.

'What?' I said, abruptly. 'Is she French?' I added, to soften my tone.

'Well, partly. She must be,' said Lelia.

'Right,' I said. I felt my face twitch involuntarily.

'I know, I know, boring academics and all that. I saw her from the window the other day.'

My heartbeat took a ragged leap.

'I waved, but she didn't see me.'

'Right,' I said again.

'I'd just been wondering about her. I was wondering how she was. I got her a pass for Senate House ages ago.'

'Did you?' I said, surprised.

'Yes.'

'Right.'

'It was strange. I was always worried that she was somehow a recluse. But then she referred to living with someone, and I saw her quite differently after that. I think she's just—'

'*What?*' I said.

Lelia looked at me. She raised her eyebrows questioningly. 'Well, just secretive. Not lonely at all.'

'No, I mean – she doesn't, can't live with anyone! She's just a pale-faced little spinster, for God's sake – an – a –

spinster — living somewhere in some granny flat.'

Lelia laughed. 'She does, though. Someone called Charlie. I was surprised, too.'

'Well, who the fuck is he?' I burst out, barely able to control my tone.

'No, no, it's a woman — just her flatmate.'

'Charlie?'

'Yes.' Lelia frowned. 'Well, I *assumed* so from the way she said it.' She paused. 'Oh. I suppose — Charlie. It could be either. I don't know. Perhaps she was being coy, and he's her boyfriend.' She shrugged.

'Impossible!' I burst out, my heartbeat accelerating to dangerous levels.

Lelia glanced at me, and laughed again. 'You really do think she's dreadful, don't you? A dull little virgin, like my worst schoolfriends, thanks so much. I wouldn't be so sure.'

'Oh, fuck knows,' I said, regaining a semblance of composure. 'I don't know. I don't care. How are your nipples? How's your puking? Let's have coffee.'

The *bitch*, I thought as I left to walk to work. The two-timing, treacherous, cunning little bitch. *Hampstead Heath*, I remembered. My legs weakened with a stab of lust: in a return to youthful habits, I was perversely piqued by rejection. I stamped upon such emotion. I refused to countenance it. The lying little bitch could go to hell. I opened my diary at work and began to fill it. I emailed Ren and suggested meeting him on Wednesday night. I rang my old college friend Katarina and arranged lunch. I called MacDara, who was shouty mid-deal and barked unpleasantly that he would call me back. I agreed to lunch with Sophie from the features desk, and then hacked my way through some of the work that had accumulated during my latest period of distraction. Yet I had to find out whether Sylvie Lavigne lived with some randy bastard who murmured coded intimacies into her ear while he fucked her – or a sallow-skinned no-hoper who hung her tights on the radiator and nurtured resentments over the phone bill.

After a fairly riotous lunch with Sophie, I returned to continued silence. This, I had finally realised, was her way. It had been going on for weeks, months. I pulled a stack of proofs from my desk, scanned some press releases, then found a note written in small, scratchy writing on a piece of lined paper torn from a reporter's notebook. *Hello*, it said. *It's me . . . Greeting you as you work, whatever you're doing when you find this. Love. I plant kisses on you. S.*

My breathing stopped momentarily. I paused, my mind speeding. When had she left it? How had she come into the office? I read it again. My heart gave an involuntary soft swoop. So that was her handwriting: mousy little academic girl writing. I realised she'd never handwritten me anything: she texted; she emailed. But somehow the writing looked vaguely familiar.

Lelia had said, within a couple of days of our meeting, 'How weird I feel like this about you already, and I don't know your birthday or your middle name yet. I don't even know your handwriting.'

It was true. Those indices of intimacy, soon to be known for ever, lurked there, ripe for discovery. Lelia's handwriting was now as familiar to me as my own, even if she tried to disguise it for Valentine's cards. I knew the style of her capitals, her numbers, even her commas. Then I remembered why Sylvie's was familiar. It must have been because I'd seen it long ago – seemingly so long ago – in Marine Ices, when she'd handed me her name and number in tiny writing. I probably still had that piece of paper somewhere in a ragged pile in my study.

'Listen,' I snapped when I next saw her.

I hesitated. My fabulously damning phrases shrivelled, replaced by a childish blurt. 'Why don't you get back to *Charlie?*' I asked.

Her eyebrows formed a jagged line as she appraised me with a look of scorn.

I floundered. 'Well?' I said angrily.

She turned away, her nose faintly aristocratic.

'In all this time. You never told me.'

'You never asked me.'

'I – but you never told me.'

'You never asked. You assumed.'

I shook my head faintly.

'Didn't you?' she said. 'You *assumed* that I didn't have anyone.'

I opened my mouth.

She said nothing. Her pale skin enhanced her coldness.

'Well, who is he?' I said eventually.

She shook her head minutely. 'We were together . . .' She tailed off.

'You used to be together?'

She glanced at me in assent.

'But now he lets you stay there?'

She said nothing.

'Out of the kindness of his heart?'

'I—' she said. 'Charlie's very kind to me.'

'Oh, is he? Who *is* dear *Charlie?*' I said aggressively. 'Your boyfriend or your flatmate? Fucking partner or cooking partner?' I went on, growing bolder. 'Or,' I added, remembering Lelia's assumptions, 'is it just a woman? Then why didn't you tell me you had a flatmate?'

She looked at me askance. 'Don't talk to me like that,' she said.

'Well, who is he?' I persisted.

'It's complicated,' she said.

'*Is* it? So you live together?' I asked, aware that my allotted time was running out.

'We're not together a lot of the time,' she said evasively.

'Oh right. So you and Charlie—'

'*You*,' she said imperiously, 'have a *flat*. Have a wife. Girlfriend. *Lover*.'

I paused, deflated. I searched for words. There was nothing to say. I felt a muscle in my neck twitch like an irritating tic.

'And double standards,' she said. 'Really, unforgivable double standards.' There was a weakening to her voice that she tried to disguise. She spoke more forcefully. 'It's just *horrible*. You shouldn't shout at me like that. I hate it. You can't do that. Leave me alone.'

I turned to her and saw her pale, pained face. I caught my breath. I pulled her to me.

'It isn't fair,' she said into my chest. 'You're – established. You're married. And you will marry her, won't you? I know you will.'

I pulled her away from me to kiss her, and a tear beneath the corner of her eye caught the light. She tried to wipe it away.

'Don't,' I said. 'Please don't.'

'You will, won't you?' she asked, scanning my face, and she looked vulnerable and desperate as I'd never seen her before. 'I know you will.'

I didn't know what to say. I pulled her towards me. Another tear was spilling over her cheek. She swiped at it with her sleeve. I looked at her and caught her eye, and saw unprecedented signs of panic in her, as though she were a trapped animal. I wanted to take away all the pain. She put her arms around my neck and pressed her mouth to mine suddenly and urgently. We stood there, kissing, the wetness of her cheeks mixing with the wetness of our mouths, and as she sobbed and I kissed every part of her face, in the midst of my pity for her, I was suffused by a strange sense of relief at the revelation of equality. I was now only wronging one person. Here was my conspirator, my little companion in crime: we were behaving badly together and, both culpable, we would play out our lust until one day – one day very soon – we would end it. The criminal seeks justification in any guise.

THIRTEEN

Lelia

All my life, I was haunted by the uneasy conviction that I could cause death. I was surrounded by its odours: my father on his stretcher as disinfectant stained the air; that same smell vibrating through the back of my nose and settling on my tongue after miscarriage. In France, I had to test my power, to prove that I didn't own it. The jury in my head – virtually *voices* in my head by this stage – weighed up all the evidence. Feeling like a mad girl, I wrote notes in French about birds and frogs my eye had caught in the garden, and buried the paper, experimenting on small creatures to find out whether I could cause their poor animal deaths just by writing about them. I searched for their corpses among the dew.

I prodded at the idea of death, because my father had gone there, and I could hardly believe that here I was, a stout, lively girl, moving and breathing and eating and shitting when he was cremated granules in the wind, or had vaporised to nothing at all. As Sophie-Hélène murmured her tales of pleasure in the garden dusk, we practised the rituals of adolescence: levitation, and fainting games involving hyperventilation followed by the holding of breath until blackness squiggled across my brain and made my father disapper. She whispered tales of asphyxiation in the bushes, hissing above the tumble of water. We enacted fragments of her descriptions of her daytime activities with Mazarine in a state of excitement.

'*Like this, like this,*' said Sophie-Hélène, her blue moon eyes dark above me, a finger on my neck and mouth as she told me what they had done; and I was the audience given only a glimpse of what had gone before; I was the poor second, *pis-aller*. We went higher and higher as we deprived ourselves of air and lost consciousness for seconds that stretched into darkness, just as she and Mazarine had done, the stifling pain sleeking into stars.

In the morning, Sophie-Hélène disappeared with her companion as she always did, while I was silent and alone, a woolly-haired specimen caught in a cage in a white town. My bathroom in Mazarine's house with its map stains and archipelagos turned into Africa in the bamboo afternoon light. In shadows sat pith helmets and hunters. I heard Mazarine and Sophie-Hélène coming up the stairs. I felt almost toxic with jealousy. I sometimes cried. I wanted to glimpse them, net them, keep them stuffed on a shelf in the sunlit dust and share their pleasure. I wanted his approval; I wanted him to look at me.

The mother went out in the afternoon: I saw a packet of X-rays delivered from Gien waiting for her, untouched, on the hall table. A furious whispering began on a high flight of stairs. They came pitter-pattering along the corridor. I crept to the door. I watched them mounting the stairs, quite naked. Sophie-Hélène was taller, with small cones for breasts. I looked at Mazarine. A flat chest, a neat parting where the legs met, like a sexless doll. I stared as two almost identical white bodies turned a corner.

Mazarine was a girl. The shock of arousal was so delicious and repugnant, I never stopped dreaming about it.

★

I dreamt about it while my ordinary life went on. I think I *always* wanted quite ordinary things. Or I made myself want ordinary things because of fear of failure. I would never be an actress like the blessed group of girls who ruled our school, with their TV producer fathers and modelling contracts and Suffolk houses; I would never be a criminal lawyer or a doctor, especially not a doctor. I wanted a career for myself, but I wasn't ruthlessly ambitious or even focused in one single direction. I think, unfashionable as it was, that what I mostly wanted was a home: a home in which there was a man who didn't die, and a baby.

I spent a lifetime reading, and thinking that I would be a certain kind of person, and make myself very clever, and that one day, when I was somehow evolved enough, I would find love. And when, after so many mistakes, I met Richard, the realisation was so swift that there was a moment, the day after I had first seen him, just before lunchtime, when I knew. I knew with a sense of amazing certainty, never previously experienced, that I'd met my love.

'You did,' Richard always said. 'I did. Don't *forget* it, bride.'

We first saw each other on a boat. We referred to it as the love boat after that. It was called *Glencora*, a name (fadingly painted on the prow) that I never forgot but never repeated to anyone, even Richard, out of a superstitious wish to preserve the love. We were both in Norfolk, at Blakeney, there beside the samphire beneath the prehistoric sky, and we got on to the same boat together to see the seals in the early morning. Neither of us was interested in seals: I was fleeing failed romance, and he, always drawn to the sea, viewed a seal trip as a small sop before he could rent a fast dinghy later in the day.

I was still vaguely attached to an archaeologist called Paul who had begun to bore me; who had, thank God, eaten dubious prawns in a pub the night before, and from whose combination of illness and lust I had then escaped. Richard was there on a press trip begged from the travel desk, his ancient actress holed up in his hotel. He nearly missed that boat. If Paul hadn't eaten prawns, and Richard hadn't been drawn to the window, I would never have met him. He had been lingering in bed, he told me later, hoping to seduce his ageing girlfriend into morning sex, but the flat gleam of the sky and the call of the oyster catchers had pulled him to the window, where he spotted a boat jerking at its moorings, a movement ingrained in his mind since childhood. And he had quickly shaved and pulled on clothes, and run to the quayside. He had so nearly been forced to wait, eating crab on a bench with the water-logged breeze in his hair before setting out with a different group of people. I sat alone on the far side of the boat, and as the rope was snaking from the post, Richard Fearon, breathless, his hair untidy, bounded on to the deck, and laughed as the boat left its moorings with a jolt just as he landed.

He turned to me. 'Can I sit next to *you*?' he said, a look of enquiry upon his face.

'Yes,' I said.

He sat down. 'Thank you,' he said. 'I didn't like the look of the tracksuits over there, but I'm desperate to avoid the squealing sou'westers.'

I followed his gaze as he frowned against the mud brightness. He wore faded corduroys and a nondescript mac, against which his eyes were bluish-green, though they contained aspects of grey and bronze that revealed themselves later. I noticed then that they were beautiful eyes.

'Look at them,' he said. 'The whole of Chiswick's here.'

'I was thinking Putney,' I said.

He turned to me and smiled, and we talked over the sound of the engine, the salt-marsh water lapping just below our elbows, droplets spraying us as the gear changed and we gouged an arc through the estuary, and he looked as though he were in an early, strangely coloured film, with the louring bright sky above us, the water churning and plant-heavy. I could smell the foam of his recent shaving, see speckled evidence of his haste. He reminded me of photographs of young men in the fifties, with his traditional mac, his emphatic nose and wayward hair and slightly untamed eyebrows, and a mouth which, when still, possessed that fatal male hint of sadness. He had nice hands. I liked his voice: it was resonant and full of laughter, and he asked lots of questions for a man.

He turned to frown at the chattering crowd. 'I didn't only want to escape the blazers and Carolines,' he said. 'I wanted to grab you as my seal partner.'

'I see,' I said, and we talked for the two-hour trip, our sentences overlapping each other's and emerging faster and faster as we laughed and interrupted and – already, even then – teased each other with increasing rudeness. We threw the seals a cursory glance. The gulls arched above us; the boat chugged diesel and hot plank; the morning air brightened. I wondered how we would we see each other again, the question drilling through my brain with growing urgency and almost silencing me as the boat vibrated among the salt marshes along the final stretch and the quay loomed into sight.

'We could both get back to London tonight,' he said. 'And then meet tomorrow.'

'Yes,' I said, frozen in terrified happiness.

'Let's meet for breakfast before work.'

'Where?' I said, for something to say.

'Soho.'

'OK. Yes.'

'Can you get back tonight?'

I nodded.

I dragged Paul the archaeologist, confused and objecting, away from Blakeney before breakfast to preserve the morning spell, and spent the day in Wells, in Burnham and Cromer so that I wouldn't bump into Richard and make him disenchanted with me, with my wind-pinked skin or unchallenging boyfriend or sudden inarticulacy. I still glanced at boats in different harbours in case Richard was on them, and cut short the long weekend as we had both arranged to do by returning late that night in the face of mounting suspicion and objection from Paul. Heartlessly, I stored the argument as ballast for our break-up.

Richard and I met at eight the following morning, and we wandered round town, never stopping, alighting on café tables like impatient birds, then upping and leaving and walking miles and miles; and both of us skipped work and arrived back full of excuses after lunch, by which time I was a welling creature, a tidal wave inside me. I cried that afternoon, because there was no other way to express the emotion. I saw him that evening. I moved in with him after a fortnight.

That winter, when Richard began to come back late from work and barely had sex with me and forgot about our baby, his neglect was the fulfilment of what I'd always feared, while hoping that the fear itself would protect me from the reality. I had always assumed that this restless, confident, tiringly energetic person would slowly grow blank towards me, because I was just an obscure little nothingness from the suburbs. And worse than that: I was cruel, there were those aspects of myself that I couldn't face and couldn't explain to him. Every year, I promised myself I would think about it: by the end of January; by the end of summer; and by the time November arrived, that promise tipped itself into the following year, my round of old worries dismissed as paranoia, and still I never told Richard what I feared.

I felt as though I had burrowed into a hole and was lost there. We suffered secrets.

The phone in the flat rang, and I took it downstairs.

'Catrin!' I said.

'Hi,' she said.

'I'm really sorry. I called you back, but then you were away. It's been weeks, hasn't it?'

'It's OK,' she said. Laid-back, passive Catrin.

I glanced at my stomach in the mirror, to see how much it was growing. I stroked it.

'And . . .' I said, desperate to tell someone new. 'I'm pregnant!'

There was a pause. Languid old Catrin was incapable of rising to the occasion. 'Oh!' she said finally. 'Wow,' she added flatly. 'Congratulations.'

'Thanks.'

'I—' she said. There was silence.

'Yes,' I said. 'I've felt so *sick*. I—' I waited.

'Yes,' said Catrin. 'I mean, well, what I was going to say was . . .' She paused.

I waited. 'What were you ringing about?' I said patiently, slowly, as if stirring mud. I raised my eyebrows at myself in the mirror, raised them higher to see how far they would go.

'I don't know. I – well . . .'

'Really?' I said, suddenly curious. 'You know – you've called a couple of times.'

'Are you coming to MacDara's birthday party?'

'Yes, yes, I think so. I'm pretty sure Richard can. But what were you going to ask me?'

'Oh, that. That,' said Catrin. 'Sorry. I was just ringing. I had to – I have to get an idea of numbers early.'

I paused. I laughed awkwardly, through my nose. 'Wasn't there anything else?' I said eventually.

'No,' said Catrin, now distant, as though her mouth was further away from the receiver. 'No, no. Just that. I hope you can come.'

FOURTEEN

Richard

The phone started to ring as I threw my coat on the sofa. My shattered nerves raced in unison. Catrin had returned sometime before to London, yet Lelia had said nothing more about her. I steeled myself, as I still did every time the phone rang. It was MacDara, pestering me for an answer to his birthday party invitation.

'Yeah, yeah, Mac,' I said.

'Well, you git. Are you coming?' he bellowed above ringing phones.

'Next month's pretty busy,' I shouted, rapidly running out of excuses. 'I'll try.'

'You'd better bring me a fucking good present after this,' he said.

'I'll adopt you a hippo from the zoo or something,' I said, and burped.

'Two,' barked MacDara. 'A mating couple.' He put the phone down.

Lelia wasn't there. I walked over to the window, threw it open, and paced around the flat. It seemed bigger without her. Chilled air sliced through the window, and I let it flood over my skin. It felt as though I were tacking through a high wind. I glanced at the gardens. The extreme coldness would end at any minute, and the unreal state in which I was suspended would melt and collapse. It made me feel sick.

'Darling!' said Lelia, walking in. 'I thought you wouldn't be here yet.' She dropped her gaze.

We hugged. She looked tired, genuinely tired: there was no trace of the Blessed Virgin expression.

'Sit down,' I said. 'How are you?'

'OK,' she said. Our eyes met. There was knowledge in her gaze. Fresh panic gripped me. But I knew Lelia. She kept a lot to herself, my Cleopatra with her denial: I sometimes suspected that she was even better than my mother and my mother's war-generation friends at repressing troubling facts, but with a matter like this, she would inevitably confront me, shouting and weeping the moment she heard.

For a moment, I almost relinquished control and said, 'Oh look, let's talk about it.' I heard my own voice forming the sentence in my head. It would be horribly easy to echo it out loud. I saw myself pulling her to me and laying my head on her shoulder and telling her, and the sobs and the lancing and the mess.

She caught my eye again. The hurt there was blanketed. Madonna of the Rocks had expired. We knew each other too well. For a moment, I wanted to say it out of recklessness, to throw a hand grenade into our relationship and watch the interesting explosion. Beyond that, I wanted to rid myself of the repulsive tension with which I lived. The moment passed.

'MacDara's party's on the fourteenth,' she said.

I hesitated. 'Is it?' I said. 'Oh yes.'

There was a small silence. 'It'll be her anniversary,' she said, pointing to her stomach. 'Fridays.'

'Of course,' I said, and I kissed the stomach and stayed there, bowed, for a moment, and as I rose, my head felt granular with treachery.

'And then − spring. And then June,' I said awkwardly. Neither of us had mentioned our marriage.

She nodded.

'June the twenty-sixth,' I said.

'Let's talk about it later,' she said.

By the day of MacDara's party I was still in merciful, terrifying limbo. I dressed and shaved and grimly prepared to face my fate. Just before I left, I received an email from the Hotmail address.

The Hindoo could recite screeds of verse by heart as I could, and knew much of foreign lands, and when I saw her kissing Emilia, I wanted to claw her and choke her, or bring her to me. But Emilia was my maiden, and we twined and flew together to places that even the Hindoo couldn't reach. It was all practice, practice, practice for the time, one day after that, when I would hang myself for my Mama, or when I would save myself another way. And so we worked and starved and stifled with much discipline.

I skimmed the email, deleted it, and joined Lelia on the stairs. She was dressed in colours and lavishness, and she looked beautiful. The journey to MacDara's reminded me of the taxi ride at Christmas − in a different era, so long ago − but this time, we were not in the grip of sex, I was not about to meet a mouse, and I knew now that there was a baby growing inside her. Something bothered me. Just as I sometimes woke in the morning with a sense of unease and had to search my brain for the source of anxiety, I was unsure of what it was that disturbed me. Then I remembered. It was Sylvie's novel.

MacDara let us in. I steeled myself for my encounter with

Catrin. I had planned and rehearsed my entreaty, and at the first possible moment I would throw myself at her mercy, abandoning all pretence. The prospect was alarming. I chucked MacDara his present en route to the kitchen, and started drinking.

This, I thought, standing under a row of concealed spotlights angling on to a glimmering pale blue Smeg, was what it was to be rich. I felt a spasm of jealousy, followed by grudging admiration. I had spent my twenties faintly pitying MacDara his lack of artistic impulse. Now here were the rewards for the course he had chosen: a thundering great four-storey early Victorian number in Islington stuffed with modern classic furniture from Heal's and a couple of mother-fuckers by Ren, and carpet that was so thick, I wanted to get down on my knees, chew its fibres and choke on it. I would never have all this. I no longer found it quite so funny to live in a garret. I had, with my lofty and imprac-tical ambitions, fucked up. All my grand plots, hatched with earnest passion in youth, had been at best semi-realised in a haphazard fashion. And then there was *Ren*. Ren, who had toiled all these years before turning his hobby into a commercial enterprise without a squeal of artistic agony or any apparent sense of compromise. And suddenly, quiet, unassuming Ren in his suburban semi was raking it in. With a sense of panic, I warded off feelings of inadequacy. I might live in a ship's cabin of a flatlet, I thought, but I had my security – my love, my Lelia – and that was worth infinitely more.

Then I remembered.

A shock of realisation juddered through me, as though I had lost my foothold and the world had tilted.

I lost my glass and fumbled for another – no stacks of serrated plastic for MacDara – and I chucked down wine to fuel myself for the confrontation with my enemy Catrin. Someone turned the music up. I hid, pressing myself against the faintly vibrating Smeg as I kept a watch for her. I was relatively safe: I could see the sitting room through the arch of the kitchen, and only the odd waster like me would dive into the fridge for beer, since MacDara, the rich cunt, was bound to have the bath full of champagne on ice to demonstrate his nonchalance, his munificence.

I saw Catrin. She crossed the room, pale and wholesome as ever, yet trailing a whiff of madness beneath all her cool Celtic calm. My heart was banging like a lunatic's. I took another swig, felt its fire suffuse my head, and bravely lurched into the sitting room. She turned from her guest, but she didn't even glance at me.

'Catrin,' I said, too quietly. She continued to ignore me.

I looked at Lelia, at her familiar and dearly beloved features. She was worth the rest of them put together. I started to walk towards her, but Catrin moved in the same direction, as though planning to engage her in conversation. '*No!*' I wanted to squeal in panicked falsetto. I hesitated, almost spinning on one foot in indecision, and then bolted between them. Catrin turned away, still ignoring me.

'Darling,' I said, barely able to breathe.

'What are you *doing?*' said Lelia, laughing at me.

I put both hands round one of her shoulders and pulled her to me. She looked surprised. Catrin fiddled with a dimmer switch, and the room became darker, and then the bell rang. Excitable cries were audible from the hall. I kissed Lelia on the cheek that was near me, and encountering that smooth plane of flesh with my lips was a surprisingly unpleasant sensation, our most casual greetings involving a brush on the lips. I felt like an abusive Edwardian father. I turned her mouth to me and kissed her again. Her lips didn't move.

'I love you,' I said.

Her beautiful tilted eyes betrayed nothing, but I knew what lay beneath them. I had hurt and displeased the person I most wanted to protect.

'Look, I *love* you,' I said almost angrily, sinking my nose on to the springy depths of her hair.

She said nothing. I kissed her head.

'You've been distant from me,' she said.

'I know, I know,' I said. 'I—' I shrugged.

'I don't like it,' she said, her tone unchanging. She turned from me. She gazed ahead, as though I wasn't there and she could live an independent, quite different life without me. *She might leave me*, I realised, and I understood it properly for the first time, my scalp shivering with a contraction. The fact that I could lose her had seemed the mechanical, story-book result of infidelity, and as impossible as the state of limbo in which I was frozen.

I asked her about the baby. She brightened. The possession of such power felt akin to cruelty.

I stroked her tummy. She held my hand, though she wouldn't look at me. I kissed her again. Every aspect of her was so carved into my consciousness, her earrings instantly recognisable though I had never knowingly seen them.

'Listen,' she said. 'It can't bite you through my cervix, you fool.' She turned from me again with the cold expression that changed her face.

I would have to give up Sylvie. She was my last, pathetic stab at freedom: a childish act of late-flowering rebellion before I committed myself for ever. Just as I sometimes wanked over the idea of Nicole Kidman, or over the mature and womanly sadists who had littered my youth, in particular the married minor actress, once beautiful in a vampiric manner, a sighting of whose press photograph briefly resuscitated old fantasies:

just as such women drifted harmlessly through my night-time thoughts, half known about and laughed over by Lelia, so Sylvie Lavigne would have to live as a frustrating sexual spur in my memory alone. I had never planned to be the kind of man who has affairs.

'Are you going to marry me?' I said, but even as I asked her, even as I attempted to appease her, the terrible knowledge that I might not be able to give Sylvie up hit me. My heart sank at the acknowledgement of addiction. Perversely, the almost unbearable existence of the unmentionable Charlie continued, despite my anger, to stimulate a new strand of interest.

'Will you marry me?' I said, taking Lelia's hand. I pushed Sylvie to the back of my mind, and stamped on the image.

Lelia hesitated.

'"*Yes*,"' I said.

She hesitated again. Her mouth twitched in resistance, a gesture I dreaded.

'I don't know what to say,' she said. I wondered whether her eyes were shiny. She looked away. It sent a pang of sorrow through me.

'"Yes, yes,"' I said.

She paused. I saw a thought occur to her. Amusement flooded her face. Relief sank through me.

'Yes,' she said, and I pulled her more forcefully towards me. 'But I don't know.'

'What?'

'I don't know whether it would be a good idea.'

'Why not?'

She buried herself in my neck, and we clasped each other, suddenly talking, finishing sentences, words, kisses for each other. I spoke loudly, so that she couldn't answer my question.

I found a bottle on the window-sill and poured more wine into my glass. I tried to pour some into hers.

'No,' she said, putting her hand over the top, like a slap.

'Why not?'

She looked at me. Disapproval, or pity, tinged her eyes.

'Fuck!' I said. 'I'm crap, aren't I?'

'Yes.'

'Sorry, sorry,' I said. 'I've got amnesia. I'm a victim. You've got to look after me until I come out of my coma.'

'You fool,' she said.

'Actually, I want to look after *you*, missus. Let's go on a little trip. Let's get away from here.'

'I can't till the holidays,' she said.

'Throw a sickie. A long weekend.'

'OK,' she said. 'Are you ever going to understand that I'm pregnant?'

'Yes,' I said solemnly. 'I'm really sorry.'

I looked around. Catrin, whose movements I had been tracking while I guarded Lelia, was not in the room. I saw MacDara mid-bluster, gesturing at a woman I didn't know. He looked animated; his eyes were fiery. I wondered whether she was MW, about whom he was so unnecessarily and irritatingly vague.

'Imagine MacDara if Catrin were pregnant!' I said rashly. 'He'd be *far* worse than me. He'd be doing deals with Japan all night and sloshing rum into her coffee.'

Lelia winced.

'He'd forget to turn up for the birth!' I continued, ploughing on in the face of her silence. 'Look at him, the clumsy great bull.'

'If you were like him,' she said calmly, 'I'd have thrown you out in the first week.'

'But I'm a blundering buffoon who can't get baby dates

into my thick head. Just remember I've got a brain tumour. Oh, let's bugger off and go somewhere romantic. A windmill in Norfolk? *Norfolk?* Or that pineapple house? Come on, let's. Or a hotel nearer London. Damn the expense. Will you come with me?'

'Let's see what happens,' she said, and she looked away. When she turned back, I caught her with a kiss, and then we hugged, and I knocked back more wine.

'Taste it. Cheat! Taste it on my lips,' I said, and kissed her. 'Do it again,' I said, and took a covert mouthful of wine, which I siphoned into her mouth when she opened it. She spluttered and laughed so that wine dropped on to my legs; I licked drips from her chin; she started to cough, shaking her head, and I tried to pass her another mouthful. She pushed me away, then tried to make me laugh so that I would spurt it out, but I swallowed it, and coughed and snorted, and she whispered in my ear, and I guffawed, and we began to bitch about the people at the party, using muttered shorthand to discuss disastrous clothes and covert gayness and assumed class categories, adopting our own strangely evolved language to talk about someone sitting right beside us.

I often thought, if asked to explain the codes and rituals that had sprung up between us by some mysterious organic process during our years together, we would sound totally disturbed. And that if in another world we were inexplicably separated – by aliens, say – we would recognise each other decades later through a muttered half-reference to any of our secret rituals, such as the menagerie of animals – or, more accurately, animal-animal and animal-human hybrids – that seemed to make an appearance just as we were falling asleep. Entirely non-sexual, these creatures had their own voices, so that the half-horse-half-squirrel called Piebald that was Lelia spoke in what was largely a neigh, interspersed by the odd scampering noise as she scrabbled around, ate proffered nuts, and displayed a rudimentary character. A speaking tadpole resided in our bath for a few months before we forgot about him, while I had somehow become a furry half-tiger-half-human called Pierre with a rich forties actor-style voice and a universe of his own, including a kind-hearted trainer, a group of circus pals, a selection of dietary preferences and, eventually, a repertoire of songs. Yet our main mode of communication was through donkey sounds. I would often bray on greeting when I picked up a call from her, just as she would mention my hooves and refer to supper as oats, and every few months we would suddenly hear ourselves afresh amidst wide-eyed spurts of embarrassed laughter.

I eey-ored into her ear and then kissed it. Catrin came past. She still refused to look at me, the sadistic dipso. I froze. She walked over to the other side of the room and started to change the CD.

'Just going to the loo,' I said to Lelia, and even a tiny falsehood – infinitesimal in comparison with the vast lie of omission under which I lived – hurt as I sullied her with it.

I wandered across the room, hesitated, and then walked swiftly towards Catrin, stumbling a little.

'Catrin, can we talk?' I said.

'Not now,' she said coldly.

I hesitated, humiliated.

I glanced at Lelia, talking animatedly to a friend of hers, and a fresh surge of panic hit me at the prospect of her loss.

'*Please*,' I said to Catrin.

'I don't want to talk about it,' said Catrin, and walked away. I strode after her.

'Look,' I said, coughing as she started to walk upstairs.

'Yes?' She turned to me from the top step with an expression I had never previously seen.

I walked up the remaining stairs two at a time. The rage of the Celt was terrifying.

'Look,' I said in a hiss, turning round to ascertain that we were alone on the landing. 'I'm sorry. I'm really, truly sorry.'

'You shouldn't be saying sorry to *me*,' she said, her voice rising.

'I know, I know,' I said, half-whispering, half-hissing as I tried to hush her with conciliatory tones. 'Listen, Catrin, I – I fucked up. I won't do it again, ever. You know that.'

'Won't you?'

'Never. Let's just talk. Please – please don't—'

'I don't want to talk about it,' she said, the disgust palpable in her voice.

'But—'

'I tried to tell her. She didn't return my calls. Now she's pregnant. I'm not going to upset her.' She turned her back and walked into a bedroom.

'Catrin!' I called, the relief of salvation fanning through me and nudging the panic into a subsidiary position, but she shut her door. Confronted by its panelled white silence, I simply didn't dare to knock. Appreciation – *affection* – flooded through me.

I found a loo and stood there, breathing deeply as I let out a long piss stream. My abdomen, or my stomach – indiscriminate entrails, ulcerous and churning – felt ragged. I stood very still, slowly processing the news that Catrin was not going to reveal my crime to Lelia. '*Thank you, Catrin, thank you, Catrin.* I muttered like an idiot. I leaned my head against the wall, a framed painting rocking alarmingly as I caught it with my ear, and felt I could shout with relief and misplaced gratitude. I bashed the black-and-white tiles of the wall a little, hoping I might accidentally crack an expensive surface, and enjoyed the feeling of pain. I could start again. One day, when our child was born, I would somehow admit to Lelia that I had snogged a woman, and clean the slate and live happily. In the meantime, I would try hard, so very hard, not to see Sylvie. I would attempt to keep away from her in the most mechanical and methodical fashion, transferring her work enquiries to my assistant and religiously refraining from contact. Chance encounters would be met with civility and brevity. I let myself picture Sylvie, mourning for one more moment before beginning my harsh training in self-discipline: I murmured her name into MacDara's tiles, feeling my breath mist their surface and briefly return its warmth to my face as I stood there for rich, elastic seconds, the thudding of music somewhere below me buzzing at my feet.

I heard her voice.

It wound through my memory as I rested my head against the wall, the noises of the party muffling speech until one voice would emerge above others with individual clarity; and although it took a few seconds for me to understand that Sylvie's voice was real and not the fantasy I supposed, the realisation hit me with a jolt.

I jerked my head from the wall. My heart was racing. What on earth was she doing here? I would have to lock myself in the loo until I could ascertain her whereabouts and then avoid her. I waited, the vaguely nauseating sensation of too much alcohol already rolling inside me as I hid myself from Sylvie and Catrin. I tried to think about other things. Our baby. I couldn't. It was a pug-faced alien in pickling fluid, or it was a nothingness. I waited. I wanted, more than anything, to pull back the lock and breathe in the scent of Sylvie Lavigne. My skin was clammy as an addict's as I made myself wait, the time measured out by the beat of my pulse. I waited. I could no longer hear her voice, all sound now merging on the floor below. Slowly, I pulled back the bolt.

She was leaning elegantly against a chair on the other side of the landing, and she smiled at me.

'I thought I might find you here,' she said.

'What are you doing?' I said abruptly.

'Waiting for the bathroom.'

'Why? Why are you here?' I said, our voices meeting with hushed clarity on the landing.

'Ren and Vicky brought me.' She smiled again. She looked slightly more polished, in the way that women sometimes do.

'You're always everywhere,' I said wonderingly. 'Or nowhere at all.'

'I wanted to see you. MacDara and Catrin don't even know I'm here yet.'

'What?' I said.

'Someone else let us in. I was hoping it might be *you* at the door – I wanted to see your face!'

'Sylvie, you've got to go, before Catrin sees you—'

'Come here,' she said. She held out her hand.

I didn't take it. Without saying anything, she turned and began to walk up the next flight of stairs, and I followed her. I simply followed her, barely questioning the impulse. She guided me, a slender wraith always ahead of me as I travelled in slow motion, the boom of my own blood filling my head. Away from the party, the house smelled different, as other people's houses always do: adult, with alien cooking and cleaning products. Somewhere, far away, a lavatory flushed. We passed a richly curtained window. My mind tick-ticked with a mechanism divorced from thought. I caught the faintest tinge of her skin scent, and like a hound, I followed her silent walk. My legs were shaking. Her skirt was brown, and possibly slightly tighter than anything I had seen her in, her small rump visible as she lifted her leg on each stair. I wanted to enter her from below, to taste the divine leverage it would give me. Her shoes were pointed, with straps, like a girl's, but they bore a small, narrow heel. The simple fact of the heels got to me, primitive that I was. I walked higher and higher, away from Lelia. What if she looked for me? Sense tugged at me and then disappeared. My mind seemed filled with a thick substance that allowed no reasoning. Sylvie climbed up to the top of the house, never looking behind to see that I was following – knowing, knowing that I would follow as if tied to a wire – and there behind a bathroom was a smaller flight of stairs, rising at an angle.

'Look, I found this,' she said.

We moved silently, her head dipping, my head crouching, as we climbed the ladder-like stairs towards the ceiling.

'How?' I said.

'I explored, by myself,' she said.

To the left of the top step was a small dark section of loft – dusty splintered joists, single pane of window framing trees and chimney stacks – containing the water tank. A few bolts, now rusting, had been screwed into the rendering on one side. A furred loop of string and a calendar hung there. The images floated before slotting together in the gloom. 1994, I read. The window was bathed bright orange by a street lamp directly below. In that silent dusty warmth, she turned to me.

'Now,' she said. 'We're alone.'

The catch in her voice resonated in the air, its after-effects

181

buzzing against my skin like little drills. I could just make out the outline of her thigh, hinted at through the cloth of her skirt.

An ambulance streamed past outside.

At that moment I thought of Lelia, honeyed and vibrant on a sofa several floors below, waiting for me to return. She would be wondering where I had gone to, or she would have given up, cold-faced and resolved, and started talking to someone else. A visual memory of the intense pooling quality of her brown eyes with their intimate knowledge of my ways and thought processes snagged at me. I thought of her voice, her habits, her body, all our history together, and I felt sickened at myself. She was a live thing with a living baby inside her, in contrast to the ghost before me.

I had to say something. I felt like a clumsy giant in that little room, stuck for words, about to make myself leave.

She lolled against the water tank, seemingly amused at something.

'Do you remember us on a park bench in the snow?' she said simply.

'Yes,' I said, and nodded, and the lower half of me automatically melted.

'*Sullied snow*,' she said.

'Yes,' I said.

'Well,' she said.

'Yes,' I said again like an imbecile.

'Why don't you sit there?'

She turned to a shelf that ran below the window. For lack of a decision, to remove my giant's head from the splintered rafters, I lowered myself on to a layer of snagged fluff and leaned against the pane. Objects radiated strangely in the orange light.

'Come here,' I said instinctively as I detected her scent and its effect spread through my body, soothing and electrifying. My voice caught. I coughed. The water in the tank swirled and gurgled above me.

'I will,' she said. 'Not yet.'

'Oh really?' I said. 'But we're going to have to end this, aren't we?'

'We will,' she said. 'Not yet.'

She knelt beside me. Her face, her limbs, her hands were cast into glowing brown silhouette, as though she moved through sepia. We sipped hot, brushing kisses, like tiny spasms. I mustn't, I thought. Her head slanted, her hair falling to one side, making her look more womanly, and I kissed her neck, and her skin smell slalomed straight through my body. Her lips parted as I kissed her, then she pushed me back against the glass.

'No,' I said with momentary resistance, but bathed in her smell with her fingers grazing the skin of my neck, I couldn't maintain my resolve. I could no more stop than I could make myself fall from the window behind me. Final flares of panic erupted in my mind.

She pushed my shoulder back lightly with her fingertip.

'I've waited all day for you,' she said quietly. Her voice lapped over me, as though it bathed me in a chemical to which I was addicted.

'But I haven't seen you since . . . when? Two Mondays ago,' I said.

'We can't always see each other,' she said.

Her mouth was in front of my eyes, perfectly sculpted in the light.

'I knew I'd have to wait until tonight,' she said. She undid two buttons of my shirt, and stroked my clavicle with the back of her nails. I reached out and touched her cheek, but she caught my hand and pressed it down on to my own thigh. 'Remember, you mustn't move. You did last time, and I stopped. I'll do that again.'

I half-laughed in protest.

'You must be perfectly still,' she murmured. 'Richard. You must lie there against the glass.'

Tremendous excitement instantly rose inside me. She moved closer. She did nothing more. She knelt above me, looking down as solemnly as a studious girl concentrating on her work, her dark questioning eyebrows slanted, and her warm breath, scented with her, travelled to my stomach, making the hairs ripple as the muscles of my abdomen tensed. My every exhalation carried a barely audible moan.

She sat back neatly on her calves, her skirt resting on the floor, the outline of her surprising heels visible, and very slowly, with delicate fingers, she began to undress me. Instinctively, I reached out and caught her waist. She stopped. She waited. I pulled my hand back, and she began again, circling, breathing over my nipples.

I remembered that I was wearing a greying vest, and cringed. She pulled the top of it with her fingertip. It simply radiated dull amber light.

'Imagine if I were a cat stroking you, rubbing you, licking you,' she said, her voice a cobweb in the darkness. The shadows under her eyes that I always found worryingly appealing were subsumed by darker shadings as she dipped her head.

'Listen, you,' I said, rising from the shelf. I bent over her and put my hands around her waist to lift her. 'I want you *there*. I—'

She slapped me. My cheek rang with a wasp sting of pain. I gasped. No one had ever done that to me before. I stared at her.

'You can't do that,' I said.

'You're lying under water,' she said, and she ran her finger-tips over my stomach. 'Lie down. You're in green water. Fronds passing and tangling.' Her fingers travelled up to my chest and under my armpits, whispering down the sides of my body as my cheek still rang. 'Here are fish, leaping. Porcelain bubbly fishes, around your legs and kissing your neck.'

'Sylvie,' I said. I moaned.

She pulled my sleeves from my arms with small deft fingers. She held the shirt, breathed it in, then threw it into a corner. She pulled off the shameful vest.

'Lie back. As you lie there – don't move. As you lie there, the currents of the water bubble and twist. All the water-weed, rushes, bend and stroke you. Richard. Glassy twists rippling over your skin.'

She inserted her fingers under the top of my trousers. I tensed my stomach muscles. She bent and kissed the skin. I stroked her hair. I moaned. I could not be silent.

'And the bubbles blow and bubble, tiny bubbles blurting from under rocks to cling to your skin,' she said, the compo-nents of her voice echoing in my ears so that I barely made sense of the words themselves. She pressed her fingers further down. I gasped. I thrust my hips forward, desperate for any touch, even the tightness of seams against me. She suspended her movements.

'Little bitch,' I muttered. She smiled.

'Roses float,' she said.

'What?'

'You see, little rosebuds beneath water, they spurt bubbles, up, and up.' Her fingertips pattered up my thighs and her hand rested on the button of my trousers. She undid it. My muscles tightened, every hormone and sinew instructing me to jolt up to my feet and take her. 'Lie,' she said, and brushed her nails over my crotch. I pressed my back against the window and listened to her voice, my breath hoarse and shallow. 'Roses fattening in the water.' I felt myself swelling, rising, frantic. She undid my fly. Silently, she pulled the trousers off, hooking my pants down in one movement. I sat on the ledge, my cock pressing against my stomach, and she embraced me fully clothed, pressing her skirt against me, enveloping me with her voice, her hair, her breath. She murmured into my ears; we kissed, we bit, we moved frantically about each other's faces, and my hands reached down and touched her breasts.

She sat back down on the floor.

'For God's sake!' I said. 'I have to—'

She raised one eyebrow.

'Sleep with you.'

'Sleep with me?' she said calmly. 'We don't sleep with each other. You sleep with someone else. You want to fuck me?'

'Yes,' I said.

She shook her head minutely.

'For God's sake,' I said loudly, sinking on to the floor beside her.

On top, she was all demure, a ruffled blouse thing covering her breasts and her small waist. One of her legs was propped up, her skirt falling down and revealing a part of her thigh in the blurred orange light. She was wearing stockings secured with a simple, lacy band. Casually, she wore stockings below her dull girl clothes, like a disturbing adolescent from a Balthus painting. I looked down again. I caught the faintest scent of something familiar, yet different, warm and mushroom and private. In the brown-furred darkness, I saw then, at the top of her thighs, a black shadow like a pool of blood. I caught my breath. I stared. I gazed, absorbing every detail that emerged as my eyes searched in the fragmented light. I moved nearer her and held her. I kissed her thigh. I dipped my head towards that delectable scent, up, up to its slick sweet origin, to where she was opening to me.

She pulled her leg away.

'Only if you sit,' she said in her calm tones.

Like an animal, rearing and foolish, I did as I was told. She knelt in front of me, and my hand reached under her skirt, feeling the rough edge of the surprising stockings, meeting an airy warm space before the even more surprising lack of underwear, and my finger found her and moved, slid back and forth across the metallic slick of liquid, her every secret curve and pocket of warmth a revelation. I bathed my fingers in her, rubbed, slipped, teased.

'I need to *fuck* you,' I said in jerks.

'No,' she said.

She raised herself above me, and she rubbed herself against my fingers, up and down, clasping my shoulders with a hard grip.

She rose and fell, emitting sounds that aroused me still further. Her movements were fluid, her small hips circling, her hair and thighs so wet that I opened out my hand against her, cupping, sliding, inserting my middle finger inside her as I moved.

She threw herself against my shoulders and pressed herself into my body, my dick against her stomach, rising, rising, tightening as her movements made me gasp.

I grabbed her hips and pulled her harder towards me.

'Have to fuck,' I said, and pulled her into my lap.

'No,' she said, her breath faster.

'What the fuck?'

'Not until . . .'

'Jesus.'

'You're an attached man,' she said.

'*You* are—'

'It's not the same.'

'You won't?'

'Not until—'

'*Fuck*,' I said. 'Hampstead Heath.'

She was silent.

'Come *on*,' I said. 'Oh, please. Come on, darling.'

She shook her head, biting into my neck as thinner juices fell on to my hand. The sea-life indentations were warm inside her.

I had to have her. For a fraction of a moment I imagined raping her. I pictured myself pushing her to the floor and pumping into her, spending my terrible, welling explosion of desire. I shocked the image away from me. She pressed herself harder against me. I felt the spasm of orgasm taking root in my groin.

'Run away with me,' I blurted out. 'Run – away with me.'

She gripped my shoulders with urgent pressure.

'A weekend. Wherever. For ever.'

I felt the shudder go through her, long and deep and propelling her far away from me to some distant place where her mouth was parted and her eyes were dark and the voice she cried in was barely her own. I followed her moments later, and in that moment of exquisite pleasure, I knew what I was capable of doing for her.

FIFTEEN

Lelia

We got married on a Tuesday. I couldn't imagine a less auspicious time of week on which to make a commitment, but my father's birthday fell on that day, stopping me from choosing any other. I had always had a horrible, creeping suspicion that we would keep to our wedding plans in spite of all that was lying and terrible about us, and on June the twenty-sixth I married Richard Joseph Fearon in Marylebone Registry Office. I was, at least, a knowing fool.

Before leaving the flat that morning, I had glanced at Richard's computer and nudged the mouse to clear the screen-saver. Something had been minimised, a trick I'd only recently been shown by a colleague. Curious, I clicked on the square in the corner, and an email from an unrecognisable address sprang up.

The creature has come. Its caul did not smother it; its cord failed to strangle it. Beneath its bonnet and binder I saw traces of wax and fur and blood, as though it had been spat out with a monstrous tearing: a plump little pupa pulsing beneath yellow skin. *In sorrow thou shalt bring forth children*, I thought, but its mother knew no sorrow. In a cloud of chloroform, she kissed and stroked that creature.

I unravelled the infant's flannels and pilches when its nurse left the room. An echo of a male part protruded, like a circus freak's, from its stomach. Below it coiled a true male part. If the creature had been more winged and filmy, I could have splintered it with a hiss, but fat filled out its casing, and it panted like a fish with vigorous pink muscles. The further it emerged from that webbed half-life in which it was curled, the more firmly its milk breaths would bloom. All that we had thought of seemed insufficient. I would, I knew, have to make myself still stronger.

The email filled me with a rage of curiosity even as it revolted me. It was slightly obscene. A kind of numb panic filled me. After I had minimised it again, I felt a twinge in my stomach, as though a period was about to tug through my body. I went to the loo. When I stood up, I thought that I saw the faintest pink smear on the paper. Sickness shot to my throat. I rubbed frantically again, twisting the paper and pushing it inside me. I held it to the light. It seemed to me to be the colour of the inside of a sea-shell. Tears sprang to my eyes. I began to howl, alone there in the sitting room. I rushed to the phone and picked it up, but Richard, who had gone to work for the morning, was not available. I went back and rubbed again, but this time the paper appeared a clear white. I didn't dare to ring the hospital in case it was true. I would wait; I would beg; it would go away.

I was sick for the first time in three months, and then I felt better, and trembling and hungry. I set off to my mother's alone: I wouldn't see Richard until we arrived at the Registry Office. How strange that we, who so casually assume we are liberated from convention, find ourselves drifting towards it, having never paused long enough to invent an alternative.

So I left our flat alone, the bride returning with her small case of clothes to her mother. On the Tube, my head nodding with tiredness, I felt as though I had left him, or he was a gentleman farmer who had ventured to the Colonies, and I would never see him again.

My mother was keen for me to dress at her house and to visit the hair-and-beauty salon she had favoured for the last thirty years, with its suburban North London ideas about bridal make-up. To please her, I arrived there shortly after ten in the morning, guilt washing over me as I stepped into the flouncy shade of her small house. My failure to take the easy journey up the Northern Line for some months made me feel prickly with excuses. My mother hugged me, giving off pride and disapproval in perfectly balanced measures even on this day.

I went to my bedroom, pausing to check for blood on loo paper first. There was nothing. My heart thumped as I pressed my forehead to my hands and wondered whether I should phone the hospital. I pushed the thought to one side. I was now six and a half months pregnant. I would not miscarry; I wouldn't go into premature labour. Remnants of the queasiness that had followed that email still clung to the outside edges of my mind.

In my bedroom, I touched walls. The wallpaper was so familiar, it was almost unfamiliar: its pattern cruder and chalkier than in my memory. I avoided looking at the photograph of my father, and then kissed it. We had a silent moment of communication on this, my wedding day. I said I was sorry. My weight shifted my bed's unstirred air. I lay back and gazed at the fake cornice, the metal window-frame and the faded Laura Ashley curtains, once saved for by me and hemmed on the school sewing machines. As I opened my wardrobe to find a hanger, I saw something. On a shelf, among my childhood collection of ceramic animals – Whimsies, they were called. *Whimsies!* – was a squirrel that was taller than the others, its glaze bearing a duller sheen. My eye rested on the dusty hollows of its mouldings, even its features reminiscent of a different era and a brief girlhood in France. Sophie-Hélène, knowing of my childish liking for these crude models, had kindly bought me a French mismatch in Briare before I left.

Had I thanked her when I wrote to her? I couldn't remember. I couldn't remember what I'd said or when, because I'd never heard from her again: she had simply declined to answer my letters. It had made me sad, and resigned, and then, somewhere in my heart at night, frantically worried, because I remembered the atmosphere when I'd left. I'd been bundled back to England without ceremony on the appointed morning by grave-faced adults. I was confused, and guilt-sick, and terrified that I was the source of their disapproval, but what really tore at my heart was that Mazarine had failed to meet me to say goodbye. When, eventually, I found the Clemenceau surgery's number through Directory Enquiries and rang it, I was informed that the Bellière family had moved. So my incubus had left me, and her spirit only returned to me in nightmares.

My mother helped me with my clothes downstairs. I glanced at the tablecloth of a garden that had once appeared as a dancing expanse of green. A photograph of me with Richard smiled through the doilied gloom – *why* did she keep her curtains semi-drawn in the day? *Why* so unnaturally clean? – and I felt once again some menstrual gravity in my thighs. I tried to steady my breathing as my mother twitched my dress into shape. I could say nothing to her. Richard wouldn't understand. I wanted Sylvie. At that moment, I knew that only Sylvie Lavigne would look after me.

Making excuses, I removed myself from my mother and checked again for blood. Then I phoned Sylvie and asked her to my wedding party. A confused Richard would scoff and tease, but she would disappear into the crowds, and perhaps he wouldn't even notice her. She would look after me. On the way downstairs, I fleetingly remembered the baby in France. I threw up again in the loo. My stomach rumbled. My mother stared at me as I made a pile of toast. The smells that I had once associated with old ladies were creeping into her life – fire lighters, custard powder, Dettol, tinned salmon, hand-washing flakes. She had begun to leave things for too long in the fridge, to thaw meat from her ice box under dish-cloths through hot afternoons. She offered me some fizzy yoghurt.

Then I succumbed to the hairdresser's will in pain and sulphur-scented heat, and quietly tamed the results every time my mother glanced out of the taxi window. And my mother looked so neatly tailored, but still poor, *poor*, that I wanted to pull her to me and break down all our old hurts and barriers and kiss her and mess up her white collar by sobbing on her neck. I wanted my father with us, so desperately, on that day. I think she did too.

Richard was waiting, looking beautiful in a suit, at the Registry Office. He was smiling, and gazing at his feet, and looking very solemn, and then turning to smile at me. I married him.

SIXTEEN

Richard

'She's *here*,' MacDara hissed.

'Who?' I said. I grabbed his arm as he stumbled towards a table.

'I don't fucking believe it. How's she *got* here?'

'Who?' I said. His eyes were wide, stubble already shadowing his face.

'Who do you *think*? You fucking idiot. You imbecile. Who do you *think*?'

I shook my head.

'*Her.*'

'You mean – MW?' I said at last.

MacDara widened his eyes further and gave me a series of big, drunken nods. 'Her. What the fuck's she *doing* here? You hardly bloody know her. What's she doing at your fucking wedding, for Christ's sake?'

'I know her?' I said, even more confused. 'Where?' I said, looking around. 'Where is she?'

'Over there,' MacDara gestured sideways. 'Behind me to the left.'

'Steady. Where?'

'I can't *look*, idiot,' hissed MacDara, his words now emerging in a flat stream of spit and air. 'She was over there.

By the flowers. Whatever you call them. Food place. Talking to – that bloke you work with.' He darted his head round. 'She's gone. Where is she?'

'Mac,' called Catrin, seeing him turn. She ignored me.

'But who is she?' I said as MacDara stumbled over to Catrin. 'What's her name?'

MacDara shrugged, half-turning his head and mouthing 'Fuck' at me. His back disappeared across the lawn.

Our wedding party started in the early evening after the private marriage ceremony. I had wanted a garden party, but since our garden was two square metres of asphalted roof, accessible through a skylight merely for cleaning purposes, Lelia had managed to secure us Gordon Square Gardens through the university at nominal cost, and we had hired a ridiculous marquee at considerably more expense. I felt crass and ordinary for resorting to a marquee, and somehow touched at the same time, as though the swaying striped cliché were a home to shelter us, Lelia and me. She was mine. I would deal with all the rest later, during our long marriage.

It was a chilled, sun-sharp June day that slanted slowly into night. A couple of outdoor heaters radiated wasteful warmth; headlights swung low through the dusk spaces in tree tangle; an occasional passer-by peered through the railings like an interesting spectre in the twilight, tempting me to call out rash invitations. The bleached faces in the blueness reminded me of Sylvie. By late-evening, guests ran wild and drunk through the garden, exploring its crannies, its pergola and bushes, and reappearing on lawns that were sown with the light-points of half-closed daisies. I loved my friends, I thought with a soar of affection as I watched them meander through the circular rose garden in the middle of the north lawn. Even Catrin (small nod of greeting, icy congratulations) I could no longer hate. The Georgian houses on either side of the square were dark, only four or five office workers still toiling in lit windows among anglepoises and unpleasant pot plants. An orange light high up in a roof sent brown-silhouetted images from weeks before quivering through me: I rocketed after her, crying out in MacDara's loft as I came. I lingered mentally over the phrases in some of the letters and emails she had written to me since, during an inexplicable and deeply enraging absence in Edinburgh, putatively for study purposes. Though now wise to her excessive evasiveness, it never failed to outrage me. I stamped on her phrases. They drifted back. In my mind, I took out some Cook's Extra Long matches, lit a fire, and burnt her letters. I saw the flames lick and singe the words. They were gone.

MacDara passed by, darted me a look, walked on.

I went to find Lelia, my wife. She was pale. She looked more beautiful than I had ever seen her. She was in some kind of a state.

'Are you *regretting* marrying me, wife?' I hissed in her ear. She shook her head.

'What then?'

'Nothing,' she said moodily, as I knew she would. I sighed.

'You're very agitated,' I said. I kissed her.

I had a quick look round to ascertain the identity of MW. The only guests who fitted her vague description and were barely known to me were a couple of Lelia's colleagues. I searched again for MacDara, but he was standing beside Catrin talking to another friend. Ren was nearby, the extreme politeness of his tones reaching me, other guests spilling wine and swearing, the occasional adult snog clearly imminent.

Lelia was nervous. She stroked her stomach. For a split

second, I forgot again that she was pregnant. Then I remembered.

'Hadn't you better sit down?' I said.

She shook her head. She smiled at me. 'Happy wedding day,' she said.

'Happy wedding day, Mrs—'

'Don't you *dare* say it!' she said. 'Even as a joke. Mr Guha.'

'OK, OK,' I said. The voice of Pierre the night-time tiger came spontaneously into my head, and I whispered his words into her ear. I pinched her bum, she rammed her hip into my thigh, and I put my arm round her shoulder. 'I want to make a *speech* about you. Right now,' I said.

'Oh, Richard. Bloody hell. I thought we said we wouldn't.'

'Yes, but we knew we would. Anyway, people will demand it. They know my skills as an orator. I want to declare to the world that you're mine to fuck.'

'Chance would be . . .' she said.

'*What?*' I said sharply. 'No muttering on your wedding day. Shall I start bashing a glass to get attention now? Should I shout? Let off an enormous fart? MacDara will lurch into a speech any minute if we're not careful. Look at him.' He was restless; his hair was wild, as though he had been fingering it. His stubble now darkened his chin apishly under the lamps strung around the marquee. I nearly burst into laughter, looking at him. He stood near one of Lelia's colleagues, a skinny redhead who could possibly have been MW. He shot me a glance.

I raised one eyebrow at him.

I made my way through the cooling night towards the tent, where friends were helping themselves to food, shepherded by Lelia's mother. I circulated happily. Evening-damp earth and traffic fumes merged in cool strands of air; jasmine scratched my face above gravel paths, where bluebells were listless and tree-shaded. What I had really wanted was a barn dance: a chokey cloud of straw, a yokel yelling do–si–dos into a microphone, and a general atmosphere of regressive hilarity. This was not, as Lelia had to remind me, possible in central London. Moreover, I was over-romanticising my teenage-hood, with its cheap cider, its boredom and dung-splattered motorbikes.

And yet this, I thought, as the drunkenness and loudness and running between trees intensified, was the kind of wedding party I had hoped to have if barn dances were relegated to fantasy. The daisies radiated their whiteness over the night-stained lawns. People were sloping off to an incongruously rural garden shed which someone had discovered was un-locked. Laughter and sudden silences emanated from it. I had vaguely nurtured fantasies of well-dressed displays of sexual intercourse in bushes that would provide scandal to fuel days of gossip, and much general drunken bad behaviour, reliably stoked up by MacDara. A few work people and the odd surprise friend of Lelia's were snorting in the loos. I was delighted that standards had degenerated so early. Only Lelia bothered me. Moody though she was, something was making her unhappy. I looked around for her. I couldn't see her. In fact, I hadn't seen her for some time. I searched again, widening my eyes to try to make her out in the dark. I felt frustrated. I asked Ren's wife Vicky to find her.

The cold breath of petrol-tinged grass streamed from the ground. One of my sisters was apparently squabbling with my brother beneath a lime tree. My father loitered, the elected parental representative as a result of God-knows-what procedure, my warring progenitors too mutu-ally antipathetic to attend the same event. I missed my mother more than I'd ever imagined I would. I wished very deeply that it had been her attending my wedding instead of my old man. Their divorce, the culmination of years of essential incompatibility, had been so vicious that we were forced into painful side-taking, and I had spent well over a decade trying to compensate my mother for the fact that her emotionally stunted husband had forced her to leave him because of his impossible behaviour. I wanted to protect her for ever from the slightest hurt. I stopped, and sent her a hasty wedding-day text.

Sylvie Lavigne crossed the lawn in front of me.

Pain shot through my chest. I thought I might have a heart attack. I stared at her for protracted seconds before my paralysed body started to move.

'What the *fuck*?' I said.

I moved towards her. I carried on walking past her, into the rose garden in the centre. She lingered behind a little, so I had to turn to speak to her. She stood several feet away from me, in a floaty dress.

'I'm not going to denounce you, *Jane Eyre*-style,' she said. 'Don't worry.'

'What the—' I gazed at her. I softened my voice.

'I knew you'd be surprised,' she said.

'How did you get here?'

'Lelia invited me.'

'Lelia?' I said wonderingly.

'Yes,' she said.

'But she can't—'

'Ask her.'

'Sylvie. Sylvie darling. You can't be here,' I said, my voice emerging gently, the faraway prickling sensation of tears coming to my eyes.

'I knew. I know. But I can. There won't be any trouble. I love you. I give you my blessing, beloved Richard,' she

199

said, and she smiled at me, a look of pain passing over her face, and walked away.

I stood very still and took huge gulps of air. A terrible writhing of conflicting emotions fermented in my brain with the wine. I burped, loudly, into the night. I caught a glimpse of Lelia again, near the marquee, strode across the grass, took her by the arm and said, 'I want to talk about you. You.'

She smiled. Her hair looked different. 'It's fun, isn't it?' Her voice a lightness in the air among the lamp-lit laughter.

I clambered on to a table and bellowed. A crowd began to form, the outer chattering edges still straggling among the trees. There was Lelia, so utterly beautiful in a dark pink curving something, her bump much more visible to me for the first time. There was Sylvie, appearing from the row of lime trees on the other side of the garden. MacDara, standing nearby, looked at her. Then he looked away. He gazed steadily at the tent.

A thought plummeted through me and settled in my bowels. The sky froze: the orange-inky clouds were still; the film of the party juddered to a halt. I opened my mouth; I took a gulp of wine. Sylvie was standing near MacDara, holding a glass and looking about her with ease. MacDara, the world's hammiest actor, his mouth tensed, averted his head from her as though his facial nerves were paralysed. My hand nearly compressed my wine glass into splinters. The fucking bastarding motherfucker of a cunt. My brain must have something wrong with it, I thought. Dementia. Chronic stupidity. That handwriting: tiny, irritating, self-conscious; she had even put a Shakespeherian fucking quote in MacDara's diary, for Christ's sake. I calculated the trajectory of a lobbed glass of wine towards his face, and decided the distance was too great. I began to extemporise – a reckless, kamikaze poem of a speech ignited and made brilliant by fury – then I climbed off the table, to the sound of shouts and cheers, with one vast, leg-collapsing step, grabbed MacDara's arm, jostled him behind a tree, and drove my fist into his face.

I had always wanted to do that to someone. The crunch of my knuckles against hard flesh was an invigoratingly satisfying sensation, almost sexual in the pleasure it afforded me. I would for ever remember the fibrous impact. Blood shot out of MacDara's nose.

'Richard, what are you *doing*?' screamed Lelia, running up to us. Blood caught the hem of her dress. *The multitudinous seas incarnadine*, was all I kept thinking, repeating it in my mind like a madman as I turned to her, my mouth open.

MacDara was reeling. Snot bubbled out of his nose. A drop of blood spread over his collar. Guests were beginning to gather around us. He was uncannily silent. I wanted more. I lifted my fist again. But MacDara lifted his at the same time, and Lelia stepped between us.

'You idiots!' she said. Her voice was high. She was crying. 'Stop!'

I hesitated.

'How *can* you?' she said.

'Keep your fucking hands off her,' I shouted at MacDara.

'What?' said Lelia. I took her waist.

There was a noise from the people around us. Several gazes turned from MacDara to Lelia in slow motion, cartoonish amazement scrawled across features. I watched them. A thought arrived slowly in my brain. Scrabbling for salvation like a man about to be hanged, I clumsily took advantage of the situation.

'Just fuck right off out of it,' I snarled at MacDara. We stared at each other, panting. My head was tight with incandescent rage towards him. Blood covered his chin. Finally, he wiped it away.

'*What?*' said Lelia, no longer crying but looking at me with an expression of fury.

'MacDara's a total cunt,' I said flatly. 'He shouldn't—'

'Not on our *wedding*,' hissed Lelia. 'Whatever this is. Tomorrow.'

'Listen,' I said. 'He's just stepped out of line.' I caught Lelia by the shoulder and turned her around.

'What are you *doing*?' said Lelia as I dragged her away from the tree.

'He was eyeing you up,' I said in desperation, my lie emerging with the smooth, hot quality of a child's.

'No he *wasn't*.'

'Yes, the git.'

'He quite patently was not! Richard, don't be such a fucking idiot. MacDara has never seen a hint of sexual promise in me in his life.'

'I think he fancies you,' I said, ever more pathetically.

'Whatever you say. *Whatever* you say, Richard,' said Lelia sarcastically. I looked at her in surprise. The sounds of cheering came from the bushes. I glanced up. I couldn't see Catrin anywhere. Nor the bitch Sylvie.

'What's the *matter* with you today?' I said.

'Well,' she said, and a splinter of terror cut through me as she paused. 'As well as you doing that – what on earth was that about? I've *never* seen you hitting someone. God, Richard – as well as that, well, I've been bleeding.'

'Yes, I know, I'm sorry. MacDara's swinish nose. It's revolting. I'll try to wash it off.'

'No. Bleeding. I've been bleeding a bit.'

'Oh,' I said.

'Yes, well.'

'Oh, but that's OK. I'm sure that's OK, darling.'

'How do you know?' said Lelia.

'Well, it's probably just something – natural. Some juices coming down. Bit of a period.'

'I just don't believe you. What does a *period* mean? I'm pregnant. I don't believe you,' she said, shaking her head. She was trembling.

'Oh, Lelia, I'm sorry. But you know what I mean. It's probably perfectly normal. Something from the womb.'

'Well, exactly. Something from the womb. Think what that was last time, Richard.' She paused. A sob caught her voice.

'Oh, darling,' I said, pity suddenly taking hold of me. 'Oh, darling. It's probably all right.'

'Are you a gynaecologist? Are you?'

I shook my head. 'Darling—'

'Bleeding – any bleeding – can be the start of miscarriage. *I* should know. I'm twenty-eight weeks; it's too early. I just—' she said, catching an in-breath, 'I just knew you wouldn't understand. At all, you know. Not at all.'

I took her in my arms. My radar, still barely consciously tracking Sylvie, knew that she wasn't around. MacDara had disappeared somewhere, probably to staunch his stinking blood. My poor Lelia felt broken in my arms.

'We can go to the hospital,' I said, holding her and stroking her head. 'What's all this stuff in your hair? It's just around the corner. Shall we go?'

She shook her head. 'Only if there's more.'

'Yes, darling. Well, if there is, just tell me, and we'll race straight over there. It's two streets away. I'll carry you. You'll be OK, darling. I promise. I'll look after you, and there's all this medical help so near.'

'Why? Why did you do that?' she said.

'Oh,' I said, swiping a hair from my forehead with my sleeve. 'I'll tell you later. I promise. He's been being stupid, and I suddenly got pissed off. It's all right. He's drunk. I'm a bit drunk. No one gives a toss.'

'Of course they do,' said Lelia, her voice distant in the still air. 'They just pretended not to. They think you're mad.'

'Well, fuck 'em,' I said.

She appraised me.

'I thought he was eyeing you up,' I gabbled disastrously to break the tension. My forehead sweated. 'I got angry.' I could hardly even enunciate the feeble words. My voice tailed off.

'Richard,' she said. 'The man is clearly having an affair.'

She turned her back on me. I thought about killing myself. I pictured my arm picking up a flint from a flower-bed and plunging it into my own chest, and then, in my death throes, swiping at MacDara. The blood. The spurting pain. The demented pleasure. I muttered strangled obscenities and decapitated a shrub with my foot, and ground its medicinal-smelling leaves under my shoe until its juices bled into the earth.

Lelia was now behind the marquee talking to her queeny friend Enzo from university. The blubbery milksop was probably consoling her by telling her that *he* – *he*, the screaming poof – had never thought I was good enough for her anyway. Well, it was a bit fucking late.

Where the hell was Sylvie? Slowly, as if collecting and distilling in my brain, my anger began to turn towards her. The shocking little traitor. She was not what she seemed. She was not at all what she seemed. Charlie. MacDara. My God. Another thought slammed itself into my brain. Had she actually fucked MacDara? No. No. She was – I slithered around in my memory – still holding off; as of the week before she'd buggered off, she was still resisting. Just as she had with me. But now she was back. When had she come back? I would never know. MW had supposedly been in Canada with her husband during that time. I had felt unspoken, half-amused empathy with MacDara while Sylvie was holed up in Scotland. The treachery of it made me feel breathless. I was a brain-dead fool. My mouth fell open like the slotted aperture of a puppet's.

I began to walk. I walked faster, half-running through the dusk, swerving under the shivering line of lime trees. The lights in the houses were now all dead but one. That sole glow gave me a nasty taste. How on this earth could MW be Sylvie? MW was some bewitching married blow-hot-blow-cold sex symbol, not a chilly little nonentity inexplicably fancied by me. My mind span. *Married*. Sylvie was not married. I nurtured a moment of hope. But it was Charlie. That was who he meant. Oh, God. I stormed through the garden. Nothing. She had disappeared, just as she always did. I asked a couple of people if they had seen her. Only Peter Stronson seemed to know that she had left. Slowly, it dawned upon me that Sylvie had been talking to him. She had spoken to him and a couple of other editors who were there. I punched a lime tree. Its bark stubbled my hand, woody fragments lodged in the punctured skin.

We spent our wedding night with a scanner attached to Lelia. The ante-natal unit wanted to keep her there, waiting, scanning and waiting, until the early hours of the morning when they discharged her with warnings to rest. We walked in silence along Torrington Place, through the bird-stirring light before the dustbin vans had appeared.

At home, we climbed into bed, and soundlessly we found each other, half in despair. She was curved and scented and hot-skinned. She slid smooth heat over my torso; her breasts were compressed against my chest. A different scent, one that pleased me and reminded me of inexplicable happiness – strands of the past, or youthful lust, or simple *completeness* – clung to her. I began to remember what the smell reminded me of. It was somehow an echo of Sylvie's smell, that fragrance that hooked me into helpless addiction.

'You smell different,' I murmured into her neck.

She moved her hips against me and we lay together. I felt relieved that she didn't want sex on her wedding night.

'You smell different,' I murmured again. 'What is it?'

'It's all that hair stuff,' she said. 'Shhh . . .'

'Mmm,' I said. I kissed her. I gave in to it. I chased the scent of Sylvie. That was all it took, I thought. I suddenly fancied my wife. It was easy. This was the way it would be for ever.

'Use it, I like it,' I said, a pang at my own treachery making me hug her harder.

I held her from behind, and kissed and kissed her, and tried to battle away the angry questions about MacDara and the thoughts about Sylvie that ran like acid through my mind. I pressed myself into her neck and smelled her Lelia smell and told her that I was so fucking happy that she was my wife.

She slept. I began what seemed to me to be my life sentence as an insomniac.

In the morning, as I hung up my wedding jacket, I found a note in small writing in one of the pockets. *Wanted you*, it said.

SEVENTEEN

Lelia

I like to think about it all now. How we met. How we loved. What we thought when we first glimpsed each other.

When we went out for coffee the day I discovered I was pregnant, and when she arrived at my flat with baby clothes, she affected me by being reserved; or perhaps I felt shy because she had already begun to move me. She read me *Angel* as I lay on the sofa, and then I slept. When I woke, I wanted her to stay with me and carry on talking to me in that foggy little voice of hers. Eventually, her reticence left her, and we talked, on and on, as I'd only ever done in a London bedroom with friends of a particular age and time, and one French Easter by a stretch of river. I wanted to carry on talking like that all night. She played with my hand as she spoke.

Later, we wandered around Mecklenburgh Square gardens. We stopped by a horse chestnut, then paused again by the gate, carrying on talking while our bodies were poised to leave. I felt the embarrassment that goes with the knowledge that a great friendship has just started — the meeting of kindred souls, with a lifetime to discuss so many urgent issues — and though we spoke at length, we could hardly meet each other's gaze in our awareness of that discomfiture.

I kept glancing at the street in case Richard was walking back. I tried to make myself leave before he saw me and wondered what I could possibly be doing with a supposedly dull semi-stranger on a dark winter's evening. Then, after all our procrastinations, we parted abruptly, almost rudely, with a jerky leaving, a backward wave, another embarrassment that I replayed in my head.

'What are you thinking about?' Richard said when he returned and I was sitting on the sofa sorting through some timetables.

'Nothing. My schedules,' I said.

He narrowed his eyes at me. 'Liar,' he said. 'You're worrying about something, aren't you? My worrywart . . . What's the etymology of that?'

'Ask C. T. Onions.'

'One day, I'll find something you don't know about me,' he said, and then, totally uncharacteristically, he reddened.

I raised one eyebrow at him.

I thought about all the times I'd seen her. I'd caught sight of her once in John Lewis and, flustered, I'd chosen to ignore her just because it was easier to do so. I'd seen her twice on the street, and once I'd even spotted her on our square from the window, and I'd felt strange about her, as though she ruffled me but I didn't know why. There was an intensity to our friendship, even at the beginning, that was absent with other women I knew.

After we had walked around Mecklenburgh Square, she sent me a text. I was touched, and flattered; I texted her back, and then something else occurred to me, and I rang her that very night, slightly pushing myself to call her so soon, while Richard was on his computer. She sounded noticeably pleased to have been rung.

She texted me a couple of days later. I texted her. The electronic beep of my mobile at intermittent points in the day made me smile. I rang her one morning on the way to work, and arranged to meet her after a seminar in the canteen at Senate House. A couple of my students were still with me when she arrived, and we sat there together in a high net of noise above the trees of Russell Square.

'I keep thinking my phone will beep and it will be you,' I said to her while my students talked together.

'Me too,' she said. 'But when I'm not talking to you, I miss that.' She paused. 'I even seem to talk to you in my half-sleep.'

'Do you?' I said. Her intensity sometimes disarmed me.

A colleague came over with her tea tray and sat down, and then my snatched meeting with Sylvie became a social event in which students, all volume and nerves, made the standard undergraduate attempt to please yet mildly shock us with their irreverence. Sylvie said very little, but her silence, I knew, came as much from self-containment as reserve. The students talked, the lively, light-toned speed of their speech registering with me through her ears – had *I* once talked like that? – and Sylvie occasionally made a comment or simply looked to one side, complete in herself; and suddenly, I saw her for the first time as a *being* – a vibrant physical presence – who was somehow rare and needed to be courted.

Before her next visit, I cleared up. I was nervous. I worried in case the ease of our conversation in Mecklenburgh Square had disappeared, and we were awkward again, and everything was stilted. I was unusually flustered: I flitted from room to room, removing piles of paper, switching on lamps.

She arrived at twenty-five to five, in a narrow black dress

with her hair back, which made her look more striking. She smelled strongly of cigarette smoke, and I teased her.

'How's the baby?' she said. She reached out and cupped her hand over my stomach.

'The baby's lovely,' I said. 'Well, she's *there*. She's growing.'

'Is she a she?'

'I don't know. I feel like I arrogantly know.'

'A daughter,' she said. 'She'd be plaity and sweet – strong and fierce – a little you.'

'Oh!' I said. 'I always think of plaits.'

'Has she got them already?' She bent over and lifted up my top and pretended to look through my stomach, her delicate fingers cold on my skin, and then kissed it.

We wandered around, talking. 'And *another* thing . . .' we kept saying. 'And another thing . . .' As we walked from room to room and picked things up, pausing and talking, I felt once again a heightened awareness of her – of her breath and her voice, of the quiet magic of her, the hidden cleverness of her mind. There was an understanding between us. Its flow was very clear and strong. I knew that if I felt this with her, then other people would too: it would not be unique; she would have the same effect on others once they looked beyond her understated exterior.

The lamps all shone, little pools splashing the dark floorboards and wintry walls of the flat. I left the heating on high, not wanting to leave the room at the front where we talked to adjust it. I had cooked cakes for her, and they scented the hot air. We talked still, we paddled over objects with our fingernails as we spoke. She looked at me in glances. There were further pauses. A terrible tension was beginning to form. The radiators seemed to tick with dust-scented heat that sat on my throat. I lifted my hand to pull my hair away from my flushed forehead.

'That's lovely,' said Sylvie.

'What is?'

'That. Your hair. How it falls.'

'Thank you,' I said. I tried to picture my own waves moving. Would they catch the light, then? Is that what she would see? The tension hummed: it was almost audible. *She is going to kiss me*, I thought with a shock. This *woman* will kiss me. My heartbeat escalated in panic. It beat faster. Seconds passed. I wanted to shout, to puncture the tension. She would move towards me. I would resist her, or –

'I—' she said.

I stuttered. I was frozen in silence.

We caught each other's eye. Cars edged past on Guilford Street, distant sirens, the throb of a taxi. I tried to look out of the window to calm myself with normality. There was a whole world out there, the floodlit tennis courts, the pale battlements of the Brunswick Centre.

We stood there together in the bedroom. The tension was noisy in the air, but somewhere in its centre, I floated. I felt so alive, it was as though I had been dying and not known it. Excitement trickled through me. It seemed to be the excitement of a long time ago: of sex first starting, and obsession, and betrayal. Adultery, delicious adultery. Sex with someone *illicit* – a teacher, or a friend's father, or another girl.

Richard turned off Guilford Street and crossed the road. He looked handsome in his winter coat with his big dark green scarf.

'He's coming,' I said, my voice betraying my feeling of urgency.

'Is he?' she said.

I watched him walk towards the flat, the way his feet swung, the way he hurried against the cold. I knew his emotions. I loved his flawed, lovely soul, just as a part of me literally hated him for being so distant from me and my pregnancy. I thought of his shoulders, of that beautiful area of flat musculature between the pubic bones and the hips, of the fact that, should he want to, with his strength and weight he could pin me down or flip me over in sex. I had never really wanted to kiss a woman. But she was so unlike me: smaller, slighter, and discreet and restrained. She felt like a different creature altogether. I wanted her to want me, to choose me above other people, and then I would know what to do.

'Yes,' I said, looking out of the window. 'There he is now.' I moved away into the centre of the room. She joined me.

'It's time for me to go home,' she said.

Without thinking, I pulled her head towards me so that it rested on my shoulder, my hand lingering just below the crown of her hair. I was shocked at what I'd done. She felt delicate in my arms. Is this the way men feel upon holding her? I wondered. We stood there, moments ticking past.

I listened for the street door. I felt her breathe on my shoulder. Her own sweet smell drifted beneath the layers of cigarette smoke that came from elsewhere: a pub, or perhaps a party from the night before. I had to say something.

'He'll be up in a moment,' I said.

We heard the flat door open. We looked at each other. Our gazes met with terrifying directness. He banged about a little downstairs.

'Lelia!' he called. I opened my mouth to answer. She moved her head away from my shoulder. I was silent.

She reached up and put her fingertips on my cheek, just above my jaw. *She's going to kiss me now*, I thought. That is what is going to happen. I saw it clearly before it happened. I froze in the panic of the moment.

She didn't.

The feeling of her fingers remained on my skin.

I heard the loo door open and bang shut.

'Goodbye,' she said rapidly.

'But—' I said. 'No.'

She looked at me questioningly, her dark eyebrows curving. She smiled. 'Next time,' she said. 'There'll be more time.'

She slipped down the stairs. I followed her unsteadily, banging into paintwork as I went. She opened the front door while the lavatory was flushing, and slipped out.

I ran into the main room and threw a ciabatta into the oven, which was still hot, and sat trembling upon a pile of cushions, and blindly tugged my hair up into a pencil, and when Richard appeared at the doorway, I looked up from my work and smiled at him.

Later, later that June, I felt a strong and unwise desire to invite her to my wedding. I had dreamed for weeks of the possibility of her being there, but my excuses were all too baffling. It was only the blood that made me certain.

She arrived there late, half-hiding in the growing darkness in a layered lilac dress that was less formal than her usual style but still bore that characteristic restraint. I embraced her when I saw her in the shadows on the gravel path. Her mouth was more visible; her eyebrows were dark and defined against her pale face in the dusk.

'I want to congratulate you,' she murmured.

'Oh, thank you,' I said, embarrassed and moved. I saw myself pressing my hands together. 'Thank you. It's – nice of you. Not nice. I sound like a – it sounds stupid. Did I do the right thing?'

'I don't know,' she said.

There was silence. I stared at her. *Why did I do this?* I thought.

She gazed back at me.

'I'm bleeding,' I whispered.

'Oh!' she said. 'Lelia.' She put her arm round me. She drew me to her as I had known she would, pulling my hair from my cheek and kissing my ear. 'Sit down,' she said, and she led me to a park bench on the side of the path where the lime shadows thickened. 'What have you done about it? We should phone the hospital.'

'Yes,' I said.

'Is there more?'

'I don't think so. I keep looking.'

'Is this – is this how it was last time?'

'Yes, but it was much earlier. There was – well, more pain.'

'And you're not in pain? Sweet love.'

I shook my head. 'I don't want to go to hospital. I want to be here with –' I looked at her – 'my friends. Richard. You.'

She pulled me to her so that my cheek was resting on her shoulder. She played with the hair at the back of my neck. 'Darling Lelia,' she said, her voice close and warm in my ear. 'You'll be all right. It doesn't seem to be getting worse. I'll look after you.'

'Oh – God. I knew that you would.'

'If you're not all right, we'll go to the hospital together.'

'Thank you,' I said. I breathed slowly. I sat against her. We looked at the orange sky above the leaves of the limes, and I kissed her palm before I left her, and she hovered in the shadows as a slim lilac figure at the edge of my vision while I talked to my other guests.

Later, I found her again. I saw her near the old hawthorn where the jasmine fell in a black-green surge over the fence.

It seemed that Richard hadn't, so far, noticed her in her quietness, or she had been keeping in the shadows. He was talking to MacDara by the marquee, his tie already loose, and he ran his hand through his hair, which flopped a little on his forehead. A feeling of disbelief came to me as I watched him and realised that he was my husband. Whatever I did, he was officially married to me. I felt panic creeping up on me at that moment – what had I signed away? How was I trapped by the law? – followed by a pang of guilt that he didn't deserve. Our guests ran around, shouting, behaving like children. I smiled slightly at the sight of them. So many daisies sprinkled over the lawns, their little white heads now closing. The deep red Alice roses were blood-black in the darkness.

'Now,' said Sylvie. 'Now . . . what? Because after this . . .'
She took me by the hand.
'Yes?'
'I want to say now. Say it. I love you,' she said.
'Oh!' I said. 'You know, I'd—'
'Shh,' she said, and placed her mouth against mine to quieten me. Her lips left a pattern of pressure whose imprint I tasted afterwards.

There was a bang by the marquee. Silence. Laughter. The band began a new tune.

'I've found a little house for us. This is our first home – our last home,' she said.

'Oh, Sylvie,' I said. I swallowed a kind of sob. Although I had always guessed that there were other people in her life beyond Charlie, just as I was aware that she had guessed that I knew, at that moment, I only wanted to stay with her; I wanted to guard her, to protect her, primarily, from me. Why did we end up marrying men? In another life, or another mindset, I could have eloped with her; I could have married my slender, subtle best friend, and we could have lived in a little house somewhere and talked all night, all nights.

She took my arm. She guided me away from the marquee and through the gnat-hung shade of an overhanging beech where the ground was soft with dampness and longer grass.

'Look, it's a shed!' she murmured. 'It's a gardener's shed for us.'

'A shed?' I said dumbly. I let her lead me through the night and away from my own party. I was driven by the childish thrill of conspiracy, of inappropriate behaviour instigated by another.

'Let's go in there first, or other people will discover it,' she said. 'It's open, you see. I just gave it a little push, and it's unlocked, specially for us. I made a place for you to lie on and look beautiful.'

We lowered ourselves and sat very close, our temples together as we talked. I felt I could decipher the thump of her blood, the minute crunching of flesh and vein as we pressed a headache into each other's brow and traced each other's thoughts.

I had never in my life known a friendship like this one. Not Sophie-Hélène before Mazarine. Not my primary school love Cally, nor my old conscience Enzo, nor Suzannah, the great friend and confidante of the last decade and a half. We had a romance, an entanglement of the mind, of books, of shops, of perpetual conversation. We phoned each other when Richard and Charlie were asleep and discussed Fontane or Sarraute or Flaubert in our nighties and laughed over inconsequential matters and talked ceaselessly about the baby.

She hadn't kissed me in the bedroom at Mecklenburgh

Square, nor in the days that followed. I was largely keeping to office hours that term, with more moral tutoring obligations and an education sub-committee that demanded my time. As I sat at work, thinking about her as I guided some intense undergraduate through a tutorial or tackled files of mind-numbing admin, I noticed that there were bubbles of disappointment trapped in the relief. She contacted me subtly: she left snatches of music on my voicemail, notes in my pigeon-hole, texts and work emails, their unspoken aim to communicate with me while bypassing Richard, the subterfuge at first disquieting. Each morning I woke to invent new plots as I lay recovering on my bed after the initial bout of vomiting.

'I'm going to train the pigeon on my window-sill,' she said. 'It's going to become a racing carrier pigeon, bringing notes to you across Bloomsbury every day.'

We carried the baby with us. It was both of us who nurtured that girl: my womb enclosing her, Sylvie's mind and imagination protecting my womb, so that even in a park in winter, in Russell Square in the big glass café when the surprising snow fell, I was warm and I was cared for. We traced the growth of my baby: she had a book, she said; she knew the average rate of a baby's development, and each week, each Friday, she showed me. She bought me rulers in newsagents and wrapped a ribbon around the relevant centimetre mark, or bought me a book or a card or a flower the very same length; she knew when organs grew and the fingernails developed and the baby could see light. I took her to my twenty-week scan: I didn't even tell Richard about it.

'Her eyelids formed this week,' she said. 'Imagine that.'

The revelation of Sylvie was something I kept secret: my friends would not understand. I barely understood it myself.

Drunken female undergraduates now routinely kissed each other for effect, I realised, but in our time as students we had never even considered such behaviour. If I asked her, tried to press her with coded Sapphic enquiries while blushing as furiously as a teenager, she would simply say, shrugging delicately, was anything so straightforward? Could human desire be categorised? She spoke lightly and casually, as though she was a senior lecturer considering the hypothetical, and kept her own cool distance. Into that detachment leapt my excitement.

Tell me, I wanted to say, to beg. Tell me everything. But not everything.

The world was different. Trees smelled of sperm; pavements smelled of dog excrement; a passing mention of Asian food made me retch. Coffee tasted of burnt oil. I gagged; I threw up on to the pavement, against trees, in rubbish bins, but every session of sickness was proof of the miracle that the baby was held tight by my hormones; it was an expiation for the past miscarriages, for my father's death, and for other problems I may have caused. Except that it would never be.

Pigmentation scattered itself over my skin, like the archipelago stains in Mazarine's bath. My nipples widened; my stomach plumped; my mind pitched. I bought new clothes, avoiding maternity shops until the very last minute, and plundering my old favourites with fresh levels of passion. Sylvie's presence was everywhere. I could sense her after-effects in the flat, I could almost smell her scent there, anxious in case Richard detected that same subtle alteration of the air. I looked out for him nervously on the streets of Bloomsbury, and there were times when we missed his return home by moments.

One evening when he'd gone out with MacDara and

stayed later and later, Sylvie had remained with me, and then caught sight of him on the square as she left. He hadn't spotted her, she said, but she'd had to hide. She slipped into the shadows by the gate to the gardens, shivering, the snow hanging on the trees above her, and watched him enter our flat with a feeling of sadness. And once, when Catrin seemed to want to talk to me at MacDara's party, I had the distinct impression that she had guessed what was happening.

'Do you feel guilty?' Sylvie asked me, teasing me with laughter, gazing intently into my eyes and holding my temples between her hands.

'No,' I said. 'Not very.'

'Good.'

'I don't know why.'

'I *do*,' she said, and indeed, in the face of Richard's abandonment of me and my baby, I barely felt guilt – I who was so guilt-ridden I couldn't look at my father's picture without the old hot panic beginning to form. I watched the development of my own duplicity with wonder as I kept him at bay with the odd guileless comment about the mouse girl, Sylvie herself so coolly, patchily amoral that I was easily, even happily, infected.

When she and I kissed for the first time, we kissed urgently. A storm was brewing, roughing the trees in Mecklenburgh Square, the leaves that mounted the fence streaming and vibrating. The sky was so grey, it was going to tear with rain. Our hair blew horizontally in spitty gusts and we had to hurry home, we had to part, but there was so much left to say, and suddenly we were gasping in the airless wind and kissing, words and coldness and the warmth of our mouths mixing as we leaned towards each other to shout goodbye against the gathering gale. The surprise of the contrast – the electric jolt of her mouth in the running air, the human intimacy – was a shock that had the power to excite me whenever I summoned it.

In Gordon Square, we had to jam the shed door. I could not be a pregnant bride caught lying in a corner of a shed with another woman on her wedding day. I lay in a sliver of moon, a mist of street light. The sounds of the party drifted near us like sea. The idea of death was coming to me again; I imagined standing up to discover a hot dead pool of blood seeping into the straw, and I was desperate to hold on to life. If my baby died, I wanted her to die here while her mother died, with someone else who cared about her and honoured her, unlike her father, who had never even known her shape or size, or on what day her weekly age changed.

Sylvie fixed the door and came back to me. I held out my arms, and she lowered herself to the floor in that dull lilac petal of a dress and we embraced. We kissed – the silken softness of kissing a woman after years of stubble still shocking to me; the way it would look from the outside more shocking still – those first girlish sips of hers mixed with whispers. She would look after me, she said.

I felt I was sealing my love for Sylvie Lavigne, as though I was making a scrolling testament to her. And then I would attempt to save my marriage, my one-day-old marriage. But the idea of losing her made me want to cry, just as the idea of losing my baby made me want to die.

'You're my best friend,' she said as she stroked my shoulder, subtly edging beneath the neck of my dress. 'I found you.'

It was damp, that shed. It smelled of moist potting sand and tiny pearly mollusc shells, of sodden spiders' web amongst the brickwork. When I exhaled, I could taste decaying fern. I could make out spades and piles of canes in the darkness.

Let my baby live, I thought. Let this be a Beatrix Potter shed of tabby cats and galoshes for her to play in, not a mausoleum.

Sylvie pulled a blanket on me, or I thought she did. It was her coat; it emitted a shadow of her own fragrance. I shivered. She cupped my face. She was above me. 'Let me look after you,' she said.

I nodded.

'Let's make her live,' she murmured into my neck.

You can't say that, I thought in panic. I dug my fingernails into the cloth beneath me in superstition. My baby's life must be my own private ritual.

She kissed me.

We three. My daughter. Sylvie. Me. All men had gone. We lived here, we three, preserved in time, as we never would again. Perhaps one day I would say to my daughter whimsically, 'See that old shed (now a burger stand, now an internet café). Once I loved someone there.' I would never betray the date or the circumstance: it would be part of her mother's misty innocent past. But I would want to whisper, *You were there too; I was in love at that time; it was my wedding day.*

She kissed me on the curve of my clavicle, her head quite still, only her lips lingering and mobile.

I was so aroused, I was filled with alarm. I didn't want to be excited.

'I want my baby,' I said. Tears ached behind my eyeballs.

'So do I,' she said. 'Don't bleed. Relax, my love. Lie down. Let me love you. Let me make you relax.'

Her skin was fine and white like a spirit's in the shadows; I touched it to reassure myself of its human warmth. The brushstrokes of her brows were like a Japanese painting in the darkness, her eyes black, her mouth containing its own separate beauty.

She moved her tongue to where the wetness of my tears streaked my skin. 'Shhh,' she said, and I kissed her hair, and she moved across me, strong and certain in all her lightness, and my breath emerged shallowly, like a moth in my neck that couldn't escape.

Our murmurings rose through the semi-darkness, as though we imagined we were magically protected by the shadows that would drown them, yet I could picture my mother, glinty-eyed and silently aware of where I was. Sylvie and I hushed each other, turning to strangle the sounds. I resisted her; I panicked about the baby; she stroked me, and I arched towards her, wanting more, pushing her away. Where was Richard? I didn't know. In another place, another planet, urban and social. I remembered love among girls. That shocking little cleft of a pubis. Mazarine was a girl after all.

'I *found* you,' she said.

Her hair fell on mine; it lingered together, snaked across the cloth we lay on, and I kissed the cool skin beneath her neck. Her palm skimmed my foot, my leg, and she paused to contemplate me with dark eyes, her mouth still and passive in the shadows, and then slowly she moved as Mazarine had once moved.

'Do you remember, then?' she said.

I laughed into her mouth.

She laughed too. She hushed me with her lips. The image chased me as we moved. Two girls, making love. She made love to me. She soothed me. My baby swam inside me as I moved. She remapped every inch of me, my nerves rippling under her, crying out and protesting, climbing higher, sweat breaking out on my forehead. Richard had once licked every inch of my skin, but she drew upon me as a man never had.

I smelled it now: the sap-rich countryside in a Bloomsbury square and the scent of Sylvie Lavigne, and Clemenceau and the chestnuts by the Loire, and as the grass scents twined with her hair, I wanted to lie here rising and rising without stopping.

'I love you,' I said at last.

'I love you, always,' she said.

I kissed her cheekbone, and it was wet. I echoed her with a sob. We were half-crying as we talked. The night was so dark, the sounds of my wedding larger and sharper in my ears, her arms circling me, holding my neck to her.

I remembered a broad river, the terrible panic seeping into pleasure. Her body was hot on top of mine. We were tangled and open, our flesh a mess of heat and liquid. If my baby died, I would die as well, because I could never survive it. I would die in orgasm. She moved her hands down, across my body, my abdomen a curve in the moonlight.

'This will be the very end, won't it?' she said. She looked directly into my eyes from above me. A spasm caught heat and rose.

'No,' I said. A sound came from my mouth, from outside of me. I heard Richard's voice. I was high on a cliff ledge in the darkest blue night. I couldn't breathe. Heat gathered inside me, then it spread, and raced. I lay in silence as the glory paused, spilled, widened, and saturated my bloodstream. 'No,' I said.

EIGHTEEN

Richard

MacDara. The snivelling paunchy cunt. MacDara bothered me almost more than anyone. More than my wife or my mistress or my failing fortnight-long marriage. I squandered valuable hours at work frantically calculating the sex that he and Sylvie Lavigne were or were not having, and then spent considerably more time weighing up the intensity and potential humiliation levels of their disgusting conspiracy. I flailed through old undeleted emails searching for clues to Sylvie's identity, embedded like a worm in his illiterate messages, but MW had always seemed to me someone else entirely: married, glamorous and above all, normal.

I missed him. I hated him more than anyone in the world.

My first instinct on the Monday after my wedding was to storm over to his office in a fury, shake him up a bit, and squeeze out every last drop of information about Sylvie Lavigne. *When?* I wondered. How? I could recall them together only once since that first night, at dinner in my flat with the shouting Fearons. She had been invisible; she'd drifted along the edges, shunning alcohol or conversation. And then, with a jolt, as though nailing the criminal, I recalled MacDara taking some lengthy work call in my office.

Had she been with him? Had she? Had she sneaked her way into his life that night?

I went to the roof at work the following morning and gazed over to the east towards the tower blocks where MacDara spent his waking hours, and every instinct in me wanted to jump into a taxi, to crash in there and wring the truth from him until he begged me for mercy. But I knew better. I could not risk further damage to my marriage. The cretin was clearly ignorant of his mistress's other activities: my outburst of violence towards him was attributed, hilariously, to an over-developed sense of protectiveness towards an innocent and little-known family friend whose honour I had defended with my fists. Thus his hammy, indignant pleas, his justifications and sudden snide bouts of conjecture were all met by a disciplined silence as I ignored his emails and told him in simple terms to fuck off whenever he rang.

'Let's go *now* on honeymoon,' I said to Lelia after a few days of marriage that were so tense I could only disperse the silence with proclamations.

'How?' she said simply, and I considered our work commitments and reflected miserably upon the stupid mistake I'd made in agreeing to postpone our honeymoon until her university summer holiday to protect her maternity leave. I should have swept her away right then and left the mess of our lives behind. And yet perhaps, in our secret minds, neither of us had wanted to go after all.

'Please,' she said. 'Talk to me.'

But I dreaded her confronting me, just as I cringed at our terrible new inability to communicate. We had barely spoken since our marriage, we who could never stop talking even at the expense of sex and sleep. Only the subject of MacDara came up with horrible regularity, as though he had somehow become the bogus focus for all our unspoken griefs, my flimsily embellished explanations failing to calm her distress. She slept badly; she rarely referred to her pregnancy; she no longer irritatingly grabbed my hand to feel baby kicks that never materialised, a rapt and patient expression on her face that I was supposed to echo.

'Are you still – are you having your ante-natal check-ups?' I wanted to ask her, but I feared that the question itself would be an inexplicable source of fury, and I failed to find a way to ask it.

This, then, I realised, was what crap marriages were composed of. All those snapping couples who seemed to hate each other; pensioners silently reading over hotel meals; couples seething with a decade of resentments, their squabbling pale-faced kids in tow. Our oldest arguments – formed, I now realised, in the first year of our relationship – were endlessly recycled, sprouting new and nasty tentacles that barely disguised their repetitive nature. An imagined tone of voice could set off a well-rehearsed chain of accusations and counter-accusations that culminated in a round of defence and tears. And yet the shouting and the silence and the tension served merely as a barrier, and in the thick of explosive arguments, we swerved away from the very questions that might reveal the truth, and we crept around each other and buried ourselves in work before tailing, late and exhausted, into bed.

One morning I looked at her face, now faintly freckly with July sun, the skin beneath her eyes tired and strained, and she looked older, and reduced in ways I couldn't describe, as though with my infidelity I'd damaged her at some essential level. A pang for her welled up inside me.

'Sorry,' I murmured into her sleeping neck. 'Sorry.'

★

Sylvie Lavigne herself was nowhere to be seen. I had looked forward, upon waking the morning after my wedding, to scorning the treacherous little cat; I had wanted to wield the easy power of banishing her from my pages, ignoring her entreaties, punishing her as she deserved. But I should have known better by now: elusive as she always was, she had disappeared. The idea that she might be shacked up with MacDara somewhere (trips to his furry loft; subtle assignations in City bars) made me fantasise about crashing my fist into his face again, but harder this time, so that his shattered jaw produced a comedy trowel of a chin resembling Desperate Dan's that would induce pity and mirth. It felt as though I was developing a stomach ulcer.

Where are you? Dearest love, I miss you.

She haunted me even as I tried to exorcise her. I loathed her now, as though allergic to her, and yet she stayed lodged in my mind, sending tendrils of lust and old unsullied affection through my memory when I was caught unawares. I found notes that had been planted by her at unknown times under piles of books at work, or in my drawer, and once even in the flat. I switched on my computer to her fragments of novel. I received a letter at work and foolishly opened it. *She's fucking with my mind*, MacDara had once said to me, weeks ago, months ago, when he was still my friend, and MW was some amorphous tart, and all was right with the world.

There is uproar in our house. The Hindoo enchants me, but she must be kept from my Emilia. She cries for her dead Papa when she thinks no one sees her. The infant whips his arms about his crib if I so much as hollow my hand upon his chin. Once I pulled his head-flannel hard upon him, and he hissed at me like a wild goose and mewled for Mama, who is *his* Mama. The nurse came clattering along.

One afternoon, I thought I could drop him from the maid's room in the sky to the barrow below and there he would die, as though the catsmeat man had pocketed him. But what if I failed? We had a few weeks, perhaps, before the infant could betray us by turning to us with his saucer-pool eyes and hinting to the world what we had tried to do. The mother and I no longer contemplated each other when I returned late from the day nursery, and God looked upon me and upon my sinful passions with sorrow. I had made myself so small, I was invisible at last.

As Mama smoothed the baby's quilling and gave her body to him, Emilia and I practised on each other, our fingers crooking and finding, a black roaring gathering inside my head.

I delected her emails, barely read, just as I made myself throw away the letters she sent me. I found a love note planted on my desk that moved me, and yet I screwed it up and threw it in the bin before I walked home from work. And much as I hated her, and MacDara, and Charlie and all of them, the odd phrase caught me unawares, slicing across the rhythm of my breathing or rocketing through my blood, yet Lelia was the one I loved. The idea of losing her during that terrible fortnight filled me with desperation to cling to the flawed yet glorious thing I'd once had. I wanted her more than anything else. I knew it one day very clearly. I understood it, finally.

I came out of Safeway's, and I saw a woman and a child at the bottom of the steps. As I left the shopping centre, the woman fell over on the pavement, catching her foot and sprawling on the ground, and in her humiliation, in the mess of exposed thigh and hurt ankle before an audience of strangers, I felt such an embarrassed lurch of pity for her, the urgency of the situation stripping my mind of all but empathy and horror as it revealed in one flashing fragment the priorities of my life. I ran towards her. The child clung to her on the ground and put its face against her waist, offering flailing child comfort even as it opened its mouth in a silent scream, and I was shocked at that moment into knowledge of what it was that mattered.

Lelia. I wanted her, and our life together. I wanted to protect her and that unimaginable child inside her. In that oblique epiphany, I made a simple promise in my head, more binding than any marriage certificate.

I walked home. I didn't truly want that child. I didn't not want it either. What I desired was her. I wanted her, and with her came our child, and like all slack and useless dads I would make an effort and grow to love it.

I looked up at the front window of our flat, and I knew as my gaze met the darkness that if only I could win her back through the toxic silence that had engulfed us, then every-thing was perfectly simple at last. I wanted to commit myself for always to the lovely person I'd married. The revelation, the relief of it, was almost overwhelming. It hurt my throat. I glanced at the dark room again, warding off a trickle of fear, and I rushed up the steps thinking, thank God, thank God, thank you, God, for warning me. My heart hammering into my neck, I double-stepped to the top. Whatever happened now, I would never betray her or the baby. There was silence. She should be there, she should certainly be there.

'Lelia!' I shouted.

I called out again, and ran in and saw that things were neat and altered.

NINETEEN

Richard

I put my head in my hands. I dragged my fingers across my scalp, trying to gouge out silken dandruff as proof of my living body there under my fingernails when I felt like death.

When? I thought. *How?* When had she found out? When? When? Who? Or had she guessed, with her terrifying female intuition, just as she had known about MacDara? Or had she simply despaired over living with a distracted and monosyllabic madman? A burp of nausea lodged in my throat. The note she had left on the kitchen table said that she was staying at her mother's. That was all. There was a kiss scrawled at the end. In my moment of shock, the kiss was a perverse token of comfort and true hope. I kicked the table leg, purposely hurting myself as the table leapt and whined across the floor. Had Sylvie herself somehow confessed to her, Sylvie who was nowhere and yet obliquely everywhere?

How to kill a baby? I didn't know. I hefted its plump weight and dropped it from high. I could not do it. I thumped it, pounded it like the nursemaid did when it coughed and retched on its milk. I pounded it harder. It drew in its breath in a silent spasm before it stormed the air with its screams. I pitied it then.

I rolled him once, roly-poly, roly-poly, from the top of the stairs to the rug below the night nursery. He tumbled quite softly on his puffs of flesh, but at the bottom he knocked his block-head on the wainscot and bawled and spewed as though a monster possessed him.

I became patient.

The Hindoo girl who was visiting my Emilia came daily to our house. There she glided, like a figurine the heathens idolised, scattering her hooks. Her charms lay in her loose curls, which she spread like rings. Her eyes too inspired idolatry – big brown stones found in the desert, and set at a tilt. Even my mother smiled on her. She rubbed ointments all day into her skin in her bath tub, keeping close to where she could hear Emilia playing, and sobbing silently for her departed father. I wanted to be with Emilia and the Hindoo when they went home together at night, and wrap myself in their scents until I embraced the warmth of the Hindoo's skin. Everything the Hindoo had, I wanted to take: her charm, her laughing beauty, the harsh orphanhood that shaded my own secret abandonment. I wanted her home in that glittering city of which I had read. I wanted the Hindoo's life.

As I skimmed the latest instalment on my computer, the suspicion that had been bothering me burst into certainty. That creepy little vixen was writing about Lelia, whom she barely knew. The woman who had infiltrated my life was now infantilising my wife in her demented tatters of fiction in order to intrigue or punish me in some obscure way.

'What *is* this novel?' I had finally asked her in the dark

corner of a café. She had merely cast me a chilly glance, and then, in her habitual manner, declined to answer.

I deleted the email, crashing down on the key, and called Lelia's mother, the only person in London with no voicemail. The phone rang and rang until BT cut me off.

I had never masturbated quite so frantically as I did during that time. I had never slept as much since my student days, nor allowed my hair to become so dirty, nor spent so much money on takeaways. I roamed the flat at night, a roaring insomniac, then wanked myself helplessly back to sleep, barking out my pain and sweating into sheets that I would never change until Lelia came back to me.

I phoned Lelia at her mother's, to continued silence. I wrote to her. I frequently turned up at the house in the early morning, rattling up there on the Northern Line before work to surprise her into an explanation, to no avail. I began to suspect that she had gone elsewhere. Lelia's mother, the mighty Joan, steadfastly refused to give me any hint of where or how her daughter was, even though I arrived in time to catch her on her way to work. Lelia was 'fine', she was 'safe', I was informed. Lelia was married to me and carrying *our* child, I reminded her in turn. Despite her habitual reserve, she managed to shoot me a withering look, then old-lady walked down the street to work. I watched her back with painful and reluctant admiration, returned via the university in case Lelia was in there marking, and yet still I failed to bump into her.

Her mobile was nearly always turned off. I texted her; I pestered her mother, called her aunt, her department, her affrontingly loyal clique of friends, and frequently turned up at the university, but term had ended and there was a sense of hopelessness to my missions, of empty halls and filed papers. I even lowered myself to contacting her yapping guard dog Enzo. I begged her mother again; I swore at her friend Suzannah; I rang her department, where a surly holiday administrator kept me skilfully at bay.

'I asked you to leave me alone,' she said, the only times I ever managed to speak to her on the phone. She was polite and distant, and her voice sounded weary, a tone that filled me with panic.

'Where *are* you?' I shouted at her. '*How* are you? The baby?'

'Bye, Richard,' she always said, and refused to talk further. 'Bye, darling,' she said once, causing a hammering of my heart.

Gradually, the flat metamorphosed into a cesspit. The table's burden of toppling paper and silly objects, now so precious I couldn't face looking at them, became the mere bedrock for an unstable and catastrophic collection of detritus. Dry plant leaves were sandwiched by bills and adverts which magnetically attracted dust and traces of plaster crumble and unidentifiable flakes of desiccated matter. The piles that had always littered the staircase took on a creeping life of their own, like kudzu, to ensnare me. In the dark I had to remember the hairpin manoeuvres required to negotiate the stairs: where I had to take two steps, where I had to grip the banisters as I clung to a narrow edge and then hopped over a pile of papers. Once I slid, and cursed, and banged my toe in a throb of pain, and I sat there sobbing in the hall like a maddened bullock.

My dear mother, sensing there was something amiss before she was treated to my full and ranting confession, rang with increasing regularity. How I looked forward to her calm, concerned calls; to her practical advice, equally

scorned and lapped up by me, and her refusal to countenance my panic, just as I had once leapt upon her chatty
postcards during a soggy German exchange in some
Godforsaken farm where I had smoked and tinkered with
motorbikes all day.

A week went by without contact. I 1471-ed every time
I came home; I rifled through Lelia's desk to find
phone numbers, wincing at evidence of former times when
we were enchanted and excited and could do no wrong,
and rang other old friends of hers, my apparently casual
enquiries sounding wildly false even to my own ears, until
I abandoned all pride and began barking out terse and inappropriate confessions to semi-strangers. Masochism somehow tangled pleasingly with machismo, and I was briefly
soothed by the drama and ensuing sympathy. I rang other
numbers: Lelia's relations, so movingly sparse and scattered,
who tended to be referred to as aunts and cousins even if
distantly related, were barely in contact, and my wild bouts
of research unearthed nothing. In free lunchtimes, I went
straight over to the university in case she was using her office,
only to have embarrassing conversations with a department
secretary, and to be barred by the electronic gates in the
Senate House library.

She rang me.

'Honestly, Richard, I do need to be left alone for a while,'
she said, then enquired about my health and her post.

'Where are you?' I said rapidly.

'At a friend's. I'm fine.'

'How long do you want to be away for?'

'I don't know,' said Lelia, her answer intensifying the pain
that hit me the moment I heard her guarded tones.

'Look—' I snapped, but to no avail.

I went to bed and ground myself into the mattress with

my mouth open against the pillow, and even as I mourned Lelia, an insistent thought flickered perversely through my mind: I could now have Sylvie. For the first time, I could legitimately bring her back to my pigsty and fuck her stupid.

Where are you? Dearest love, I miss you.

She ghosted through my existence, inciting streaks of sexual fury. In my despair, my hostility even swung to its opposite extreme: I could go with her, perhaps, throw my lot in with this strange, treacherous being with her un-expectedly beautiful little body who turned me on and snared my mind. I shuddered at the notion in the morning. All I wanted to do was to eradicate her from my mind and life. Yet whatever I desired, Sylvie Lavigne herself, like MacDara and Lelia, had quite gone.

Increasingly, I found her in other people's newspapers. I picked up a new anthology of short stories that had come into the office, and there she was. I flung it down on the floor and stormed upstairs to Peter Stronson.

'What's happened to Sylvie Lavigne?' I said to him, coughing as I spoke.

'Sylvie Lavigne?' he said, attempting to look blank. 'She's doing the Atwood for me. I think.'

'That's not for a while.'

'I think she's editing her novel.'

I snorted.

'She's been speaking to an agent about it.'

'What?' I said.

'You know – Lachlan.'

'Really?'

'I suggested him.'

'*Why?*'

'She didn't seem to know anyone.'

I laughed, inappropriately loudly.

'He's an old mate,' said Stronson, looking embarrassed.

I stared at him for a fraction of a second to scare him a bit, and glanced at his wedding ring.

'What do you think of her?' I said, enjoying myself.

'She's very good. Authoritative. Colourful.'

'No – *her*.'

He paused for a fraction of a beat. 'Well—' he said. 'Socially.' He laughed. 'She's wallpaper.'

I laughed again.

'Isn't she writing for you?' he said.

'She hasn't for a while. I haven't spoken to her,' I said. There was a silence. 'Where is she?' I said.

'Where is she?' he repeated, as if caught. 'I don't know. She seems not to – at home, I suppose,' he said.

I raised my eyebrows at him deliberately, and walked off.

A new week began. I wrote to Lelia in Golders Green, again alluding to my crime without delivering a full confession, and outlining, with honesty that was painful to summon, my guilt and love. The idea that she was now heavily pregnant and might need money troubled me on a daily basis. I sobbed and cursed and hit walls for her. The fact that she had left me made my jaw feel heavy, as though I had been punched with grief, and I would do anything for her bossy ways, for her growing bump with its intangible baby kicks, and her dear familiar voice in my ear. I stretched out, laying my arm across the cool pillow as though I might find her there. I wolfed down Indian takeaway and burped and farted; the more evil and protracted the farts, the more satisfying. Cereal stuck to the oily spillage on the hob. I arrived at work unshaven.

I could shag anyone, I realised. During a short-lived angry fantasy, I even managed to blame Lelia for my own infidelity as I mulled over the possibilities. There was a neighbour I'd always quite fancied, and the assistant in the health food shop on Marchmont Street was a well-known local fox: I'd once dragged MacDara in there to cop a look. I could seek out my lunatic actress of a former girlfriend and spend an energetic afternoon in a hotel for old times' sake. Such plots kept me briefly sane as I chewed them over at three in the morning; they were laughable by the time my alarm rang.

On Saturday, I woke in the afternoon and switched on my computer, like a tic. The Hotmail address was there.

I tried to stop the poison that was running through me, but I could not staunch it, and then I thought that I must cry until my heart punched out its own life. All that I had ever wanted was a family: a family that would look after me and take me to its breast and be mine, like other girls seemed to have.

Yet I had dreamed of institutions. I had read of Lowood with its loves and tuberculosis, and early in my girlhood, I was sent from my own home to a girls' high school. And then later, when all the world was in turmoil and dressed in black, I was to be banished to another place: a harsher place, an institution for girls such as myself, over whom God despaired, and whose evil had brought only abandonment. It would be no better than a charity school for foundlings with its diseases and foul air, and there I would live out my earthly years.

I would not go, I screamed. They bound me. They forced sal volatile and punishment upon me. I screamed and screamed until I injured my lungs and spat phlegm. I would not have *nothing*.

Where was Sylvie? Another chilling thought inched up my spine and spread over my scalp. Were they all together somewhere: Lelia and Sylvie and the baby-to-be? Was she, caught up as she was in her own obsessive little mental world, planning to harm Lelia to punish me? For the first time, the distaste that had been accumulating spilled into fear.

In my agitation, I had to move about. I had to do something. It was too hot. I caught a taxi on the square and asked it to drive along Endsleigh Street. Sylvie's windows were high and blank behind their metal frames. A sole pigeon nodded on her balcony railing. I took the taxi round Gordon Square and then back again, ghosting the streets that she herself haunted, the leaves on the trees sooty, the grass paling. A memory of addiction came back to me as I gazed at the windows. I switched it off.

I coasted through Bloomsbury, then asked the driver to return. If I went back to the flat, Lelia might have rung in the meantime.

I glanced at our own windows, half-thinking, in my eternal lunatic's optimism, that she would have arrived while I was out. If she had, I would walk into her arms, and I would want nothing as much again in my life. As I paid the taxi driver for my fruitless round trip, I scowled at Lucy, the local slapper. She gazed blankly back at me, her eyes blackened with make-up, her skin mottled with unsavoury blemishes.

'Seen my wife?' I said flippantly, to fill the void with the presence of Lelia.

'Yeah,' she said.

'*What?*' I said, turning to her.

She emitted a bitchy little snort and shrugged. 'With her post.'

'She came to collect some post?'

Lucy nodded.

I waited.

'Where did she go?'

'She's left you, hasn't she?' she said, a malevolent smile spreading over her face and further tilting her small sharp nose.

'Yes, she's left me!' I shouted. '*Where* was she going?'

'I don't know,' said Lucy.

'Was she on her own?'

'No.'

'Who was she with?' I asked. I felt unsteady.

'A friend.' She shrugged again.

'Who?' I almost shook her.

'*I* don't know,' said Lucy indignantly.

'A woman?'

'Yes.'

'Right. No one you know, then?'

'No,' said Lucy, as though insulted to be asked.

'Listen, Luci— Lucy. Don't you know where she was going?' In my mind, I reached into my pocket and pulled out a twenty-quid note as a bribe. 'Do you know anything?' My voice rose.

'Nope. Sorry. Better run after her, mister,' she said, giving me a sly look as she disappeared down the steps to her flat.

An unknown tabby cat was sitting by the geraniums in the area. The novelty of its presence lent me a surge of hope. When I reached the top of the stairs, the stillness of the flat in smeared sunlight filled me with the worst loneliness I could ever remember experiencing. The weave and dust on the collar of Lelia's winter coat were picked out by a shaft of light. The fear that she'd actually left me took a fresh grip. A pile of proofs to read sat beside my computer. I went online for comfort, sweating in the heat. I would look up news and desperately Google anything that occurred to me; I almost felt like joining a chatroom. The madwoman had emailed.

Once I lay in wait for the Hindoo, to frighten her. Emilia had gone visiting with her mother, and the orphan was taking the air. I lay so long, I became cold in my roost of grasses and I began to cry over my missing father, and all that my mother and I had lacked, and the poor failure of my life until now.

A parting of ferns. A neat little shoe. The Hindoo stepped down by the river where the water ached and swirled. I watched her slender back as she came. I thought of clasping her there, to worry her a little, but I couldn't punish her after all for soiling my love. Instead, the Hindoo and I talked of shameful things – of the gentleman and the maiden, and how they embraced and stifled the other until their breath was taken away and they flew to a place like death.

The Hindoo was beautiful. That day, I wanted her for mine. She spread her charms to me; I showed her new worlds. I began to love my old enemy. She was cold by the river, and so I warmed her. She lay back, her curls sleeked with light as she bent her head just so, and our words flowed and softened as the grasses parted and darkened.

We talked then of my sorrow. I almost sobbed. I said, 'I will die, that baby will make me die.'

The Hindoo placed her hand upon my arm and tried to comfort me. Her mouth, that pretty curve of a mouth, became tight as a coin. '*No*,' she said. 'You must not speak in that way.'

'I want it to die instead of me,' I said.

240

TWENTY

Lelia

She had got to me. She was so sexy, so beautiful, so damaged, I had entered her world, and yet a part of me had already begun to dislike her.

'Let's leave,' she said to me in the second week of July, after we had attended my midwife check-up together and Richard had failed once more to ask about our poor baby's health.

'Leave?' I said.

'I mean, let's be together,' she said.

I'd recognised her at the beginning, of course, though I had only seen Mazarine for longer than a few moments perhaps six times, two decades before. There she was again, surely, that androgynous French child from the big shuttered doctor's house, sitting at MacDara's table. I knew her voice.

It made me think – what was it that had once happened with her there, by the Loire? I could never recall it all, just as later I blocked out memories of the night before I left France.

My third week in Clemenceau, I'd talked to Mazarine at last. Sophie-Hélène had to help her mother with the toddlers, and I was mercifully excused such duties. I wandered out of town past the raincoat factory, and dived down a lane that led to the old canal that ran parallel to the river. As I walked, I had a playful instinct that some-where in the course of the day I would chance upon Mazarine. I was so fine-tuned by then to the feverish concealment of Mazarine and Sophie-Hélène that I would be able to detect them. I passed a woman herding her animals, the cows patterned plates of late afternoon sun. The vegetation frothed across the river, and in a slant of light I came upon Mazarine, crying in the long grass and nettle. He – *she* – wore a skirt instead of the usual unisex long shorts and aertex shirt. She looked vulnerable, like an almost pretty girl with her large hazel eyes and pale fine skin.

She was crying; she was snotty and blotched in the leaves. She was as humiliated as she would have been had I stum-bled upon her naked there. She was weeping, and I knew that it was about her mother and the baby. I watched her and she turned from me, and I thought about the grief that parents bring – not loving you, or leaving you by dying; and I cried too and tried to hide the tears flattening over my face.

After a long silence she said, 'I'll show you other things.' She wouldn't look at me. She led me along the old canal, and we scrambled up a bank and along an avenue of planes that widened into a ring of horse chestnuts.

'I'll show you more,' she said; she would say nothing else, and we clambered over small bridges on to the old *écluse*, and there was the Loire in all its thundering width, vaster and more sinewy than anything I had seen. The houses, shutters, locks were stunted before it. 'Like the Mekong,' she said. 'The Plain of the Birds.'

She gazed. 'Look at the river like a sea where it divides,' she said. 'It's a world out there.' I felt flags rise, fluttering. I felt sails, a gala, a wind that could lift me up. 'There's an island,' she said. 'You could live there almost. We could live there.' She said nothing more. She turned and we left.

It was as though, that afternoon for the first time, we loved each other. We walked back; we stumbled; she led me. How could that slight, straight body, the smooth little mound, the small hands, give another girl such pleasure? How how how when she wasn't a boy? My curiosity made me light-headed. She began to speak to me again. We spoke in English. Of course, I realised, it was inevitable that she spoke nearly faultless English. She spoke to me calmly, her tone almost monotonous, about everything she did with Sophie-Hélène; she half-glanced at me; she held my arm so lightly, her hand sometimes catching my waist, and I had the strangest sensation that in her mind – in *my* mind, which was her mind too – she was talking about us, about our own bodies astonishingly, improbably intertwined.

I felt then as though she would lead me by the hand and I would walk and we would disappear together, runaway children never found, living in the grasses. We made each other little promises in hints and shy ellipses. I chattered brightly, self-consciously, trying to fill in her silences and please her clever mind, because when the roofs of Clemenceau came into view, she would belong to Sophie-Hélène. We created new delays and grassy loops. We talked on our knees, lowering ourselves so slowly that we dis-appeared into the grass together. The weed petals and green blades arched above us, rustling and concealing us. We emerged much later, in the early evening.

She whispered into my ear. She knew, now, despair, she said. We spoke, frowning, heads huddled and almost pressed together as we walked, about the baby. I sometimes tried to remember that conversation afterwards. I couldn't, though; I couldn't exactly.

★

When I saw Mazarine again, I had the sensation of waking in confusion from a dream. Newly pregnant, I felt the ghost of her arrive. I saw, sitting there, someone I'd thought for years would turn up in my life again, and I knew then that my image of her had become skewed, and I realised how wrong, how unreliable memory is. I had half-looked for her all my life, the taste of frustrated childhood desire and shame and anxiety having never left me as I imagined for a moment that I recognised her in certain girls, in particular women on the streets over the years. There was always the flare of recognition that must then subside as a stranger passed by.

I even, just once, tried sleeping with another woman. I had split up with my older man; I was feeling hurt, and care-free and single, and I was introduced to a woman at a party. Something about her restrained manner had reminded me of Mazarine, and with terrible curiosity, in a fit of nerves, I had gone back with her. I'd wanted to re-create something in my mind, but it wasn't right. Nothing caught fire; it disturbed me, and I left with ashamed apologies in the night.

Mazarine was at the other end of MacDara's table, and apparently her name was Sylvie. I felt immense excitement and anxiety, as though I might be sick. Yet this woman wouldn't talk to me; I suspected a desire for self-reinvention; I tried to catch her eye, but she was a shadowy figure in a corner who barely looked up. She knew, she told me later, that she would find me again through Ren.

The second time I saw her, I was less certain; I thought it was possible I had made a mistake.

'Mazarine?' I said, half-muttering her name. She looked at me blankly, unsettling me, since I'd only seen her a few times in my life after all; I would have recognised Sophie-Hélène more easily.

'Mazarine,' I said again later, testing her, though I was

equally afraid of the past, but she simply ignored me in her cool, controlled way, as though I'd never spoken, and after a while, I understood what it was she wanted. Whoever she was, she wanted us to know each other afresh, to discover each other as women. It was like a delightful exercise in adulthood.

'I really wanted to know you again,' said Sylvie eventually, after so many weeks of wilful silence in which she only hinted, just slightly, at the presence of the past. 'I wanted you to know me, not that terrible child.'

'You weren't a terrible child. Is that why your name's different?' I said.

She said nothing. 'My mother gave me my name,' she said at last.

I had only five days left in France by the time Mazarine talked to me and touched me. I had never known such pleasure in my life; I wouldn't know it again for years. My morals became muddied: we slipped out when Sophie-Hélène was helping her mother with the toddlers, and I, already so absorbed by the idea of boys, could somehow seamlessly accept the fact that my lover was a girl, the surreal revelation of her gender only piquing my extreme excitement. She made love to me; she dived far into my mind; she showed me tricks that Sophie-Hélène had already sketched for me, controlling my breathing and my consciousness and my pain levels, and I entered that black world almost innocently, only shocked at myself years later.

Mazarine stayed away from the new baby, and we snatched moments and hours together, already addicted. On my last night in France, we sneaked back to my room above the garage. I was in love with her by then, my every waking moment spent in a fever of longing for the troubled child who'd been my rival just a week before. We couldn't stop. For eight hours that night, we said, we became each other's bride.

Mazarine left before dawn, and when I woke, the happy atmosphere of Sophie-Hélène's cottage had unmistakably changed. I was barely given time to exchange kisses with my penfriend before I was ushered out by distracted adults and hurried to the airport by a mother who had clearly been crying. I never knew whether our underaged Sapphic activities had been discovered, or whether something else had happened. I didn't want to think about that something else.

What broke me – I could still nudge the scar two or three years later and feel the after-effects – was that Mazarine had promised to meet me behind the garage door to say goodbye. She would kiss me there in the oil-scented darkness, I knew, and excite me with her pained, ungovernable mind. The appointed time went, and I waited there, loitering and scuffing my shoe on grit in growing distress, until I was called from across the stream into breakfast. I wandered past the kitchen window whenever I could, clutching my napkin and muttering about needing the toilet, to check for movements of the garage door, and then I pretended I'd left something in my room and ran outside. Mazarine was not there, and I was sent back to England with a raw new strand of mourning.

After my wedding, I had to get away from Richard, from his increasingly obvious infidelity and his lies and the way that he made me feel. More truthfully, with a hurt and competitive pride, I wanted to leave him before he left me. And more truthfully still, I could no longer keep myself from Sylvie Lavigne. I was too in love, too drawn to what a part of me had always wanted, and the sick mind it enclosed.

The solution was not a glamorous one, but it suited our purposes well. A cousin by marriage of my father's, my old Aunt Nanda, had been taken into hospital and there was the possibility she would then go into a nursing home. My sweet mother, understanding me now in my moment of need even as she gazed at me in a silent, fault-finding way, that may not, after all, have been as critical as I'd always imagined, had procured me the permission, had arranged for the keys to be available, and had kept Richard at bay for me, comprehending in a few brief sentences the state of our marriage.

As we entered that concrete-balconied old-lady flat in Southwark with its scoured melamine kitchen, its lingering scent of other people's long-gone toast and muddy river views, I felt a terrible pang for Richard. I yearned to be with him, back home. The flat's phone had been cut off; post was gathering, and damp beige pensioner underwear was rotting in the washing machine. I wandered to the window, where the sound of roadworks far below vibrated through the glass.

'Richard,' I murmured into the glass. I *love* him, I thought with an unexpected new rush of emotion.

I felt my bump. I gazed at the river. The cramped flat was on the twenty-first floor of a sixties tower block, the river swirling beyond the ledge of a balcony. Cranes swung on the horizon, glinting with summer light; the sound of the road drills rose a pitch. I remembered the fact of Richard's mistress, that unknown threat polluting my life somewhere in London, and I swallowed a sob of panic. My baby shifted.

Sylvie pulled my hair back and whispered in my ear, and as the afternoon progressed and we moved around the flat, throwing open windows to the cry of the seagulls and drills, tentatively arranging our possessions and setting out food and anemones brought by her, we were girls together again, the growing baby treasured by us, and I felt as happy as a child playing at houses.

The tide lapped each morning with its own breath, muddy and noisy with seagulls; helicopters emerged through the heated river smog. On free afternoons after term ended we walked by the water, finding parts of London entirely strange to me, as alien from my old suburban life as a different country; or we went to bed, the blinds blocking out curious neighbours and the distant clamour of bus brakes beneath us. Richard came to me in sudden shadows, my heart racing with a thought about him.

'I sometimes thought I'd never see you again,' Sylvie said when we had been there for over three weeks and I was increasingly wondering, against my own will, when Richard would turn up. He was not the sort of person to accept defeat. All my confidence had gone: I wanted him to stride around town until he found me, and then I would know, and yet I wanted to put off that moment for a while longer and spend however long I had in that strange sex-filled limbo with Sylvie. My hand kept reaching for my mobile, since he had been texting me, unanswered, several times a day, but I'd left my phone in my office when I went to collect some books. I felt naked without it, perversely abandoned by Richard if I couldn't read his messages. I went to Mecklenburgh Square once, to collect the post that had gathered in my absence, and he'd left me a letter on the table which I read several times, and then Sylvie hailed a taxi and played with the hair at the back of my neck, and she continued as we travelled back over the river.

Sylvie and I had begun to talk about the past, to refer to incidents her fierce avoidance had always made impossible to mention, and so we treasured each new section that could be illuminated: Clemenceau, and those early days in London.

'You know how I heard about you again?' she said.

'I thought you saw me by chance . . .'

'It was when I was in Edinburgh. I went to an exhibition that featured some of Ren's paintings – do you like those paintings?' she said, shaking her head and frowning earnestly. 'I loathe such— But he was there with Vicky and I heard your name mentioned.'

'Oh!' I said.

'"I used to know a Lelia," I said casually, my heart going. I asked the surname, and it was you.'

'You remembered.'

'Of course I did. I knew then that I might see you again.'

'Why?'

'I wanted to come to London—'

'Why did you?'

'Oh – it was time for me to leave,' she said, briefly dropping her gaze. 'Ren and Vicky were very kind to me. They let me stay with them for a few days when I moved to London, and I didn't have any money for rent or know anyone. And then they arranged for me to stay with friends of theirs and—'

'Who?' I said.

'Oh,' she said, the shadows under her eyes lending her an intensity that drew me to her. I wanted to open my mouth against the fragrant surface of her skin, but she wasn't touching me that afternoon. 'I can't remember—'

'But—' I said, frustrated. I stopped myself, having learnt, so long ago, that curiosity alienated her. The ends of her hair fell on my lips as she moved, but she drew her head back, and my nerves seemed to flicker still with the sensation of hair brushing as it passed.

'I longed to see you. And you know,' she said, circling my wrist with her fingers but still barely touching my skin, 'twice I saw you crossing Russell Square, before I ever met you again through Ren. I thought you were beautiful: I loved to look at you. I loved all your clothes. I put your face to your name even then, and I watched you walking.'

'Oh,' I said, shocked. 'Why didn't you come up to me?'

'After I'd met you,' she said, sitting up and twisting her hair off her face, 'I even followed you − once − I wanted to *see* you so much. I followed you when you went to the doctor's, and waited outside for you.'

'Oh!' I felt disconcerted. 'I thought . . .'

'And I was so excited that you were pregnant.'

'I know.'

'I think about her all the time,' said Sylvie, her cheek just grazing where my baby kicked: the baby who had survived, after all, through blood and scans, and shifted like a dog in my womb, and punched and hiccuped.

'She's yours too,' I said. 'You've looked after her.' I tried to kiss her ear; she pulled away.

'I want her,' she said, her breath cool on my stomach.

'You've fed her her fish and broccoli . . .'

'I think I love her.'

'She loves you,' I said. 'But why didn't you come up to me when you knew it was me near the university?'

'Wouldn't that be weird?'

'No.'

'Oh,' said Sylvie.

'It's weirder *not* to,' I said, frowning.

'I sometimes think,' said Sylvie, and I caught a glimpse of the pain I so often saw in her now, hidden in our earlier days, 'that I don't know what's "*weird*". Is it because I'm not English?'

'No,' I said, laughing at her. 'It's because you're you.'

'Oh, don't.' Sylvie jolted as though I'd slapped her.

'But I *love* that,' I said, holding out my arms to her. 'Why did I love you? You were a strange little girl. I loved you! And I wasn't even your first,' I said in wonder. 'Not even your first.'

She smiled at me, her mouth tilting at the corners.

'Yes. But I was in love with you, from that day. I always wanted, wanted, longed to see you again,' she said, and she idly lifted just the hem of my dress very slightly, then let it fall. The baby kicked.

'Oh, hold me,' I said.

She gazed ahead as though she hadn't heard me. 'You have to *eat*,' she said, glancing at my bump.

'It's too hot.'

'No, you have to eat.'

'I don't feel like it this evening.' I was desperate for her to hold me. She lay stretched out beside me, the slender curve of her hip lit by a broken wash of sunset, looking at me as though appraising me. I caught my breath. My body felt light, almost bilious or stormy. The evening drifted through the blinds in furred shadows, and the city seemed suspended, as though a brief silence had fallen before the sounds of night arrived. Sylvie reached out and skimmed my upper arm with the back of her nails, and I was in her thrall, as I always was, pregnant and on heat, my body ticking like wood. Please, I thought; I lay back a little, my legs resting open, my belly rising above me in one astonishing swooping curve, and she still held me in her gaze, a severe little eyebrow faintly raised, as though testing me with the perfect discipline she knew she possessed. Please, I thought, because only she was rough with me, so swift and certain and hard in a way I wouldn't want a man to be; because she alone could take me into a kind of darkness I'd never experienced, my brain liquid and battered, where I saw something disturbing or even evil in her, disturbing but addictive, pumping the breath out of me. She controlled me; she played me; I gave myself to her, shocked and sore, desire just stirring again the following day.

'When the baby is born, my love, we'll see all the broccoli and mackerel and apricots I fed you in her pink fingernails. In her bright brown eyes.'

Through the cloth of my dress, she trailed her finger over my linea nigra.

I breathed out through my nose. 'Again,' I said.

'Do you remember our last night together in France?'

'Of course.'

'I know you do, darling.'

A feeling of unease hovered as a light pressure on my forehead. She stroked my leg. 'It was delicious, wasn't it?' she said.

'I never stopped thinking about it,' I said. I watched the pools of last sun that highlighted her hips convulse.

'I thought about it too,' she said.

'I kissed my arm for years afterwards, trying to make my mouth feel that,' I said. 'My skin was alive. I didn't – have sex – for so many years after that. Not till I was – well, I was nineteen. A shameful virgin. But I'd known that time with you.'

'I know.'

'I thought I'd see you on the street one day,' I said. She pressed my shoulder so that she was above me. 'When I went to Paris, I was sure I'd see you.'

'I wasn't there.'

'Where were you?'

'Never really there. I'd like to be.'

'Where were you then?'

'I . . . I sort of – I suppose I hid from people. While you were living, being a student, falling in love, using your mind.'

'And you didn't? Didn't do that, I mean?'

She gazed at me, then her eyes seemed to wander, the hazel-green depths darker in the evening, and I suddenly sensed in her, as I had perhaps twice before, something slightly unclean, almost seedy, as though she was a slender, knowing little prostitute with shadowed eyes and an eroded soul.

'Do you remember what happened that evening?' she said.

'What do you mean?' I tried to make myself look at her.

'We escaped,' she said.

'Yes.'

'Well?'

'I know. I don't feel well,' I said.

'Why?'

'I don't know. I just feel different. I need the loo. My stomach hurts.'

'Oh,' said Sylvie, pausing.

I stood up. When I moved, I felt impossibly heavy, as though my changing centre of gravity was finally beginning to defeat me. I came back. 'Tell me different things,' I said. 'Tell me stories. I feel strange.'

'How?'

'Like – it's a bit like period pain.' I kept shivering.

'Braxton Hicks!' said Sylvie.

'Is that it?' I moaned. 'It's tight on my tummy. It hurts.'

'It's just little practice contractions,' said Sylvie, swivelling round on the bed and placing her hand where the baby lay.

I breathed out.

'Is that all right?' asked Sylvie gently.

I nodded.

'You can practise now, and when she comes,' she said, stroking the hair from my forehead, 'we'll be ready.'

I don't know, I don't know, I wanted to say.

'She'll be handed to you, and to me, and we'll love her.'

'I don't know,' I said weakly.

'What do you mean?' said Sylvie. Her face turned paler.

'I don't feel right.'

'Darling, come here.'

I lay beside Sylvie. My skin, always hot in pregnancy, had begun to prickle. The area between my breasts started to sweat, and yet I was cold.

'In France—' she said.

'You know,' I snapped, 'I shouldn't have been there at all. I was in a state. My mother should have kept me at home.'

'You *had* a mother,' she said. 'She loved you. Look what she'll do for you still,' she said, raising her hand towards the flat. She smoothed my bump with her hand.

'I did. And you . . .'

She raised her eyebrow at me.

'I don't know if I ever saw you together,' I said.

'I saw *you* together, though. She chatted to you in the hall. I even saw her stroke your hair once as she passed.'

'Oh, Sylvie,' I said, pity softening me.

'She drank too. Did you realise that?'

'Did she?' I said, the blank-faced doctor coming back to me with adult eyes.

A tightness gripped my womb like a belt. A sound escaped from me. I had an image of a rubber slimming device from the fifties, a vibrating rubber girdle slapping against the fat of a smiling woman.

I moaned. 'It's too *early*,' I said.

'Breathe,' she said. 'Do your NCT breathing. It's just your practice contractions.'

'How do you know?' I said sharply.

'She loved her drink,' said Sylvie. 'That was all.'

The belt tightened.

'*Richard*,' I said, my voice louder.

Sylvie turned to me, her face above me, her mouth a small circle.

'What?'

There was silence.

'I—' I thought I saw tears begin to form in her eyes. My eyes prickled in response.

'*Breathe*, Lelia.'

'Yes, I—'

'*That* was what kept her from me, I thought,' she said fiercely, her mouth still altered and open, 'as well as she loathed her reeking little runt of a daughter. Her fucking, *fucking* daughter.'

I flinched.

'Every evening, she drank,' she said in a low voice. 'All through her pregnancy. I thought the vodka might kill the baby. I didn't make any fuss, because she might lose her temper. I *read* all day, didn't I, Lelia?'

'You had sex,' I said. 'You were a child who had a girl-friend.'

'When Sophie-Hélène was there. And other than that, I read. There was nothing else to do. She was too inebriated, I thought. I thought she was *incapable* of loving anything. And then—'

'But she worked so hard,' I said, shivering. The tightness subsided. I tried to breathe slowly.

'Oh I know, I know. She was brilliant. She worked like a hound. She could do both. She couldn't in the end – they started noticing. I thought she only loved that stuff. All those ruby-red vintages. Oh! Her fucking vineyards. My dear departed father's fucking vineyards. And then – surprise – she didn't only love that. She loved her bottle, and she loved her baby. She loved the infant through the fog like a mother demented.'

'You sound demented,' I said.

'Shut up,' said Sylvie.

'You do,' I said, recoiling.

'Wouldn't you?' she said, feeling my leg.

'It was hard,' I said, 'for you.'

'I wanted what you had,' she said, embracing me and pulling me to her.

We lay holding each other. I still loved her smell.

'I always wanted what *you* had,' she said at last, her mouth warming the top of my breast.

'What?'

'I always wanted you to share that with me.'

I shrugged, half-laughing. 'I didn't have a father, or siblings. I was chubby. We didn't have enough money; I was thwarted, and aspirational.'

'But at least your father wanted you. My mother even liked *you* better, because of course she did, because of course you were so fucking charming, your skin and your mind, the way you spoke French. You—'

'*What*—'

'Everything. A home. Look. Everything else. You got it. Oh, we fast-forward a few years, couple of decades, and – Lelia the beautiful has her cock and her baby.'

'Oh, *please*,' I said, trying to push her away. I stood up. I began to walk around the room.

'And what did I have?'

She caught my arm.

'I don't know,' I said, still walking. It was a relief to walk. The baby felt slotted low inside me.

'No.'

'You didn't tell me. You don't tell me.'

'No,' she said.

'I don't know what happened to you later. You don't ever—'

'That's because you don't choose to know. Just as you don't choose to know a lot of things.'

'Please, Sylvie,' I said.

'I might just remind you of what we did on the last evening. Who did we look after?'

The baby. I always remembered her, Mazarine's little sister, quite newborn. She was the most moving, most beautiful thing I'd ever seen. She was a shock in human form. She smelled of warm milk and baking. Her arms lay above her head like a teddy bear's. Sophie-Hélène and I frequently went downstairs, unable to keep away, fascinated by the tiny scale of the perfection. The frowning doctor had become a lank-haired, soft-faced woman in love, quite transformed and barely recognisable as Mazarine's mother.

Mazarine kept upstairs and rarely even appeared for meals, a shadow of the shadow she had been. She was excessively thin; she was white; she was nervous and withdrawn. She had made too many cards and gifts: notes and pictures filled the room with crayoned declarations: *I love the baby* and *Welcome* and *You are sweet.*

I saw her downstairs one morning, and her face reminded me of a very young child who has got lost, who bobs between strangers in a frenzy of panic. Her eyes were deeper and darker with pain than any child's I'd ever witnessed. Her forehead was scored with tiny lines. She looked like an old man. In her eyes I saw terror and misery that I didn't know existed in children. Stunned as I was with grief at my father's death, I understood then that even very young humans can suffer pain which makes them feel as though a part of them is dying.

'Talk to me later,' I murmured to Sylvie. 'Please . . .'

'You can sleep,' she said gently. 'Try to sleep now, because you might need your strength.'

The old cardboard breath of Aunt Nanda's flannel bedcover had taken on the invisible scrawl of Sylvie's scents, the comfort smell of my own grief and hair on the pillow overlaid by traces of her. I kept listening for the door, for Richard, in case he had somehow found me and turned up.

Sylvie touched my neck. She curled up next to me. I pulled away from her. I saw myself as a mollusc, aroused before it recoils.

'I can't sleep,' I said, but I realised I had been drifting in and out of consciousness, the contractions subsiding. The sounds of lorries thumping over the speed bumps, the sirens and night buses accompanied my brief half-dreams of Richard, of Sylvie, of pain. Police boats trawled up the river. My waking dreams were overlaid by girlhood, like an airless veil. It was too hot. I didn't feel well, or I felt very well, but my body wasn't itself.

'I couldn't sleep that night either,' she said.

'What night?'

'The night before – the night before we spent the whole night together.'

She curled herself against me in a spoon, so much paler than me, so much slighter. I kept my back to her, and I breathed slowly, trying to avert further contractions. The shape of an unfamiliar wardrobe spread in front of my eyes, growing turrets and battlements in the hot darkness. If I kept very still and calm, if I slept and breathed, the baby would settle down again. She wasn't ready yet.

'I knew that night I wouldn't sleep, because already, already, they were talking about sending me back to school.'

'Were they?' I murmured.

'Do you remember? Just before you left?'

'No.'

'Yes. Well. The term hadn't started yet, and they had been wanting to send me back to Paris. There was someone there – a former colleague of my mother's she wanted to send me to, like the children with parents in the colonies.'

'That's so sad,' I said. I stroked her.

I turned my face to the pillow where I mouthed a frantic prayer for my baby's safety.

'I thought about wanting to die,' said Sylvie. 'I couldn't sleep, all night. Have you ever had that? It's quite different from staying awake till the early hours and then falling asleep. Especially if you're a child. It's like a torture, a small death.'

'I'm sure—'

'I had to do something,' said Sylvie, her speech rapid, and sounding more French. 'I went downstairs – I went down to the kitchen, and on the way I heard my mother. She was up – she was up with the baby! I don't know where the maternity nurse was. My mother, who was usually too drunk at night to do anything, was lying with her baby. Then I heard her singing to the baby. Crooning. That was what did it. That magical sound, like mermaids. She was singing. It was so beautiful. I'd never heard that sound before. I wanted that so much. I *wanted* that so much. And I knew then – I have nothing to lose. Nothing! I was liberated.'

'God, Sylvie.'

'I hit my head a few times. It was the only thing I could

do. I thought about running and crashing it into a wall, a particular section of wall beside a window, the top flat part of my head. That was the image I had when I lay there and couldn't sleep and the lines of tiredness were growing in front of my eyes.'

'Sylvie,' I murmured into the semi-darkness. 'Don't.'

'I crashed wooden spoons instead. I pinged teaspoons against the skull until they bounced. They vibrated. My brains jellied a bit. I needed to do that. I did it harder and harder until the pain was bouncing and running into itself, and I did it faster, and it felt right, I was punishing myself, I was a runt, a cunt, and I did that, but I began to be scared. I tried to stop myself.'

'Oh God, Sylvie,' I said, almost crying.

'The next day, the next evening, I went in there to see the baby by myself. It was your last night in France, my love. Her shutters were closed; she was on her front, her hands tucked beneath her. I'll always remember that. She was the loveliest thing, really. That was the only day I realised it. Her poor blood must have run with Pouilly Fumé. I breathed in her milk-hot breath, her uriney nappy, for the first time. There was something peaceful about her. She had a little blister on her top lip. I wanted to kiss it and press it against my mouth. She was so lovely, lovely, no wonder my mother wanted to pick her up. Pick her up and drop her? No, I didn't think so.'

'Sylvie!' I said, protesting. 'No.'

'Why not? Why don't you want to know?'

'I don't. It's obscene.'

'It's part of my life. It's all of my life, really, isn't it?'

'No, Sylvie. No,' I said, shaking my head. I heard a train shunt over the bridge.

'You were due to come to my house that evening; we

would sneak off somehow, away from Sophie-Hélène. I thought you were the most exotic beautiful thing – from London where poets were buried. I found you so beautiful.'

'I wasn't,' I said. 'You had Sophie-Hélène.'

'Sophie-Hélène . . . she saved me all those years; she was my friend. I never stopped thinking about *you*. I wanted you so much. I wanted you very badly – it seemed to grow and grow as years went on. I wanted to lie in grass with you again so that the rest of my childhood wouldn't exist.'

My muscles contracted. I gasped. I removed her hand from my waist, where it touched my bump. The belt tightened and spread tendrils of pain.

'Breathe,' she said, kneading my shoulders.

'*Don't*,' I said. 'Don't touch me.'

I jerked away from Sylvie's breath on my neck.

'Oh God,' I said. I got up and leaned against the wall. The room was airless with August heat. I ground my forehead into the indentations of the wallpaper. I couldn't stand the smell of it.

The contraction went on for longer, taking me by surprise with its pain. 'Sylvie,' I said, moaning. 'Phone the hospital.'

'Oh, darling!' said Sylvie. 'Not yet, my sweetheart. This is just the beginning. They don't want you yet.'

'I'm *early*,' I wailed. 'This is much, much too – how much?' I stood leaning there struggling with calculations, my mental calendar dark and shifting where it had once been precise to the day. 'Thirty . . .' My brain scrabbled.

'Thirty-six,' she said. 'That's OK, my love.'

'It's not, it's not!' I cried. 'It's not as much as that – is it? Thirty-eight. I need to be thirty-eight weeks.'

'Yes, darling. You'll be fine.'

'Will I? How do you know? Phone the hospital.'

'Sweetheart, I don't *need* to yet,' said Sylvie, moving behind me and stroking my back. 'I can look after you. You're just in the very early stages. It's not even called labour yet.'

'Sylvie,' I said. I gripped her arm. 'Please phone.' I was nearly crying.

'OK,' said Sylvie, and she walked to the window with her mobile pressed to her ear. I paced around. I couldn't lie still. I lowered my head over the bath and breathed deeply. I wanted to be sick. I couldn't hear Sylvie talking. I turned on the taps. The water gushed out, furry with spray, mercifully clean and hot, unlike the rusty belches in Mazarine's bathroom. Even in the close air, I wanted heat on my belly. There was bloodstained mucus on my legs.

Sylvie came in. 'I have to time the contractions,' she said. 'Listen, darling,' she said, brushing the damp hair from my forehead, 'we don't need to go in until they're faster than every five minutes. You're probably hours off, my love. You can rest.'

'But this is too *early*,' I said, beginning to shout at her. 'I've had my show. Have you told them? What did you say?'

'Of course. Of course. They're not worried. We need to keep an eye on it, then phone them again later.'

'Why?'

'This is pre-labour, sweetheart.'

'It doesn't feel like it.'

'It never does. You're having contractions, but they're mild and far apart. They may even stop for a while again. They're going to get much longer and closer together later. You know all that, don't you?'

I shook my head.

'We can do this on our own for a while, darling.'

'I need a drink,' I said.

'Of course.'

I gulped water. My forehead was throbbing, my skin fiery.

I must look like a monster, I thought, my eyes bulging, my hair a wild wet shock. I got in and out of the bath. I sat on the loo, feeling sick, as though my body was trying to turn itself inside out. I walked into the bedroom, and I sank my head into the bed. Knots of sirens gathered outside. I breathed slowly.

'I don't want to hear any more now,' I said. I felt a rush of blood to my head.

'You do, though.'

'I don't,' I said, biting the pillowcase, the blood in my head sinking like sand. I tried to face myself: I pressed the pillow to my eyes until I saw blackness and orange owl eyes slipping through my madness. I wanted my baby. The guilt that had followed me all my life – the slow-burning fear, impossible to explain to Richard, but dismissed alone with effort as childish superstition; the vague sense of commotion at the end of Clemenceau; the grief of French adults; the Bellière family's departure – was rooting me out in adulthood. Sylvie had even once told me she'd known a death. *Liebestod*, she'd said, and I could barely breathe. I moaned into the pillow; I dribbled into its already damp surface.

'Why not, darling?' she said, kissing my neck. 'Remember?'

'No, I don't remember,' I said.

'That evening, your last night—'

'Yes,' I said.

'I watched her in her cot as she slept. She was a bit snuffly, she snorted. She'd sometimes stop breathing for a while all by herself, the silence hanging in the air, and then she would accelerate back into her little tractor snores.'

My cheek dragged across the wetness of the pillow. 'Don't,' I said. Sylvie pulled me towards her in one movement so my head was curled beneath her armpit and she was holding me, and my mouth was dark and almost sealed, pressed against the pillow as the helicopters thrummed outside and young male shouting echoed up from the street.

'I'd always fantasised about just putting a hand over a baby's mouth, as softly as a butterfly, or a little plug,' she said. 'I kept doing that, I stroked her there, but I pulled my hand away, because I couldn't do it. I kissed her forehead. At first she didn't even wake! She wriggled a bit; she frowned. But then she started crying, and I lifted her from her cot, to comfort her. She was spitting and wailing. I kissed her mouth. I almost loved that baby then, even though I hated her so much. We came from the same place. I held her tightly against me, pressed her to my shoulder, pretending to be its mother and rocking it. I kissed her. I was waiting for you to find me, to come to the house all rosy and shy and sweet.'

'I feel—'

'You came in; you found me in the baby's room. Do you remember? You said — stop it. Stop cuddling the baby like that, you're holding her too tight, you'll squeeze the life out of her. My mother called you and you went to her.

'This overwhelming love came to me. I was clinging to her and rocking; I was crying, and kissing her. I was sorry for her by then. Vodka puffed her stomach, it ran through her brains. I just kept cuddling her. I couldn't begin to hurt her by that time, because I'd started to love her. I kept on soothing her and cuddling her, pressing her to me and talking to her. She and I could be together, as sisters. I kissed her, kissed the top of her head tens, hundreds of times, in superstition and love. It was hot and wispy and half-bald.'

'Oh,' I murmured from somewhere beneath her arm, her torso. Tears shot into my eyes. They ran, fast, all over my skin. My mouth opened in a sort of voiceless shouting retch.

'Eventually she seemed calmer,' said Sylvie. 'I put her back in her cot. Poor baby. I left, and I heard my mother getting ready to go out. The nurse still wasn't there. I joined you. You looked so lovely.'

'No—'

'You were. I always thought that I'd find you again and we'd be together again. One day, when we were grown-up ladies and very elegant. But by the time I heard about you, you were taken. And it was too late. But I wanted you still.'

My muscles tensed. A heavy contraction took hold of me. I rolled over on to my hands and knees.

'*Please*,' I called out, panting and clenching my abdomen. 'This is too *early*. It's – it's a month early, or something. I don't know. A month. It's too early.'

'I can help you, darling,' said Sylvie soothingly. 'We can do this together. We can even deliver her here.'

'No!' I shouted. 'Fucking hell. No, you – ring the hospital again.'

'Your contractions are too far apart,' she said in her cloudy, calm voice. 'You won't be dilated.'

'I can't go through *normal* labour. It's too early.'

'Of course you can. They'll observe the baby afterwards.'

'But what did you *say* to them?' I shouted. 'I want to speak to someone.'

'Shh shh. Later,' said Sylvie, soothing me.

She held me still, her arm cradling my shoulder, her hand dangling over my breast. I turned away from her.

'I'm in *pain*,' I said, clambering into the bath again, my foot skidding, a wave slapping like a whale over the side. The pain drilled into my middle, its dead weight edging down my thighs. I opened my legs, hooking one calf over the side of the bath as I turned and tried to roll away from the pain. 'Are you sure,' I said, panting, 'are you sure the hospital said—'

'Yes, sweetheart,' said Sylvie calmly, looking at her watch. 'You're nowhere near five minutes yet. You won't be three centimetres for a while.'

'How do you *know*?' I said, shaking her hand from my shoulder.

'Of course I know. All those classes. You know too, sweetheart, it's just you can't remember right now. Of course you can't. That's why you need a birth partner.'

'I want a midwife. I'm scared. What if the baby—'

'You'll have one,' said Sylvie calmly, 'when they think you're ready. They know how many weeks you are. Now relax. Watch the contraction, float on it, let it carry you.'

'Shut up.'

'When the baby is born, we'll take her with us along the river,' she said in soothing tones.

'We won't live *here* by then. Oh God, my baby. Get me Richard. Phone him. Give me your phone.'

'I don't need to ring him yet, darling,' said Sylvie, dropping down and placing a wet flannel on my forehead. 'Breathe. Let's breathe together. You remember. See it like a circle — stop at the top, breathe slowly out. Now.'

'Oh, Sylvie,' I shouted, crying. 'Get me Richard.'

'Why?'

'I need him.'

'We need each other,' said Sylvie.

I stared at her. I bit the inside of my lip until a throbbing ridge formed, diverting pain. I shook my head, my cheek pressing against the side of the bath.

'I can phone the labour ward again for you if you like.'

My muscles began to unclench. I lay in the bath, panting. The heat drew out all my own familiar body scents, the smell of creased skin between breasts, and the salty back of my neck, and sweat rolling from my hairline. A pulse in my forehead banged. I breathed. I was beached but alive, ecstatic at the receding pain, shocked by what had gone before.

'They say to time you and call again in an hour.'

'Let me talk to them.'

'You *can't*, darling,' said Sylvie. 'Look at you. Just relax.'

'Sylvie,' I said, exhaling heavily. My heart raced. 'This is much too early. The baby might – it's *early*. Please. Don't you understand? I want Richard. Please.'

'Do you?' she said slowly. Her features were motionless. 'Really?' She seemed to gaze at a fitting in the corner of the room. 'But if we do this, if we do this *together*, darling – we're so strong, we can do this, both of us, we can get you through this – then we've done, well, almost the opposite, haven't we?' Her voice was light, threaded with something like amusement.

'What do you mean?' I snapped. I breathed slowly and deeply, revelling in the calm between contractions. I felt in control of my body, as though the pain would never come back. How was it possible for such pain to return? I wanted Richard. I wanted my baby to be safe. I tried to quell my panic. I reached out my arm and touched her. 'Help me,' I said. 'Do everything properly. You'll help me, won't you?'

'Of course. That's what I'm here for. I'm helping you. Whatever else I've done – and I think you'll hate me one day—'

'Why?' I said.

'Oh, you will. People – everything seems to go wrong.'

'*Why?*'

She pulled me closer to her so my head was resting on her neck, supported by her as I clung to her. 'My baby,' I whispered. 'I'm scared. My baby.'

'Whatever else I've done, believe me, I loved you,' she

said, her voice now hot in my ear. 'I wanted you to share it with me.'

'Share what?' I said, confused.

'I thought, you know, somehow, one day, you'd tell me I was silly and make it all right.'

'What *happened* to that baby?' I said, at last, panic making my voice shrill and thin.

'Do you remember what she said? *Do* you?'

I shook my head.

'My dear mother said it. Look after Agnès for the evening. Look after her, *Mazarine and Lelia*. Do you remember? I'm sure you do. We fed her her bottle together, we tucked her in, we agreed to check on her. And who – what – who wanted to go skipping over the fields, back over the fields to the grown-up room above the garage? Who? Innocent little Lelia. Tupping through the night.'

'What happened to her?' I moaned.

'Who agreed that we'd be much better off fucking each other stupid than keeping an eye on a snuffly boring little kid? Let's fuck off back to the great big bed and know heaven. Never mind the baby alone in the house and the lush out for the night.'

'So—' I said. I started to pant. I howled, long and low.

'*We* were meant to look after her together.'

I breathed out through my nose in reply. I gulped air, constricted. My head seemed lodged beneath her arm.

'You didn't say goodbye to me,' I said eventually, my voice emerging as a low-pitched groan.

'They'd already got me. They'd already decided on my future. No one would speak to me or tell me what was happening. Adults loomed above me like giants: they were so tall, so elongated and no one speaking to me. I never really saw my mother again.' She shook her head. 'Twice. I saw her twice again, much later, I mean.'

'Where did you go?' I said.

'I was sent straight back to Paris, to the woman I stayed with. Then school. And then on to another school, and . . .'

'Then?'

'We lived separately. School. School for ever. Relatives.'

I pulled in my breath.

'Canada. Back to Europe.'

I breathed out slowly.

'And then I was on my own.'

'What happened to her?' I hissed, though I knew. My mouth barely moved. My eternal fear loomed before me, poised to catch me. Her fingertips held my arm. She stroked me. I shook her off aggressively.

'Don't you know?'

'Not really,' I said. Tears were soaking my face. They comforted me for seconds, like hot rain. The skin was sore at the corners of my eyes.

'She – you know. She – the baby died in the night.' I could smell Sylvie's skin. She was trembling. 'My sister,' she said.

'Was it what – was it what—' I felt the juices of nausea fill my mouth.

'She stopped breathing.' Her mouth hesitated by my ear.

'Did she?' I said. I felt her head against me.

'Yes.'

'Because of – why?'

'No one knows. They'd call it—'

'What?'

'Cot death now.'

I burped back nausea. I lifted my head above her skin scent, her skin warmth, reaching for air.

'I'm going to throw up,' I said, and I vomited on to my hand and into the water.

'I thought perhaps you and I,' she said, reaching for my flannel and calmly wiping my mouth, 'when we became – friends again, lovers – you'd take your share. I thought, one day, we'd live together, be together, and we'd share that; you'd make it all all right. We'd make it all all right. And then you were pregnant. Somehow this would make it all right. We'd make it right.'

'Nothing can make it all right,' I said, gazing at my own vomit as it spread and floated on the surface of the water.

'Oh, my Jesus.'

'But it wasn't your fault.'

'Wasn't it?' said Sylvie abruptly.

'Of course not.'

'It was equally *yours*.'

'Yes, yes, but it wasn't anyone's. It happened.'

I remembered it. 'Look after her,' said the mother. The milk was in the fridge. The baby was snuffly and crotchety. 'Yes,' we said, but the baby started to sleep more calmly, and any minute, Sophie-Hélène might come in and join us. We were soundless with suppressed desire. I wanted that girl with the face of a knowing child to take me and fuck my father away. I wanted it more than anything. The baby blinked up at me through her bars, and I felt a kick of anxiety. I leaned over her cot, willing her to be all right if we left her for a little while. Anything I did at that time, I did out of primitive fear, my brain cells clenched with terror, riddled with superstition as I tested out my psychic powers to prove once and for all that I didn't have them.

We slipped away through the fields behind the houses until we reached the gate at the back of Sophie-Hélène's garden and let ourselves into my bedroom. 'We have to check on her,' I kept saying, in guilt and perverse excitement, but we never did, and as Mazarine took me to higher levels of pleasure, a tiny strand of my mind was exhilarated by her hatred of that poor scrap of a sister; I almost wanted to bully her myself, or leave her to her own devices and please Mazarine.

I lived with the guilt of that all my life: I had thought ill of a baby while neglecting her. But life wasn't like that, I thought: a child's fear manifest. I made myself picture her, always, as a plump, healthy girl with looping plaits and red tights toddling around the fields of Clemenceau and growing, growing up and away from my fears.

'Oh, let's make it right, darling,' said Sylvie. 'We can do this. Let's bring her here together. If we go to the hospital, they'll ask, who's the father? We can do this on our own.'

'You're mad,' I said. I seemed to cling to her sister in my mind, saving her as the dark stain of a lifetime's further penance filtered into my brain. I felt like dying. The belt squeezed me. I shouted out in pain for my baby's safety. The belt pulled tighter, fanning outwards and downwards, dragging nausea and compressing me until it seemed to torture me with its hot liquid grip.

I had no concept of such pain. I don't want to die, I thought, *I don't want my baby to die.* The idea of losing her was beyond anything I could contemplate. Now the other baby had gone. My father had gone. All I wanted was my own baby. That was all in the world that I wanted. I was in love with the baby who moved around inside me; I wouldn't let her suffer. She was trying to come out now.

'Get me to the hospital. Ring a taxi,' I said.

Sylvie smiled at me. She shook her head. She glanced at her watch.

'Get me a fucking *taxi*,' I shouted at her.

'You don't need—'

'No. Get me Richard.'

'But why, sweetheart? I don't understand why you—'

'He's the father,' I shouted.

I walked around the flat, water dripping down my back and legs. I leaned over the bedstead. I seemed to breathe in a choking ball of air. My hips began to sway.

'But—' said Sylvie hopelessly. She tailed off. 'This is our home.'

'Sylvie,' I said, shaking my head as my contraction began to subside.

'I think of this as our *marriage* home. We left, we *eloped*—'

'Sylvie, sweetheart.' My voice came out cracked and dry. 'I can't think. I don't know what – I want him.'

'But I thought – we don't need him.'

'I do. I need him right now.'

'Oh,' she said. Her mouth was stiff.

'I'm sorry,' I said, turning to her, and on her face I glimpsed the expression she'd worn when her sister was born, long ago: an older person's grief etched in her eyes and the grooves of her forehead. I began to cry for her little sister. I cried for my baby.

'Oh,' said Sylvie, her mouth still open, and then I cried for her.

'Phone Richard,' I said again.

'On your number?' said Sylvie in a monotone. 'I can't phone him at home, can I?'

'Yes. Yes. Phone him. Tell him to come here.'

'Yes,' said Sylvie.

She pulled her mobile out of her pocket.

'It's Sylvie,' I heard her saying, and then she walked into the bathroom. I heard her voice through the wall. I rocked on my hands and knees; I arched my back, sobbing; I climbed clumsily off the bed.

'Richard!' I shouted. I stumbled over there. I banged on the door.

'He's coming,' said Sylvie, and put the phone back in her pocket.

'I wanted to speak to him,' I said, crying. 'Is he coming?'

'Yes,' said Sylvie dully.

'I'm truly—' I said, shaking my head.

'You're leaving me again,' said Sylvie, her mouth still a terrible small opening.

'I never left you.'

'I thought you wanted me.'

I sat on the edge of the bed, panting. 'I need him,' I moaned. 'I can't think. Get me an ambulance.'

'I—'

'Quickly. I want an epidural now. I want Richard.'

'Darling.'

'Fuck!' I shouted. My womb was tearing out of me. 'This is − agony.'

'Let's get to the hospital now and be together,' said Sylvie.

I shook my head with a violent movement. 'This isn't right, is it?' I turned to her, begging her. 'What are you doing? Get me there. Or I'll walk. I'll—'

'God.' She shook her head.

'I'm *scared*,' I shouted.

'I wanted *this*, I wanted *us*. Our own family.'

'It's mine. My baby.'

She turned from me. 'You're actually leaving me, aren't you?'

'I don't know *what* I'm doing!' I shouted. 'This baby—' The contraction tore through me, building up, rising and knocking into me before I could catch a breath. There seemed to be no spaces between the pain.

'Breathe. Slowly. Like this.'

I opened my mouth. 'Shut *up*,' I shouted. 'Get me – get me there.'

She turned from me again. I saw her neck sag, as though her spine was failing to support her.

'Where are you going?' I said, my question rising into an involuntary scream.

'Downstairs.'

'What?'

'Just wait a few minutes,' said Sylvie.

'Oh God, Sylvie, don't leave me.'

'I have to.'

'No.'

'Just wait a few minutes,' said Sylvie, half-turning to me. 'Just keep breathing.'

'No! Sylvie!' I bellowed, reaching out for her, but the waves of pain were riding into one another, lapping and overlapping, and falling against me. I crouched on the floor, tensing and moaning from outside myself like an animal, and I heard her shut the door.

TWENTY-ONE

Richard

The phone rang in the night, and I stumbled about in a shin-crashing state of bewilderment before grabbing it from the bathroom sink.

'It's Sylvie.'

I could hear her breath through my own hammering pulse, as though she was pressing the receiver close to her ear as she asked me to meet her. There was a hallucinatory quality to her unexplained request on a phone in an unknown hour of the morning, like a dream that swung between a nightmare and merciful intervention. She was a tenuous link to Lelia, and I would leap at anything that might alter the insistent, remorseless flavour of my existence alone in the flat.

'Do you know how Lelia is?' I barked to no effect, as she told me where to meet her in her measured tones, like the manipulative little monster she was. I 1471'd her afterwards, but she had called on her mobile.

I looked down at myself. I was unshaven, old-T-shirted, waxy-eared. What if that vixen, whose seemingly vague acquaintance with Lelia had merited an invitation to our wedding, could lead me to my wife? I ran into the shower and shaved, nicking myself. There were no clean underpants.

I had very little clean washing. I found I was trembling as I dressed. I went out to the car, filled with manic purpose, lovingly grateful when the engine started, and I swung out of the square and headed towards Waterloo Bridge. I crossed the river, lit white and blue, suddenly irrationally hopeful and excited and in love with Lelia and our baby and my own trusty old car as I let myself be comforted like a poor fool with the temporary fantasies that the Thames and Sylvie had stirred in me.

The offices on Stamford Street where I'd once visited various girls on magazines rose above me, surrounded by a tangle of unfamiliar new developments, and I dumped the car on a double yellow and stood for a moment, breathing deeply. I wanted a cigarette, though I had abandoned smoking years before. I bent over a little, an idea that I was having a heart attack flickering through my mind. I gulped the river-damp air. Sylvie had asked me to meet her outside the Tate Modern, but I was twenty-five minutes early, so I wandered down to the river to sit on a bench, and gazed at the water and thought of Lelia.

I remembered the first time in my life I had seen her, on a boat. I had jumped on board, and there she was, vibrant and somehow naughty, well dressed for the country, her beautiful brown eyes holding the promise of excitement. I could sense her curves through her windproof jacket. She seemed a rare being in all her liveliness, shining out among the others. I wanted to see her again, and talk to her again, and try to kiss her. I wanted to wrest her from whatever bastard she was seeing. The water had streamed against the side of the boat as it lapped beside me on the bank of the Thames now, diluted fragments of the currents that had once flowed past her.

The tide was low. I remembered the beach beneath the

walkway, where I had once sat smoking spliffs with colleagues after subbing shifts on the *Express* in my early days in London. Tourists and drunks and Victorian pipe-hunters had always populated it until dusk and then abandoned it as night fell on that desolate expanse, so different from the arching illuminated symphony upriver to the west.

I climbed over the gate and made my way down the concrete steps. The smell soaked me: the automatic trigger of sea, of seagull-heavy harbours, that made me long for something past and ineffable. On that rock-strewn strip of beach, away from the warm residue of the day's traffic, the air was more mobile and scented with the colder depths of muddy water. I took off my shoes and walked barefoot along the sand, treading carefully over pebbles and old bottles, the bridge lights shining through the night in the distance. The river lapped and rolled, and even a trace of the waterlogged air I had once known made me think that I was mad to constrain myself in a landlocked fug of carbon monoxide. The gritty sand compacted pleasingly painfully beneath the arches of my feet. I began to feel nervous about the junkies and stray loners who might be down there. I narrowed my eyes. It was impossible to decipher the shadows that clustered beneath the railway bridge.

The concrete wall above me darkened with the sky. A police boat went past, beaming its searchlight and disappearing into the night. I began to feel discomfited, the unaccustomed London silence pressing in on me, only the river's breathing and the traffic on the far bank pumping with my lungs. Something specific reminded me of Sylvie Lavigne. A clear image of her surfaced in my head. I tried to rid myself of it. I felt as though I could almost smell her, and the memory of her scent loosened my knees for a fraction of a second against my will as I slowly walked. I banished the thought.

It was dark all around me, St Paul's rising in its haze of light on the far bank. I had never known fear here before, but as I moved along through the ink-spill shadows cast by the walkway's pillars, longing, longing for Lelia beside me right then, the quietness intensified and anxiety infected the rhythm of my breathing. If I were to shout out, no one would hear me on the walkway. For a moment, I had a feeling that someone was there. I made myself look over one shoulder. I could see nothing. The river lapped yards in front of me, its surface shadowed by the bridge.

'Hello,' came Sylvie's voice beside me.

I let out a high scream.

Sylvie Lavigne's hands lay lightly on my shoulders. I dragged air into my lungs. Even in my confusion, my heart clattering painfully in my ears, I could smell her scent all about her, the bewitching skin fragrance merging confusingly with the mud streaks of the river, the live meatiness of seagull. She was breathless and agitated.

'Richard. Shhhh! Richard, Richard,' she said, a smiling exhalation of air somewhere near my chin.

I gulped, trying to calm myself. Anger at the sight of her welled up inside me.

'How did you *get* here?' I said, half-shouting at her.

'I saw you,' she said. 'I came down.'

'What did you want to meet me for?' I said. I was taken aback by the reality of her physical presence. Even in the dark, she was instantly familiar, shockingly tangible after her weeks of absence. Her hair was somehow less sleek than usual. She was wearing a pale summer dress. I could just see the shape of her breasts beneath the fabric in the moon and bridge light. Her eyebrows were dark question marks. A surge of rage went through me at the memory of her treachery.

She turned and merely stretched her narrow shoulders back, tracing an arc in the sand with her foot. The water crept beside her shoe.

'What are you doing down here?'

She didn't answer.

'Writing your creepy fucking novels about my wife?' I said, my words emerging unevenly.

'No,' she said. 'I came—'

'Why?'

She seemed edgy, her features inscrutable in the night.

'I've been staying with a friend.'

'I'm sure you have!' I said with a cynical bark of laughter. 'The kindness of strangers. Why don't you get back to Charlie's granny flat?' I said, and felt a pang of shame at my own rudeness.

She hesitated. 'I'm not going back to Bloomsbury.'

'Oh really?'

'I don't want to see you and Lelia everywhere. Taken. I wouldn't make myself do that. I wanted to say goodbye.'

'Where's Lelia?'

'She's – with a friend,' said Sylvie quietly.

'Who?' I said loudly, turning to her. 'Where is she?'

She looked apologetic. She paused. 'She's with—'

'*Who?*' My voice travelled through the expanse of water and paling.

Sylvie gazed out at the river. She hesitated. 'I don't know how to say it,' she said. She was tense and nervous; she kept glancing up at the walkway.

'*What?*' I said fiercely.

'She's with someone else.'

'Oh what?' I said. I sounded, to my own ears, like a seal barking. 'What? What? *Who?*'

She shook her head.

'Jesus,' I said. My brain felt light and granular, as though it filtered out the horror of what she was imparting. 'How do you know?'

'I've been — we've been quite friends,' said Sylvie.

'Where *is* she?' I said, my voice now high-pitched and uncontrolled, my position as supplicant angering me in the face of her slight hesitation so that I wanted to shake her, or punish my fragrant, disturbed messenger.

She wrapped her arms around her own waist. I saw her small hand flutter as she pressed the side of her body.

She shook her head. 'She doesn't want to see you,' she said.

'But where *is* she?'

'I don't know. The last I knew, they were together.'

'Oh, God. No,' I said. I kicked a rock. It stubbed my toe. I yelped, shamefully, then kicked it again, yanking it out of its muddy anchorage and sending it scudding into the water. 'Please, Sylvie. Who is it?' I howled in outrage and pain. 'No, no. Lelia. God, no. Who is it?'

Sylvie shook her head. 'I don't know—'

'You don't even know his name?' I said. I grabbed her arm, bringing my face close to hers. She seemed perturbed beneath her show of calmness.

'No, really—'

'You've never seen him?' A gargantuan red-skinned caricature of a jock kicked his way into my mind.

'I haven't. Truthfully,' she said.

'She's *pregnant*, for fuck's· — so you know nothing about him?'

'Just about her. I think she's been — she's been very caught up . . .'

I stared at her. The temptation to kick something, to sink my knuckles into a paling, left me almost breathless.

'So it's serious.'

Sylvie hesitated. 'I – I think so,' she said gently.

'Jesus.'

'Richard.'

'She's pregnant.'

'I think – they thought they'd bring the baby up together.'

'No they *will not*. No *fucking way*,' I shouted in an explosion of possessive rage. 'Jesus – just get me to that bastard. That is *my* baby. I'll have as much fucking access as I want, and Lelia would never stop that.'

'No.'

'So she's – she's left me. Good God. Good fuck.' I started to sob, loudly and jerkily. It was the clarity of the image of her that came to me – calm Lelia, my Lelia, pregnant and animated and moody and herself; Lelia who was *mine* – that made me want to roar with disbelieving fury. She was mine. I'd had her. That was not going to change; it was a given in my life, a blessing. Someone else, some marauding animal, had fooled her into temptation. It felt as though she had died, been taken from me, snatched from me, when I loved her. A shadow passed over us, making me jump: a gull, night-flying.

'You romanticise her,' said Sylvie. Her voice thinned. She sounded momentarily vulnerable.

'What do you mean?' I said sharply.

'Everyone has flaws. Even Lelia.'

Rage caught me again. 'Shut up,' I said. 'Leave her *right* alone. God,' I said, fragments of her novel coming back to me and sticking like leeches on my brain. '*Hindoos*. Dainty-wainty Victorian maids in nighties strangling each other. Baby falling roly-poly down the stairs. It makes me feel *sick*.'

281

'Why are you being like this?' she said simply.

'She's left me,' I said, my shoulders trembling and sinking, and I began to pick my way over the stones and old cups, the sand wetter beneath my bare feet, turning to mud, to stray brick and rock as I walked faster. I felt my foot bleeding; I was pleased. Sylvie lost her balance a little as she walked beside me. She caught my arm. I let it rest there. We stumbled towards the wall of the walkway. A siren squalled along the bank behind us.

'I hate this,' she said.

'What?'

'Seeing men crying,' she said, and she put her arm around my shoulders with a tentative movement. 'It's so sad.'

'Sorry,' I said. 'I just—'

'I have to go back soon,' she said. She sounded nervous.

'Yes, yes,' I said, and I sat down in the shadows beneath the hulk of concrete, looped with swags of chain, that led to the walkway. I sank my head into my hands. My skull seemed close to my fingertips, and hard and human, and old. This is what it felt like, then, to be a man left by his wife. I wondered whether I might choose to die. There was that comfort, that despair. The Thames's muddy gleam rolled ahead of me where it lapped the shore. A couple walked across the Millennium Bridge, pressed close together.

'Please don't cry,' she said. 'I can't bear it. I'm sorry to – I'm sorry it was me who told you. You're amazing, Richard. You will always be. And then you'll have your child – the most important thing you could have in your life. You'll have that still—'

'I want Lelia,' I said, my voice low and mechanical and seemingly separated from me. A train hissed as it juddered over the bridge. I fixed my eyes on the bobbing sinister shape of a mooring midriver. The sky was vast above me, like a country sky smudged with city light.

'I know,' said Sylvie. 'I understand.'

She took me in her arms, and I rested my head against her chest so that her clavicle pressed into my closed eyelids and I could see nothing but blood pulsing against my vision, its blackness forming stars that exploded with the motion of a crazed screensaver, and beyond that, the horror of what was happening darkening and spreading like some unending night ahead of me.

She stroked me. I let myself be stroked. I thought of my mother, who'd pulled my hair off my face in lulling clean sweeps when I couldn't sleep, miserable with flu and summer nights.

I began to sob again, unashamedly.

'Where can I find her?' I said.

She shook her head, still stroking my hair. She looked at me with an apologetic expression, and her female loyalty infuriated me and enraged me, as Lelia's always did, even as a part of me admired them for it.

The air was restless in its dying warmth. I smelled her smell. It still, in itself, bewitched me for a fragment of a moment, like an electric current in the air that flickered and disappeared. It seemed faintly repulsive to me as well, as though the scent had been treasured for too long and had gone off. Its mixture of dissonance and allure settled on my senses. Sobs still rose, humiliatingly, through my chest as she held me.

She whispered to me; she breathed in my ear; she offered me endearing words of comfort, and I was grateful for them when they surfaced through the clamour of my thoughts. We sank back against the wall, beneath the wet shadows of the overhanging walkway, and held each other, and talked.

Her hand was on my chest. She kept speaking to me, her sweet comforting murmurings just reaching me, and once I thought that she was crying too. She pressed my big wet animal's head against her shoulder, and when I shifted I felt a trace of warm liquid on my ear.

'I've loved you,' she said eventually, after she'd spoken to me about all I had in my life, and all I would have, and the funny silly things I'd done, and how what I said still made her laugh, and recent books she'd read, and thoughts she'd had.

'You've loved many others,' I muttered, still soothed, not wanting to break the rhythm of the comfort she gave me as she pressed my back, dispersing tension in my shoulders and touching my neck with her fingertips, such pleasure as horribly temporary as any appeasement could be. I hadn't been touched for so long that I stayed motionless, willing the relief to continue and continue and calm my mind. Her fingers pressed the indentations along my spine, one by one, prodding tiny vibrating currents, her foggy voice small and quiet like an incantation against my skin.

She turned to me. I was close to her. I could hear the water, fingering pebbles as the tide turned. I could see only her mouth, large against my eyes. The instinct to move towards it rose as a fully formed image to my mind. I pulled back.

'Are you crying?' I said.

She shook her head.

'Don't,' I said. I pulled her further towards me. I stroked her. 'Please don't.'

'It makes me sad,' she said. 'All this.'

'Don't.'

'It does,' she said. She rested her head on my shoulder. 'I can understand . . .'

She kissed me. There was sand on her lips. It pressed against mine. It scraped against my teeth.

'We can't,' I said.

'We can't.'

Her skirt was tangled in damp ridges against her legs. Gravelly sand gritted her calves. She leaned to one side, her jaw straight and fine. She looked dead, lying against me; she looked beautiful.

I felt her teeth on my lower lip, the sudden cool wetness of her mouth. A pheromonal surge shot through me. It plucked a terrible sob in me again as I thought of Lelia.

'Shhh,' she said, stroking me, 'shhhh,' and she kissed my ear, and we held each other. Her hand drifted over my thigh. I was sobbing again, blubbering gibberish.

She gazed at me. Her mouth was open: dark lips, a dark space between; a perfect, scrolled oval. It was like a viola, blood-black against the pallor of her skin. I stared back at her. My mouth was closed. I felt myself breathe through my nose, my chest rising and falling as I was crying, cursing, almost laughing. Heat rose from somewhere indefinable in my body; I pulled away. The shape of her mouth stirred old memories. We kissed suddenly, her saliva pure and cold on my mouth. I thought of the agony to come. I wanted to bawl out my pain.

'We love each other too,' she said.

I murmured something, the kind of sound I made to myself out loud when I was imagining speech.

'It takes more than one,' she said. She was crying. Her skin scent threaded the air. 'It wasn't all my fault. There was someone else. Not everything is as—'

'Oh—' I said, frowning, confused. 'What—'

'Not now.'

We arched back against the rock, its surface damp and

hard on my spine. Stones and river detritus clustered around us in jagged outcrops in the shadows. Her mouth came towards mine as a parting of hot breath pressed lightly on my lips. There was sand in her hair. We were moving now, twisting and breathing, our mouths finding each other's necks as she cried out, and she licked my skin, and I kissed her, my lips on her mouth and her shoulder. She drew me to her. I tilted her hips. She pressed herself against me. With a flooding of warmth, I was enveloped. It was so sudden, it took a short time to realise it had happened. The moment of tightness was like diving; a fragment of heat and sliding; I fell headlong. The glory scudded, held fast, rippled in one glistening net of nerve endings.

I cried out.

A party cruise boat travelled past the far bank, distant whoops and lights carrying across the water. I pulled Sylvie to me, catching my breath, kneading her shoulders without stopping as though I possessed a useless tic, stray spasms still threading through my limbs.

'Let's go,' she murmured.

'Where?' I said, bewildered, breathing into her neck as I turned to her, my body stripped of strength and suddenly shivering. Reality was flooding back into my brain. Oh God, I thought. Lelia. Lelia was leaving me. A lump formed and hurt in my throat.

'Oh, Richard, let's just leave right now.'

'Where?'

'Anywhere. Yours. Somewhere else – new.'

'God,' I said. 'Sylvie. You know—' I stroked her.

'We can make a go of it,' she said, her eyes made immense by darkness as she gazed at me and I stared back, transfixed and slack-mouthed and batting away the shame that was beginning to pool at the base of my brain. I felt as though I had woken with a hangover, the disturbing facts of my life just beginning to re-establish themselves in my consciousness with the pain and persistence of a drill.

'Now's the time,' she said. 'We could.' She kissed my jaw, my cheek, my ear, and again she pushed hard into the ridges and knots below my neck, easing the tightness, and for a moment, pressed against her, our skin heated and wasted in the cooling pre-dawn air, I wondered whether we could after all run away together: I could invert my destiny and take a risk with this faithless, fascinating oddity who would evade me and interest me and turn me on. No one else wanted me. In madness and sadness, I could cast my lot with her.

'Let's do it,' she said with the rising, enticing enthusiasm of the inspired.

I hesitated. 'We can't,' I said.

'Why?' she said, her lips parted.

'You know that,' I said, and I kissed her. Her open mouth remained still. 'You would never quite have me. I certainly wouldn't have *you*.'

'You would, you would—'

I laughed. 'Charlie,' I said. 'Peter Stronson. MacDara—'

'Charlie's been – very good to me,' she said defensively, moving her leg, stroking my chest. 'But that was over a long time ago.'

'Was it?'

'I hardly know Peter Stronson. MacDara—'

I laughed.

'Do you think I care about MacDara?' she said, circling my wrist.

'I really don't know,' I said.

'I had to – be appealing to him – to get to you, your world, to get to—' She hesitated.

287

'To whom?'

The pit of my stomach felt queasy. She gazed evenly at me, her lips still slightly parted. She said nothing.

'This isn't the first time you've done this, is it?'

'Don't—' she said. 'Don't say these things now.'

'There's always been some entrée, some Ren, some MacDara, hasn't there? There's always some group of fools ready-made for you—'

'Of friends.'

'In one country or another.' I laughed slightly. 'To win over.'

She said nothing, as she so often did. She stroked my chest, my shoulders.

'When did it happen with MacDara?' I said, desperately, hating myself, unable to stop.

'Last – last year—'

'My God. Before – before Christmas? Me? You were – you knew him *first*?'

'He and Catrin were kind – good to me. They let me stay with them in the first few weeks here. I didn't have *money*. I didn't know anyone—'

'My God,' I said slowly. 'Sylvie—'

The river dragged its tow of sand as the tide began to inch towards us, oily and light-streaked in its darkness. The grit was damp beneath my toes.

'I loved it that he was called MacDara,' she said, looking at the river. 'I love some people's names – *Lelia*. That's so beautiful. There's an island off the Connemara coast where they celebrate St MacDara's day. He didn't even know it . . . They have an open-air mass in Irish.'

I could imagine her murmuring stories to him as he lay in her arms. Residual anger rose up inside me.

'The fishermen dip their sails in the water when they pass the island. I love to think of that.'

'I'm sure they do. What's he like? When did you see him?' I persisted.

'I never – I never truly did,' she said. A dog came down on to the beach. It trotted past. From far above us came its owner's voice, shouting.

'Never actually fucked him?' I said abruptly.

She was silent. She shook her head slightly.

With an immense and invigorating rush of pleasure, I let out a roar of laughter. My anxious post-coital shame was alleviated with a momentary swoop of triumph. I pictured MacDara's face. I laughed again.

'What else was I supposed to do when I first came here?' she said.

'What do you mean?'

'You don't understand, do you?' she said, turning to me, her face gathered and sharp and made more beautiful in the concentration of her sudden rage.

'What?'

'Charlie's isn't what you would call a home,' she said abruptly. 'You don't understand that. *You* could never understand that, could you? You with your Cornish rabble and your salary. All your bohemian chaos. Your beloved mummy.' She glanced nervously at the walkway above us.

I stared at her, stung, at a loss for a response.

'Leave with me, then,' she said, calmly.

'Sylvie,' I said. 'Oh, God.'

'I think we should. After all this . . .'

'You know – you know that wouldn't be right.'

'Once,' she said, and she paused. 'I really *loved* – I think I'd have done anything to be with you two, you three. Stay with you.'

'Don't,' I said. Pity tightened my throat. A streak of rank briny air cooled my face. 'Which three?'

'You're not going to come with me?' she asked in a small, calm voice, but she was trembling.

'It won't – it wouldn't *work*—' I said hopelessly.

'Then I need to say goodbye,' she said, close to my ear. She put her head in her hands. 'But I can't really bear to.' She rested her forehead on my shoulder. She stroked me. I could hear, now, that she was crying, her words emerging in a staggered fashion as she attempted to control her breathing. 'I thought, after all these years of looking, that finally, perhaps, it would be—'

'Look,' I said, my voice a dry croak. 'We couldn't. Sylvie. I'm so – look, I'm sorry. I'd be a hopeless tosser. Completely useless. I can't – you know. It wouldn't be right.'

'No. I know.'

'I'm in love with Lelia,' I said quietly.

'So am I,' she said.

I paused.

'Sorry?' I said. I laughed, embarrassed.

She was silent.

I frowned. 'What did you say?'

'I love Lelia Guha. She loves me.'

'What do you mean?' I said, my brain cantering un-comfortably through a series of surreal possibilities.

'Exactly that.'

'You've got a – a – is that why you're writing about her? You've got some kind of – a thing for Lelia?'

'Not a thing. She's been my lover.'

'What?' I said with a bemused laugh.

'She has,' said Sylvie. She stood up, plucking at the muddy folds of her skirt. 'Until, until today. That's it. We were lovers. We've been lovers,' she said, a small smile of triumph, or excitement, animating her face.

'How the – fuck—'

I gazed at her body. She gazed at me. She seemed like an angry, elegant child in the flat light. Her bare legs looked thin, planted on the sand. Her eyes had seen a naked Lelia; the glorious arrangement of curves that was her mouth had met Lelia's in some kind of lesbian passion; she had bestowed upon her that soul-stirring illusion of unique understanding. It seemed ghastly and alien. Perverse trails of lust shot through my shock. I stared at her, layer upon layer of consciousness opening up in my brain, and it was as though the earth had slipped, and then slipped again, while I flailed and gawped and stumbled. And I was a fool, a bigger fool than anyone I had ever met. There were facts, aspects to life, horrible truths, that other people comprehended while my own brain simply failed to work. I was a child, a gibbering idiot; I should be stuck in a jar and studied by Victorians. I could trust no one. My world had turned inside out to reveal its maw and then its secret teeth. It was as though my mother had informed me she was a man or Ren had confessed to a past as an axe murderer.

'When?' I said.

'A long time,' she said.

'No,' I said.

'I had to,' she said. 'I had to be with her. She was mine. I just – I just love, loved her.' Her face crumpled a little. 'I've always loved her.'

'Like you've loved so many,' I said in sarcastic tones.

'Only really her,' she said.

More layers of understanding slowly surfaced in my brain, as though manually slotted into the head of a robot.

'I wanted her. She wanted *me*,' she said, a combative, triumphant expression momentarily passing over her face again.

'I'm not even – I'm way down,' I said, almost laughing.

'I'm so far down your pecking order. After all that. After all you and I . . .' The full bathos of it hit me. I wanted to laugh loudly. There was a masochistic element to the situation that almost turned me on, just as the image of those two women together made me want to grab my dick even as I shouted my outrage aloud.

'So this man,' I said, 'this man – is you?' I barely had the language with which to process my bewilderment.

'There was only me,' she said in cool, calm tones. 'Me and her. That's all we wanted. We didn't need – you. Or anyone. We lived together.' She shivered. 'We looked after the *baby* together.'

Along the Thames, a barely perceptible stirring in the sky seemed to hold the idea of the coming light. She glanced nervously at the walkway.

'Did she know about us?'

'No.'

'And there's no man?' My thoughts fragmented again before they settled, and then inexpressible relief flooded through my confusion. I tried to absorb the fact that my wife had left me for my mistress. She was not holed up with some snake-hipped, moneyed, pillaging brute after all. Joy in its most distilled form shot through me. 'Lelia,' I said.

Pain passed over Sylvie's face. She glanced at the concrete steps. She turned back to me with a calmer expression.

'I *loved* you too.'

'My arse, frankly.'

'I truly did,' she said simply.

'God, Sylvie. All those months—'

'I'm leaving now,' she said.

'Where is she?'

'She's up there,' she said, and she started to climb the concrete steps in her stained dress. I followed her wet legs

292

with my muddy, bleeding feet, just as once, long ago, when she was someone else altogether, I had followed her upstairs to MacDara's loft. She pointed to a tower block rising behind the clutter of buildings around the Tate.

'It's Flat 221.'

'Thank you,' I said.

'I'm going to go.'

'Yes.'

'I really am,' she said, the strained lines returning to her forehead. 'Leave me alone now.'

I nodded. I paused. 'OK,' I said.

'Look after her,' she said, a last strand of her hair scent twining with the mud breath of the river. 'And your baby as I would. Look after it *properly*.' She suddenly seemed tearful, and anxious.

'Yes,' I said. 'Of course.'

She hesitated. She looked down. 'I – well, I made myself a life.' She looked at me. 'Didn't I?'

I paused. I attempted to suppress my impatience as I glanced at the block of flats.

'You did,' I said, and then I held her. We kissed each other.

'I do still,' she said, glancing in agitation at the tower block. 'Go up there now. Hurry.'

TWENTY-TWO

Richard

I sprinted towards the block, surpassing any burst of speed ever achieved in my adult life in my impatience to find Lelia, and I stood gulping for breath outside the stained concrete entrance. My nervous excitement at the thought of seeing her again made me feel as though my entrails were floating, bilious and untethered. The block was vaguely familiar to me, I realised: I had a distant memory of dropping something off here with Lelia in the early days, when we were greeted by a small Indian woman in her seventies or eighties who had been kind to us, to a couple newly in love and no doubt transparently impatient to walk along the river and flirt over drinks. The simplicity of that time seemed as long-gone and unformed as a version of childhood.

I pressed the bell. Nothing happened. The sound of my heart booming waxily somewhere in my ear drums seemed to deafen me. It occurred to me that it was much too early for normal people to rise. But I had to see Lelia. I pressed it again.

After a pause followed by electric crackling, an old man's voice barked, 'Yes?'

'Is Lelia there?' I said.

There was a wheezy silence. 'She's coming down,' said the unexplained pensioner in Lelia's love nest, his breathing trailing strands of electronic interference.

I waited, confused. I pressed the buzzer harder. Light was just softening the shadows along the street, every bird noise loud and vivid during those God-given moments before I found Lelia again. I peered through the wire-threaded windows of the hefty security door and as I stood watching, the lift opened.

She was there, crumpled and haggard and barely dressed under the strip lighting.

'Lelia!' I shouted. I thumped on the glass. 'Lelia!'

She was ill. She was panting and calling out, propped up by a tiny wizened man in his pyjamas. She bent over and lowered herself to the floor. The pensioner went down on his knees and awkwardly held her shoulders, an act of kindness for which I would always be grateful. I shouted for her again. In staggered movements, she made her way towards me.

'Darling,' I croaked, pulling her into my arms. 'Shit. Christ.'

'Richard,' she said. 'Rich—' Her mouth opened in a slack howl of tears as she sank against me.

'Is it the *baby*?' I said.

'You took so long.'

'She only just *told* me. Jesus,' I said, kissing her neck, pulling her closer to me, kissing her all over the wet skin of her face and ear, knowing the heaven of holding her even as the baby was torturing her. 'I'm her husband,' I gabbled to the old fellow, by now clearly overwhelmed. 'Thank you,' I said. I clapped him on the back; I grabbed his hand and shook it like a maniac. 'Thank you.'

He nodded. He took one last look at poor Lelia, then returned, head bowed, to the lift.

Lelia moaned and leaned over, pushing against me, nearly unbalancing me. She was silent for seconds, merely breathing, and I held her, talking to her in a smooth rush, instinctively rubbing her with hard and regular strokes as she crooned and shouted and cursed. A man looked up from his street-cleaning vehicle and went on brushing.

'Have you called an ambulance?' I said rapidly.

She nodded, wincing. 'The neighbour.'

'It's OK, darling, it's all right,' I kept saying, holding her and steadying her.

'I'm so *glad* you're here,' she said, her words barely audible against my chest. 'I needed you, I needed you. Richard, my baby – how many weeks is it?' She looked up at me, her expression imploring and helpless. I didn't know what she meant.

'Where *is* it?' I said urgently, scanning the street and considering running for the car. 'Let's call a taxi.' I clumsily stabbed at numbers on my mobile, and she turned over on the steps, and I rubbed her from the base of her spine as I called a cab. An orange light coasted along the other end of the road, slowing to turn the corner. 'Taxi!' I roared. I put my fingers to my mouth and let off a piercing whistle, and the cab switched off its light and trundled over to us.

I hurried Lelia into the back, aggressively ignoring the driver's protesting glances, and switched on the cold air to dull the volume.

She lowered herself on to the floor, clinging to me so that I crouched down beside her; she shook me off and leaned over the seat. She moaned.

'I know, I know,' I said in pity. 'Oh, darling, you're brave. Just keep going. Good girl. You're so brave. We'll be there soon.'

'She left me,' said Lelia, looking up at me wildly.

'Who? Oh—' An ambulance streamed past us in the opposite direction.

'She – you know – she left me, she left me there. On my *own*. She stopped me coming to the hospital.'

'*What?*'

'I don't think she called. She could have killed – it's too early – It hurts.'

'She *knew* you were in labour?'

She let out a long low cry, nodding by pressing her head into the seat. 'It stinks. This seat *stinks*,' she said, looking up at me in distress. I kissed her tears; I curved my arm and chest around her back. I wanted to merge my body with hers to absorb her pain.

'You were like this when she left?' I hissed.

'Yes,' she said.

My mind, already set spinning at vertiginous speed by Sylvie's shifting versions of reality, now jolted into a sickening counter-rotation that made me reel once more.

'She's mad; she's mad,' I said, my voice rearing into a semi-falsetto.

Lelia pulled herself up and squatted on the floor, clinging to me, gripping my arms as we swung round a corner. The driver had switched on Capital FM.

'Darling, we're getting there,' I said, holding her body tightly, supporting her weight by spreading my knees out on the floor.

'She's *mad.*'

'I know, I know.'

'Why did you take so long?' she said, her head butting against me, her eyes disturbed and imploring.

'She only just told me.'

'Where were you?'

'By the river with her—'

'By the river?' said Lelia uselessly, a groan emerging from deep inside her abdomen.

'She lied to me. She's gone. She's gone. She's left. We don't have to see her any more.'

'I was so frightened.'

'Look, she's gone. I'll never speak to her again. She's – we'll never see her, I promise. I'm so sorry.'

She moaned.

'She lied—'

'I know, darling,' I said, repositioning my hands under her armpits as she swayed. 'She—'

'*You* lied,' she said, her forehead ridged with distress, her voice rising weakly. 'Being un – unfaithful. You fucking – you – I was pregnant.'

'I'm know,' I said, shaking my head. 'I'm so sorry—'

'What were you *doing* by the river?' she said wildly, clutching at me. Her eyes were large and frightened.

'I—' I said, and I glanced at the ground, and then at her. I felt my Adam's apple rise. She knew me; even in terrible pain, she knew me.

'*What?*' said Lelia.

'I'm sorry,' I said. 'Never, ever again. She's gone now.'

She turned to me. Her mouth opened. Her skin, pallid and streaked with shadow, had paled to a new kind of yellow.

'She's not a threat,' I said desperately. 'She's a drab little—'

She let out a loud laugh, shocking and uncontrolled, that turned into a wail.

'No,' she said. She turned from me; she half-laughed again, then sobbed. She turned back to me with a rapid movement and held my arm so that it hurt. Her eyes seemed unfocused. Her mouth was loose and formed a different and disturbing shape. She groaned as she bent double, arching her back like a cat.

She was breathing noisily.

'It can't be,' she said finally in a tiny, tight voice.

'I'm sorry,' I said. I held her. I rubbed the length of her spine. I gripped her torso as we came to a swaying halt in a hospital car park. 'Lelia. My love. You too . . .' I said lightly. 'Look, we can't talk about it now. We've got for ever to talk about this.'

'Shut up, shut up!' she said. 'Not now. You cunt. Not now.' She bent towards the edge of the taxi as the driver opened the door and she staggered out.

Birth was a ritual whose sheer brutality required it to be enacted in private, in a windowless chamber where the sounds of other women's agony trailed along corridors in an echo of Lelia's. My love was wired and girdled and electronically monitored; she was injected and penetrated and medicated, while bizarrely dated machines spewed out wonky screeds of graph paper and Antipodean agency workers drifted in and out with their clipboards through the dawn, and only an unemotional doctor seemed to know exactly which dipping foetal heartbeat and sudden emission was standard or problematic as Lelia rocked and vomited her way through a session of torture.

She cried out for her baby, and for a different baby: some infant from her past who appeared in her garbled shoutings; and for a disturbing period, I wondered whether she was anthropomorphising her miscarriages. She cursed Sylvie, and intermittently cried for her; she cursed me, informing me that I was faithless and cruel and a swine; she pushed me brutally away; she pulled me to her and told me she loved me, and had always loved me more than anyone. She referred to Sylvie, and to me, to us together, and even to their own coupling, with obscenities that I had never heard her use: an alien language, medieval and misanthropic and savage. When she appeared actually maddened with pain, the medical staff and I clearly removed from her blurred consciousness, she seemed to be making peace with herself, muttering about her father, and about someone called Agnès. She gabbled a few words that I struggled to follow, saying that she was sorry, and promising to look after her baby. She appeared to be making some pledge, fragmented and monotonous, as though she muttered a liturgy.

I watched her with stunned admiration, perceiving her as a Trojan, a brave battler, the most beautiful, deranged and refined spirit. And in moments that transcended the fact of her poor pain, I thought, here we are, Lelia Guha and I, in a room together. That was all I wanted. I frantically thanked any god I had ever known, from the man with the beard so at odds with the sylvan deities and aboriginal spirits favoured by my Cornish neighbours, to some less precise mental blur that presided over me in times of need. I wept a little. Thank you, I said, and tacked on a quick prayer for the baby.

And still in my heart I felt ambivalent about that baby. I didn't want Lelia to fall for it. I knew that the further it bored its way out of her body, head scrunched and inexorably hormonally propelled, the more firmly I was shunted back a notch in her affections.

Though gripped with protective fear for the unknown creature as I heard the murmured consultations about its distressed heartbeat and Lelia's early labour; though I wanted to weep for her as I held her head and she vomited, blotched and bloody, over a cardboard container, a series of unhealthy and inappropriate thoughts threaded through my barrage of powerless sympathy, reminding me of the selfish deliberations about the timing of funerals and the necessity of flowers that emerge fully formed after a death. An absurd and parochial sense of disappointment flickered through my mind when I remembered that my child would not be born in the heart of London as planned, but here, here, *south* of the river. Less fittingly still, Lelia's face mid-push reminded me, during a cruel fit of detachment, of a fluffy tooth-baring monster on a children's morning television programme. Worst of all, I felt an almost manic desire to catch the headlines on a porter's abandoned newspaper, their link to the world at large disproportionately delicious. From time to time, I simply wanted to opt out of the attenuated drama and catch a snooze.

She pushed and growled, the team now gathered round the end of her bed, as I encouraged her with the blaring rhythm of a coxswain, and then I saw a remarkable thing. A tiny head, a dark snaily scrawl of hair on a human scalp, flashed for a second into view and then disappeared again. It was a person, a living creature momentarily emerging between Lelia's legs. The doctor put a sink plunger up her vagina; they cut her poor flesh in one brutal movement, blood blooming on the gaping wound; she pushed, and then the person descended again, slithering out with a pause at the shoulders, to a scream from Lelia and an efficient convergence by the medical staff – and it had a *face*; I was startled to the point of shock that it had a perfectly formed human face – and I leaned towards Lelia, who was panting with little gasps and suddenly smiling, and time was compressed as the doctors did something with towels and tubes over by the sink; and then there was another person in the room. A person was born. The person was tiny, and too early, but safe. I stared. I was unable to get over the fact that it had a face: it was not a bland, bald, featureless pink thing, but a wax-covered being with a face. It had felt-tip lines for brows and a wrinkled forehead and a tiny purple bud of a mouth and a slick swirled cap of hair and a little silken pumping pot-belly. Its face was so beautiful.

Lelia held her. She was a mother. Fuck, I thought. She seemed newly mature; a womanly creature subtly elevated above me, half-lost to me; an entity with powers I would always have to chase. And then there was a third person, no longer attached to either of us, who changed the room. She was a girl. I wept over her like a great male calf bellowing sobs that I couldn't control: I wept at such indescribable beauty.

TWENTY-THREE

Richard

The Hindoo was to return to that city where the bells rang along the great river. She came in the night to visit me; she flowered now in front of me. I rested my brow on her cheek and I knew by then that a tender pink portion of her heart was mine. Her eyes were tilted desert stones that lit me as we whispered. All of our destiny, we said, we would share.

I never saw that little Hindoo again. She was returned, and I was sent away. I always prayed that I would meet her when we were ladies and had quite grown beyond the parents who had abandoned us, and then we would repair all of our sins. And if I could not have the Hindoo, I would be what she was and embrace her life in London, with its poets and its garden squares and its secrets. We would make a family, she and I.

I deleted the final email that Sylvie sent me. And gradually she became a myth in my mind, the embodiment of something urgent and secretive and past. Her name could only be hissed as bloody ammunition on tension-soaked nights when such betrayal seemed impossible to surmount, Lelia's grief and fury so extreme that she stubbornly avoided discussion of her, and the unravelling of all treachery occurred in heated stabs and spurts over time. Sylvie was a half-buried subject dominated by the existence of someone else so much more pleasurable and new.

Our refusal to excuse each other's infidelity was a point of pride. At heart we could not quite forgive one another, and our life together, however happy, would always contain those scars, those dull indices of maturity and experience that would flare, and recede, and then rear up again, freshly raw. My friendship with MacDara never recovered. We bumped into each other and muttered and growled on a couple of occasions, and I scorned him and missed him. Pathetically, I treasured the revelation that he'd never quite had his way with his MW, and I noted how jowly he was lately becoming, and how disconcertingly wealthy. Stronson was wary of me and was clearly nurturing a hangdog crush on a particularly nubile workie who had been set skivvying on the arts desk. The mysterious Charlie seemed to disappear after his love forsook him, the windows of the Endsleigh Street granny flat cheerfully lit and curtained by someone else on the times I looked up on my way to Euston.

Sylvie's unacknowledged presence hovered round our home on Lelia's more private and circumspect days, when I caught a certain softened expression in her, an abstracted gentleness distinct from the one our daughter inspired, and I wondered then with a stopped heart whether her mind was with her. Sometimes I felt miserable about Sylvie. In my regret for all I'd done to her, despite her treatment of Lelia, I wanted to be certain that she had some sort of divine protection. At other times, I wished I could punish her. And on rare occasions she came to me in the hours after midnight and I smelled her and I felt her narrow pale body in my memory and wanted her.

On tired mornings as the year progressed, when grizzling feeds had kept us awake at night, Lelia and I touched each other over our baby's sleeping form as the newspapers arrived and the sun angled across the bed. She sometimes stretched to kiss me above her; she sometimes chided me, in her puritanical Lelia fashion, for lying in bed and wasting the day. The simple presence of Lelia and our baby as they lay there, their hair and eyes, the rhythm of their breathing, was remarkable to me, just as the newspapers, the taxis on the square, the rags of Lucy's glottal stops floating from the area, were glorious and lovely and tightly woven into our history, into the miracle of the mundane. And gradually, Sylvie became less and less real. All that lived on was her uncomfortable shadow: the ghost of a ghost.

TWENTY-FOUR

Richard

I caught sight of Sylvie Lavigne one afternoon the following spring in Paris. I was carrying our fat-cheeked daughter aloft beneath the limes in the Tuileries while Lelia read by the pool, and I glimpsed the back of her hair. I jolted, momentarily uncertain of whether it was Sylvie, but her hair's movement as she walked cast the tiniest hooks to ruffle my skin.

Then I realised she was holding a baby. She settled the miniature creature on her shoulder, and I looked into its face as it bobbed, cocooned upon her. Its half-open eyes contained an instantly familiar expression. I caught my breath. The baby resembled my own daughter at birth: the sight of it sent me straight back to the first time I'd seen her, because all new babies look so very alike. I followed them with my gaze through the trees, and then I turned away and we left the park.

A NOTE ON THE AUTHOR

Joanna Briscoe is the author of two novels, *Mothers and Other Lovers*, which won the Betty Trask Award; and *Skin*, which was runner-up for the Encore Award. Her short stories have featured in several anthologies. She was a columnist for the *Independent* and the *Guardian* and writes regularly for all the major newspapers and magazines.

Joanna Briscoe lives in London with her family.

A NOTE ON THE TYPE

The text of this book is set in Bembo. This type was first used in 1495 by the Venetian printer Aldus Manutius for Cardinal Bembo's *De Aetna*, and was cut for Manutius by Francesco Griffo. It was one of the types used by Claude Garamond (1480–1561) as a model for his Romain de L'Université, and so it was the forerunner of what became standard European type for the following two centuries. Its modern form follows the original types and was designed for Monotype in 1929.